W9-ANT-948

WHERE
ANGELS
FEAR

BOOKS BY D.K. Hood

Don't Tell a Soul
Bring Me Flowers
Follow Me Home
The Crying Season

D.K. HOOD

WHERE ANGELS FEAR

Bookouture

Published by Bookouture in 2019

An imprint of StoryFire Ltd.

Carmelite House
50 Victoria Embankment
London EC4Y 0DZ

www.bookouture.com

ISBN: 978-1-78681-545-3
eBook ISBN: 978-1-78681-544-6

To Daniel and Gary Brown my brainstorming team,
who encourage me every step of the way.

PROLOGUE

Friday

"Just keep driving." Fear gripped Ella Tate and she turned in her seat to glare at her friend. "Don't stop. Have you lost your mind?"

"We don't leave people stranded in Black Rock Falls." Sky's voice sounded harsh in the stillness. "There's a blizzard on the way and the poor man could freeze to death."

The idea of traveling into the middle of nowhere in the pitch black with not even a sliver of a moon scared the crap out of Ella, let alone stopping for a strange man on the side of a deserted highway. "We haven't passed a car for at least an hour. He could be a serial killer just waiting for us to drop by.'

"*Really*, at midnight on this stretch of road? It's freezing out there, and why would he have his hazard lights on if he wasn't in trouble?" Sky slowed the car.

Unease fell over Ella like a shroud and her heart raced. "Don't stop. His face is covered and I can't see his hands. He could be a psycho carrying a gun and just waiting for someone to come by so he can murder them."

"*He* could be a woman. Everyone bundles up against the cold. We don't look very feminine at the moment, do we?" Sky gripped the wheel and edged the car to the side of the road. "Even a psycho wouldn't be crazy enough to be out here with a blizzard on the way. He or she needs our help. It's the neighborly thing to do."

The same dread she experienced walking into a haunted house on Halloween gripped Ella and the hairs on the back of her neck rose. Everything her brother had drummed into her when she left for college came to the front of her mind. She could hear her brother's voice loud and clear. *Do not at any time help a stranger alone.* The advice was right up there with hitchhiking. Stopping in the dead of night on a lonely highway, miles from town, was stupid. She swallowed hard and gripped her phone as the dark figure came into view. "Offer to call a tow truck and drive on."

"You won't get any bars out here. We're too far from town." Sky's window hummed down. "Can we offer you a—"

The hooded figure lashed out and a spray of hot fluid splashed over Ella's cheek. Sky fell into her, blood gushing from her nose and staining her blonde hair. The dark figure wrenched open the door and grabbed the car keys. Heart hammering in her chest, Ella gaped in disbelief at the ax he held in one hand, the blood-splattered metal glistening in the interior light of the car. Shocked and unable to move, she stared into the black eyes of a huge man. He said nothing, just almost casually unclipped Sky's seatbelt, dragged her from the car and tossed her onto the ground as if she was a bag of trash. *Oh, my God, he's killed her and I'm next.*

The stranger laid the ax on the blood-soaked seat and lunged toward her. The freezing air hit her in the face like a slap. She cringed and leaned away from him. "D-don't touch me. I'm calling 911."

Sheer panic constricted her chest and her muscles bunched as her body's flight reaction slammed into place. When he cursed and went for her cellphone, she flung it at his face, unclasped her seatbelt and fumbled for the door handle. His large gloved hand groped at her arm just as the door swung open and her feet hit the blacktop running. She dashed down the highway, leapt a ditch alongside the road and headed into the cover of total darkness. The dead winter grass and frost-covered undergrowth tangled around her feet. Terror grasped her throat as she stumbled over the uneven ground, not looking back. A white gate loomed up and she threw herself over the top. The drop onto the hard frozen ground radiated through her legs but the terrain here was level, with no undergrowth. She lifted her knees and, gasping the freezing air, ran for her life. *I have to get away*.

With no moonlight and nothing to guide her, she stretched her eyes wide to see but only pitch black lay ahead. Each breath hurt deep in her chest and shooting pains cramped the muscles in her legs but she kept going, running blind. Something hard hit her in the chest and she bounced back, winded. Terror dragged a cry from her throat and she pushed down the panic. Caught on an invisible fence, she struggled, unable to move like a fly in a web. Barbed wire stuck to her clothes, holding her like Velcro.

Behind her, she heard a roar like a wounded animal and pounding footsteps on the blacktop. She chanced a look over one shoulder but only the headlights of Sky's vehicle lit up the highway. Wrenching the coat from the wire, she gaped in terror as the unmistakable glow of a flashlight moved in an arc and she hit the ground. Her stomach knotted in fear. He was coming after her.

When the light moved in another direction scanning the open land, she paused for a second to watch then her stomach cramped in horror as it turned her way. She had to run. The flashlight bobbed in the distance and in moments, he would be heading through the gate and in her direction. A sob of distress escaped her lips but she pushed to her feet and escaped into the blackness. As if nature was against her, the snow clouds parted and a crescent moon peeked through. Her insides twisted and she turned, searching for a place to hide.

Not ten yards away she made out a clump of trees with trunks like massive black poles and chest burning with overexertion, sprinted into their protection. On the other side of the cluster of trees, she could make out the shadowy outline of a building. Not a house but perhaps the ruins of an old barn. She turned around and heart thumping in her ears, watched the light bouncing along in the distance. Her chest ached and huge billows of steam surrounded her with each breath giving her position like a beacon. Exhausted, she bent hands on knees. There was nowhere to hide and how much longer could she keep running? He would catch up soon and murder her.

She needed to think, to outsmart him. He would expect her to hide in the building but she had other ideas. She dragged in a few deep breaths, turned around and headed back into the trees. The pines had a few low branches but high up they thickened capping each tree with lush foliage.

She panted for each breath and, fighting through the agony of torn muscles, reached for the next limb.

Trembling, she wedged herself between two of the tree's sturdy branches then straddled a thick bough. She hugged the trunk, pressing her cheek against the rough surface. *He's coming.* The heavy crunch, crunch, crunch as his footsteps pounded the frozen ground sent shivers up her spine. A shadowy figure appeared and the flashlight beam scanned the area. As if tracking her by sound, he stopped and turned his head this way and that before moving on. *Oh, God, he's found me.*

The crunch, crunch, crunch of his boots breaking the thin patches of ice on ground had gotten louder. The flashlight moved from side to side as he searched under the bushes and his heavy breathing sent plumes of steam curling in the beam. He'd come so close she could hear him muttering obscenities under his breath. And he was as mad as hell.

"Where are you, bitch?" His voice came out in a ball of condensation. "When I find you I'm gonna cut you into little pieces."

He moved away, his flashlight picked out an overgrown trail to a dilapidated building. Ella choked back a sob of relief and, to her horror, he heard her. He stopped dead and swung the flashlight around, then made his way back to her tree. He was standing directly beneath her. Her mouth went dry and she bit down so hard that the metallic taste of blood coated her tongue. Sweat prickled down her back. She prayed he would not look up and find her; then, as if by divine intervention, an owl swooped across the shaft of light and settled in a tree. The crunch, crunch, crunch came again as the stranger moved away.

Fingers numb from holding on to the tree, Ella peered into the darkness, too frightened to move. Minutes later, the bobbing flashlight was heading back in her direction. Sheer terror slammed into her as he lifted the beam into the trees. She wrapped her legs around the trunk and made herself as small as possible. She pulled the cord of her hoodie tight around her face with trembling fingers, and squeezed her eyes shut. If she kept her face hidden, he might not see her.

The light came closer. He was checking every tree. Afraid that he would see her breath, Ella pressed her face into her sleeve and breathed through her nose, but the lack of oxygen made her dizzy. Panic gripped her and she shook. Her teeth chattered. She held on tight as he scanned each of the pines, coming closer and closer. Each second seemed to last a lifetime. Then she heard a sound, way off in the distance. She must be hallucinating, it sounded like a woman's voice calling her name. No hallucination, he had heard it too.

"Dammit, I'm goin' to shut her up for good and you're next, sweetheart." The man's angry voice seemed to boom in the silence, then he spun around and took off at great speed toward the road.

Ella let out a long breath and listened. The thin, wavering, ghostly voice came again.

"Ella, where are you? Help me."

Shocked and horrified, Ella peered in the direction the man had run but trees blocked her view. *Oh, my God. He's going back to kill her and I'm next.*

CHAPTER ONE

Saturday

"Jenna, you should go see a doctor." Deputy Dave Kane handed her another box of tissues.

"It's just a cold." Sheriff Jenna Alton raised red-rimmed eyes to his face. "I'll be fine in a few days."

Kane shook his head. "It's been over two weeks and you're getting worse. Trying to cope with the horses in this weather isn't helping." He tapped the bottom of his cane on the floor. "Damn this knee. I should throw you in the car and make you go."

"Good luck with that." Jenna gave him a belligerent glare then wiped her red nose and sniffed.

Duke whined and rested his big head on the bed. His sad bloodhound eyes moved from Jenna to Kane as if he was reluctant to take sides.

Kane pointed to him. "See, even Duke knows you're ill." He threw one arm up into the air. "Okay, have it your own way. I'll go make breakfast."

Stymied, he made his way slowly into the kitchen and filled the kettle, then checked the hotcakes in the oven. Working with an ex-DEA agent living in witness protection with a new name and face as his superior had been one crazy adventure. Especially as she lived in fear of her life after giving evidence against underworld kingpin Viktor Carlos.

After leaving his job in the DC's Special Forces Investigation Command, he'd found himself working off the grid in Black Rock Falls. At first life had been difficult, living a lie. The government had created a new identity for him after a terrorist planted a bomb under his car, killing his wife and leaving him with a titanium plate in his head. He'd settled into his new life until everything changed last fall. A maniac had shot him and he'd fallen into a canyon and shattered his knee, however the plate had become an asset. It had saved his life but he'd suffered short-term memory loss, his mind taking him back to the day he lost his wife, and the memories of his time after he arrived in Black Rock Falls had vanished. After extensive rehabilitation following surgery to replace the plate, he'd found his balance again and could walk on his reconstructed knee. The pain endured since the extensive surgeries had intensified with the freezing temperatures and, over the last few weeks, venturing outside had become near impossible.

He'd been in no shape to care for himself after leaving the hospital and had taken up Jenna's offer of her spare room rather than try to cope in his cottage, set a stone's throw from her house, a massive hundred-year-old ranch house, with big rooms and wide hallways, which made it easier to negotiate in his wheelchair than the cottage. For the first month, Deputy Shane Wolfe had arranged a nurse to care for him during the day, which was a pain as he could cope fine alone and only needed her for his injections. The well-equipped gym was perfect for his rehabilitation, but he had to admit having Jenna as his coach was a double-edged sword because although he enjoyed her company, she pushed him to exercise like a marine drill sergeant.

When Deputy Jake Rowley called to offer his assistance with the horses, Jenna had gladly accepted and insisted he stable his own mount on the ranch as recompense. Now, with Jenna ill, he was considering stabling the horses in town instead; it didn't seem fair to drag Rowley to the ranch twice a day to check the horses as well as expecting him to take over the sheriff's department in their absence. He refilled the coffee pot and leaned against the counter. Moments later, Rowley knocked on the front door.

"Coming." Kane swung open the door and a blast of freezing air slammed him in the face, sending spirals of agony into his brain. He stood to one side and Rowley stamped his feet on the mat, then stepped inside, shucking his boots at the front door. Kane peered into the blizzard. "It's getting worse out there. You'll have to wait for the snowplow to come by and follow it back into town."

"Sure looks that way." Rowley shrugged out of his coat and Kane could feel the cold flowing from him and smell a hint of snow and horse on his clothes. "The horses are snug and warm. I've seen racing stables with less insulation. The double doors make all the difference and you have enough food in there to see you through June."

Kane led the way to the kitchen. "I ordered extra supplies before the snow. I remembered how it was last year." He hooked his cane over the back of a chair and went to the counter.

"How's the sheriff?" Jake Rowley pulled off his gloves and dropped onto a chair.

Kane poured the coffee and handed him a cup, then turned back to the counter and broke eggs into a bowl. "Worse and she won't go see a doctor."

"She would have a hard time getting in to see old Doc Brown, he's everyone's favorite. I hear the women prefer to go to Doctor Abigail Sneed but Maggie said her friend waited three hours yesterday." He sipped his beverage. "The other one, Doctor Weaver, has a notice in her window saying she'll do home visits." He raised a brow. "Do you figure being new in town the locals don't trust her?"

Kane added butter to a pan and poured in the eggs. He wondered why their receptionist's friend had decided to wait rather than go to a different doctor. "Doctor Weaver was here when I arrived. Exactly how long does it take to stop being a newbie?"

"Oh, twenty years or so, I guess." Rowley grinned. "Maybe you should give her a call?"

"Give who a call?" Jenna strolled into the kitchen, then coughed and turned back in to the hallway. Sometime later, she re-emerged, her face flushed and eyes running.

Kane piled three plates with eggs and placed them on the table, then pulled the hotcakes from the oven. "The doctor." He slid the hotcakes onto a plate and Rowley stood to take them from him. "I'll make an appointment for her to come here so you don't have to go out." He reached for the coffee pot.

"You never give up, do you?" Jenna glared at him.

"Nope." He set the coffee on the table and slid into a chair. 'I'm calling her as soon as I've eaten—and there's something else we need to discuss."

'Go on." Jenna eyed him suspiciously.

"We can't expect Jake to drive out before five every morning, do a day's work, return to tend the horses, and then drive home in this weather." Kane glanced at Rowley's blank expression. "He hasn't complained, but it was different when he had your help."

"Yeah, I agree, it is too much as he's handling the office as well." Jenna looked at Rowley, who was staring at his plate. "Can you move into Kane's cottage until I shake this cold? Only for a couple of days." She sighed. "I'd ask you to move in here but Kane has my other spare room filled with his equipment."

"Sure, ma'am, anything to help and it would save time." Rowley smiled. "Not that caring for three horses is hard work."

Kane gaped at her. *Oh, boy, she's moving Rowley into my cottage.*

"Great! His spare room is all made up." She glanced at Kane. "Knowing Kane as I do there will be enough food in there to feed an army." She chuckled. "If you want to cook, that is, or you can join us for meals."

"Breakfast would be a help, ma'am—I'm used to tending for myself." Rowley smiled. "I usually eat at Aunt Betty's for breakfast and have done for years now, but with the snow and all, I'm not sure I'd have time."

Kane wondered what would happen with the living arrangements when he recovered. He also had a number of questionable items in his possession left from his past life and would have to make it over to his cottage to lock two of his bedrooms. As much as he trusted and respected Rowley, some things about his life remained *need to know*.

"Well then, that's settled." Jenna picked at her food then rubbed her temple. "Kane is well enough to work from here on case files and if necessary you can call in Wolfe or Deputy Webber. Don't forget Wolfe might be our ME but he is still my deputy."

"Sure thing, ma'am." Rowley finished his coffee and stood. "I'll be heading off now. I can hear the snowplow. I'll follow him back into town."

"Leave Deputy Walters to close up at noon, and we won't be opening on Sunday. Pin a notice on the front door. If anyone needs help they can call 911." Jenna reached for her coffee. "Drive safe."

Kane refilled their cups and waited for Rowley to leave, then turned to her. "I have things in my cottage I don't want Rowley to find." He leaned back in his chair. "Enough to blow my cover."

"You can't walk over to the cottage in the snow. If you fall you'll be back to square one." Jenna squeezed his hand. "Dave, I know your injuries are killing you, and you're way behind in your knee rehab because of the head injury. The doctor told you it would take time to recover."

He gaped at her. "You're missing the point, Jenna. I have to get into my cottage before Rowley moves in. I'll walk over there if necessary. I hardly use the cane anymore."

"Do you honestly believe Rowley would be able to crack your safe or break into your computer?" Jenna smiled at him. "He wouldn't even try."

"How do you know about my safe?"

"Well, I'm capable and I *would* try." She giggled. "Oh Lord, you should see your face." She let out an explosive sneeze into a ball of tissues. "I went over to collect your clothes and stuff, remember. The safe is a bit hard to miss."

Kane heaved a sigh of relief. "That's the gun safe. I have two." He gave her a long considering stare. "I guess I can trust you with the contents of the other one now."

"I have two safes as well and you're welcome to share." She gave him a warm smile and pushed to her feet. "Bundle up. I'll drive you to the cottage and help you collect your stuff." She gave him one of her no-nonsense stares. "I won't die of pneumonia driving a hundred yards."

"Okay." Kane lifted his cellphone from the table. "As soon as I've called the doctor."

"You always have to have the last word, don't you?" Jenna collected the plates. "A long time ago, the people next door to me had this dog named Oscar. It would bark like crazy and the neighbor would call out for it to stop. It would stop then let out a little bark. No matter how many times the neighbor told it to stop, it always did the same thing."

Confused, Kane frowned at her. "You saying I'm a dog?"

"Nope." Jenna rinsed the plates and stacked the dishwasher. "But you remind me of that dog, always having the last word."

Kane chuckled. "Really?"

"Yeah really." Jenna glared at him.

He gave her his biggest smile. "Woof."

CHAPTER TWO

The night had been horrendous for Ella. After hearing a long cut-off scream then silence, the blizzard hit with force and the stranger had not returned. Torn between staying safe in the tree or braving the blizzard to look for Sky, she had peered at the sheet of snow falling around the trees and sobbed. The chances of making it back to her alive would have been zero. Wedged in the branches, she'd heard the distant sound of traffic overnight but was too scared to move.

When the watery sun finally peered through the snow clouds and birds hopped around her, she decided to chance it. The snow-covered fir had offered her shelter and the fact she'd filled her bags she'd packed for the visit had probably saved her life. Not wanting to leave her clothes behind for her stay at Sky's house for the next few weeks, she'd added many more layers than usual and two pairs of thick socks covered her feet in the sheepskin-lined boots.

Her muscles ached and her hands refused to work properly but by the time she made it halfway down the tree, the feeling was coming back into her limbs. The scenery had changed dramatically overnight. The highway had all but vanished into a sea of brilliant white. She shuddered. Close by, hidden in the snow, Sky could be lying brutally murdered.

With cautious steps, she moved from the cover of trees staring into the white wilderness for any sign of the killer. Bile rushed up the back of her throat at the thought of finding her friend battered to death. Searching the snowscape in all directions, she could not see anything resembling Sky's yellow car. The snowdrifts came up to her knees and every step was like quicksand on her way back to the highway.

The road was empty but she could see tire tracks in the fresh snow. A truck had come by recently, so the highway must be open to traffic. The roar of a motor echoed in the distance and she dived into the bushes trembling with fear then stared out to see an eighteen-wheeler bearing down on her. She had the choice: freeze to death or risk climbing into the cab with a stranger. The risk was non-negotiable and she needed to get help for Sky. Steeling herself against the rising panic, she moved to the side of the road and waved her arms. The big red truck screeched and billowed steam like an old locomotive as it slowed to a halt some ways past her. The window buzzed down. A man in his forties with rosy cheeks and wearing a fur trapper hat stuck his head out. She ran to his door, slipping and sliding on the ice-covered blacktop, and banged frantically on his door. "Help me. A man murdered my friend. Call 911."

"Murder, you say?" The man looked both ways and then back at her. "What are you doin' way out here alone? Where did you come from?"

Ella gaped at him and banged on his door with both fists. "Call 911!"

"There's no cellphone signal out this way. I'll contact the sheriff on the two-way." The man's expression turned to worry. "I figure you'd better get inside out the cold." The man's window buzzed back up, hiding him behind the tinted glass.

A sudden wave of fear grabbed her. Pushing her leaden frozen limbs forward and making the choice of getting into a truck with a stranger or freezing to death in the middle of nowhere with an ax-wielding killer on the loose, she staggered around the hood and climbed up into the cab. Heat surrounded her and the man appeared more concerned than a threat. "Please hurry."

"Okay, okay. Here, take this." The driver dragged a blanket from behind him and offered it to her then spoke into his radio. "Ten-four good buddy, over." He turned to her. "He wants to know what's happened."

She stumbled through her horrific ordeal then gaped at him; whatever coded language he was speaking, it scared the hell out of her.

"A deputy from Black Rock Falls is on his way." He turned back in the seat and the truck engine roared and moved forward. "We'll meet him on the highway. I'd stop here and wait for him but I'm late and I've given him the coordinates where I found you." He indicated to a thermos. "Help yourself to coffee."

The stress seeped out of her and she leaned back in the seat. The warm air from the heater permeated through her clothes making her sleepy. With the gentle rocking of the cab, her eyes drifted closed for a second then she sat bolt upright. *What if he drugged my coffee?* She had to stay alert and bit down hard on the inside of her cheek. Chancing a glance at him, she cleared her throat. "I really appreciate the drink and ride."

"I can't figure why you would risk driving to Black Rock Falls in the middle of the night." He kept his eyes on the road. "Are you aware of how many murders occurred in this county in the last couple of years? I know the area covers many thousands of square miles but it's all over the news."

"And from what happened last night, I guess there is another killer on the loose." Ella bit back the rush of panic threatening to take over.

"I wouldn't live here." The man waved a hand toward the road. Blue lights flashed in the distance. "There he is now." He eased the truck to a halt. "You take care now, hear?"

CHAPTER THREE

Deputy Jake Rowley took down the truck driver's details, then turned his attention to the blood-spattered young woman beside him. She had a few scratches on her cheeks, but not enough damage to account for the copious amount of blood on her face and jacket. Concerned she might be involved in her friend's murder, he opened the back door of his cruiser. "Okay, Ella, get inside in the warm."

"Don't you want to know what happened?" Ella gripped his arm. "My friend Sky is lying on this road somewhere." She pointed back down the road. "Back that way. We have to find her."

Rowley eased her arm free and urged her into the car. "The truck driver didn't see a car or any sign of anyone but you on the road, but we'll take a look." He climbed behind the wheel and pushed the coordinates into his GPS, then spun his cruiser to face the other direction.

"Hey, I recognize that clump of trees in the distance." Ella squirmed in her seat, teeth chattering. "His vehicle was here, lights flashing like he was in trouble."

"Stay here." Rowley slid from the seat. "I'll go see what I can find."

The icy wind cut into his cheeks and buffeted him with each step up and down the stretch of road. He searched for any sign of blood on the frozen blacktop, but the snow covered everything in a deceptive white powder. With regret, he walked back to his car and climbed into the warm. He shook his head at Ella. "I can't find any trace of your friend, I'm sorry."

"You have to do something." Ella's eyes filled with tears. "She has to be out here somewhere."

Rowley's heart went out to the shocked young woman. "Search and rescue will be out here in no time. We'll have a snowplow to clear the highway and men looking for her before we get back to town. Don't worry—if she is out there, we'll find her. I have the details of her vehicle and the coordinates. We'll conduct a search of the entire area." He tried to use a calming tone. "You need to be checked out by the paramedics."

With so much blood on the young woman and no apparent injuries, he needed to run the incident report past Sheriff Alton before taking Ella to the hospital, but he was reluctant to disturb her when the doctor was due to visit. She would expect him to use his initiative and call Deputy Wolfe. The ex-marine widower with three daughters had joined the department the previous year but spent most of his time working as the Black Rock Falls ME. If Ella had witnessed a homicide, as she claimed, he would want to examine her for evidence.

He reached for the satellite phone, slipped out the cruiser and walked a few yards away to call him. "Hey, it's Rowley. I'm out midway between Blackwater and town. I have a female, nineteen years old, Ella Tate. Claims a man attacked and killed her friend last night. The truck driver who found her didn't see her friend's yellow vehicle or a body on the side of the road. I checked the location as well and found zip. I haven't gotten a statement from her but she is covered in blood and likely suffering from exposure."

"Her *blood?*" Wolfe sounded interested. *"Any serious injuries?"*

Rowley kicked at a clump of graying ice and looked at Ella. "Not from what I can see. She has a few scrapes, is all. It looks suspicious. I guess the scratches down her cheeks could be from her friend's nails."

"Have you notified the sheriff?"

Rowley blinked away snowflakes from his lashes. "Nope, she was waiting for the doctor to arrive and I didn't want to disturb her. With her and Kane out sick, you're the senior officer."

"Okay, I'll call her. She'll organize search and rescue but if the injured friend has been out on the side of the road all night, they'll be searching for a body. Take Tate into custody. Not at the sheriff's office. Take her to the hospital and get her up to the secure ward. Don't allow anyone near her. We'll have to treat her as a suspect for now. I'll meet you there." Wolfe cleared his throat. *"How's the sheriff this morning?"*

Rowley headed back to the cruiser. "She'd be better if she took the time to rest but she hates being holed up in the house and wants to get back to work."

"If this is a murder, she'll want to be involved and so will Kane. I doubt illness will slow her down."

Rowley opened the car door and slid behind the wheel. "I hope so. We sure need them back at work." He started the engine. "I hope you can spare Webber. We'll need to send him out with Walters to coordinate the search."

"Nothing's happening here." Wolfe sounded bored. *"I'll send him into the office and meet you at the hospital. Let's hope we haven't gotten ourselves another maniac loose in Black Rock Falls."* The line went dead.

CHAPTER FOUR

Jenna waited for Kane to slide a heavy locked metal box inside her floor safe, then pressed her thumb on the scanner. She entered a few more digits into the panel and glanced up at him. "Scan your thumb. The locking device accepts two fingerprints to open, so either of us will have access. Is that okay?"

"Yeah, the info is secure in my box. If someone forces the lock, it catches fire." He smiled at her. "Between you and me, it's the usual: IDs, cash, passports and burner phones."

Jenna raised one eyebrow. "Codebook?"

"If I told you that I'd have to kill you." He snorted in amusement. "You know the drill."

Jenna's cellphone pealed and she growled in frustration, then looked at the caller ID. "It's Wolfe." She accepted the call and placed it on speaker. "Is anything wrong?"

After listening to Wolfe's explanation about Ella Tate and the apparent murder of Sky Paul, adrenaline started to pump through Jenna's veins. She exchanged a glance with Kane. "Of course we want to be involved, I only have a cold. I'll head the investigation from here. I'll call search and rescue and send Walters and Webber to meet the chopper and the snowmobile volunteers and coordinate the search." She sighed. "What are the chances of finding Sky Paul alive?"

"It's unlikely anyone could survive injured and lying on the side of the highway in a blizzard." Wolfe's voice sounded strained. *"The*

temperature has been dropping all day and another blizzard is on the way. We might not find her until the melt. If another four hours goes by with no sign of her, it will be a body retrieval."

Jenna frowned. "Yet the other young woman lived to tell the tale. How so?"

"Right now, I don't have much more information for you. Rowley is about twenty minutes out of town with Ella Tate. I'll head out to the hospital to meet him and collect evidence from the alleged victim shortly."

Impressed by Rowley's quick action, she nodded. "It sounds like you have everything under control. I'll call in Walters and Webber and get them out to ground zero."

"No need. Webber and Walters are making their way to the last known coordinates with a snowplow to cut a path alongside the road where Miss Tate said the incident occurred. Rowley mentioned Walters has experience in search and rescue."

"Okay." Jenna frowned. She needed to be in the midst of the action, not stuck at home, but to venture outside with a chest infection and a fever just to find a corpse was begging for pneumonia. It wouldn't be worth the risk. She had skilled deputies and issuing orders from home was no different to being in the office, but right now, no one was available at the sheriff's department apart from Magnolia the receptionist—Maggie to her friends. "Okay, if you take down Miss Tate's statement it will free up Rowley to run the office. I'll call in some help from Blackwater. Right now, we have to consider Miss Tate as either in danger or a murder suspect. We'll need around the clock surveillance at the hospital. Has anyone contacted the parents of the missing girl? She may be safe at home for all we know."

"Rowley didn't mention contacting Sky Paul's parents but I guess his main concern was getting Miss Tate to the hospital. From the blood Rowley mentioned on Tate, I doubt she is at home or her parents

would have reported the attack." Wolfe sounded concerned. *"I'll speak to him."*

Jenna exchanged a glance with Kane and frowned. "No, it's fine, you have enough to do. I'll call him now. He can go speak to Sky Paul's parents before he returns to the office."

"Sure. I'll email you a report of my findings and Walters will keep you updated on the search."

Jenna let out a long sigh. "Okay, thanks." She disconnected and looked at Kane. "I feel useless not being out there coordinating the search and rescue."

"All parties involved know what jobs they have to do. You know as well as I do the search and rescue chopper has been doing this for many years. Same with the snowmobile volunteers. They know their stuff and you have Walters out there to direct traffic if necessary." Kane shrugged. "It's not your fault you're ill. Don't be so hard on yourself."

"I've never tried to run an investigation from home before." Jenna turned her head away and coughed. "I prefer to speak to my deputies face to face."

"Then get them to drop in here. I don't think it will make any difference if you're not in the office. I figure our only problem will be if Wolfe suspects Ella Tate is involved."

Jenna rubbed her temples to ease the threatening headache. "If she is then one of us will need to interview her. Rowley is a competent deputy but he doesn't have our experience, and Wolfe will be working forensics."

"Maybe not." Kane made his way to the kitchen and poured two fresh cups of coffee. "But Wolfe is on the ball. I figure we should wait for his report." He sighed. "As Wolfe said, we're more likely to be searching for a corpse. After twelve hours or more out in this weather, she wouldn't stand a chance. The search is routine now, not a life-or-death situation."

Jenna huffed out a long breath. "Yeah, I guess but if he believes she's responsible for killing her friend, I'll want you to interview her. You ask the right questions and get inside people's heads."

"I'm sure I can drive to the hospital and back without a problem, or Rowley can drive me." He smiled at her. "Try not to worry too much. You have a capable team at your fingertips. Rest up and you'll be back at work in no time."

Jenna shook her head. "I can't right now with this case buzzing around in my head."

"Talk to me." Kane looked interested. "What have you got?"

"A theory." Jenna leaned forward in her chair. "If someone attacked Sky Paul on the highway and her car is missing, we could have another murder on our hands—or we might have the killer in custody… whatever, I'll call Blackwater and see if they can spare a few deputies to guard Ella Tate in the hospital. Can you follow up with Rowley? He needs to get over to speak to Sky's parents."

"Sure." Kane's brow furrowed. "I'll ask him if he notified Ella's next of kin as well. If not, I'll call them. It's likely, with organizing the snowplow and arranging for Wolfe to examine the girl, it might have slipped his mind."

Jenna heaved a sigh of relief. Head injury or not, Kane was firing on all cylinders, although he had become a little remote toward her since losing his memory. The incident had reopened the wound of losing his wife—for him it had happened a few weeks ago—and she recognized the signs of a man in mourning. Keeping him busy was the best medicine. "Will you be able to chase down some info on the Tate girl for me as well? We only have her word for what happened. If Sky is dead, she would be the last person to have seen her alive."

"Sure can." Kane reached for the coffee pot. "Go back to bed and rest. I'll pour you a cup of coffee and bring you a slice of Aunt Betty's fruit cake."

"That is easier said than done." Jenna heard a vehicle heading toward the house and groaned. "Did I ever mention how much I hate doctors? They always want to jab a needle in me."

"Go back to bed. I'll get the door." Kane pushed to his feet and walked to the door without using his stick. He glanced over at her. "See, I'm fine. I made it to the cottage and back without a headache. I'll be back to work before you at this rate."

Jenna glared at him. "Ha, ha, very funny." She made her way back to her bedroom to wait for the doctor.

When Kane ushered the doctor into the room, Jenna took in what she could see of her. Bundled up in a huge sheepskin coat that hung down to cover her boots, the doctor peered at her through oversized black-framed glasses that made her dark eyes appear huge and surreal.

"Good morning, Sheriff." The doctor had a distinctive English accent and when she untied the knitted scarf from around her face and then pulled off her hat, long black hair spilled down to frame her features. "I'm Doctor Mavis Weaver. What seems to be the problem?" She placed a brown leather bag on the bed and inclined her head from side to side, like a bird of prey, then looked down at her.

Jenna wrinkled her nose at the strong smell of lavender and blinked at the doctor. She looked as if she had walked out of the 1940s. A large woman in her late thirties, she dressed in a variety of unusual clothes like a bag lady. Stymied for a second, she cleared her throat then coughed uncontrollably.

"Oh, I see." Dr. Weaver opened her bag, took out a stethoscope and proceeded to examine her. "You have a chest infection. You should have called me a week ago, young lady. I want you to stay inside; going out in this weather could lead to serious complications."

Astonished by her bedside manner, Jenna blinked. "Ah, I thought it was just a cold."

"Are you allergic to penicillin?" The doctor reached into her bag, took out a small bottle and a syringe then prepared an injection.

Jenna read the label—it was in her best interest not to trust strangers planning to shoot drugs into her system—and shook her head. "No."

"Good! I'll give you a shot. Roll onto your side away from me and lift your nightie. This one goes into your butt." Dr. Weaver grinned. "It hurts like a bitch too."

"Ah… is that really necessary?" Jenna eyed the needle with suspicion. "Pills will be fine."

"Oh, you'll need them as well." The doctor chuckled as if enjoying the idea of inflicting pain, cleaned the area and jabbed in the needle. "There you go. I'll draw some blood while I'm here as well, just to check for any nasties."

Jenna rubbed her backside. The injection hadn't worried her. She sat up and offered her arm. The doctor was fast and efficient. She watched her write on a prescription pad and wondered why she ran a clinic. "Do you work at the hospital as well?"

"The hospital is all about insurance and around these parts there are people barely surviving. I never turn anyone away and I can handle most emergencies." Dr. Weaver's eyes moved over her face. "I have a few colleagues who are prepared to help out pro bono when necessary as well."

"That is very noble of you, but we do have the Department of Public Health and Human Services to assist low earners with health-care. If you provide a free service how do you pay the bills?" Jenna pressed a wad of cotton to the crook of her arm. "We all have to eat."

"Those who can pay are more than enough for my simple needs." Dr. Weaver handed her the prescription. "Take the meds and if you're not better in four to five days, call me, or if your condition deteriorates, go to the ER."

"Sure." Jenna eyed her critically. As a doctor, the woman did not fill her with confidence. She reached into the bedside table for her wallet. "Are you a Medicaid or HMK Plus provider? I'll pay cash for the visit if that's okay. If you leave my blood sample, I'll have one of my deputies drop it at the ME's office. Wolfe will perform the tests."

"You don't have to worry, my dear." Dr. Weaver patted her on the shoulder. "Deputy Kane insisted on providing his credit card details before I left. I'll email him a receipt and as I go right past the ME's office, I'll drop by on the way home. If you have someone to pick up your meds, I'll drop the prescription into the pharmacy on my way home too. I won't contact you unless the tests show up something of concern."

"Thanks, that would be a great help." Jenna's attention drifted to the door, wondering why Kane would pay for her medical treatment. "I'm sure I'll be fine in a few days." She handed the prescription back to the doctor.

She watched as the doctor shrugged into her coat, pulled on her bright red hat and purple gloves and waddled into the hallway. The moment she heard the front door shut behind the doctor, she slipped out of bed and marched into the kitchen. "Kane, why did you pay for her visit? I had cash here."

"I told her you were insured and she asked for credit card details before she left, so I gave her mine." He sighed. "Friends do that for each other, it's no big deal."

Jenna balled her fists on her hips. "Uh-huh. I would have preferred to go into town to see Doc Brown. She was... weird."

"Sorry but I didn't have a choice of doctors." Kane gave her a sheepish look. "I don't know any others who make house calls. It's like she stepped out of the fifties."

Jenna rubbed her butt. "You can say that again. And she gave me a jab. I hate needles." She went to the counter and refilled the coffee pot. "When she sends the receipt, I'll reimburse you."

"If you must, but it's not necessary." He took down coffee cups from the shelf. "It was my idea for her to call."

Jenna gave him a sideways look. "Maybe, but now it will be all over town we're living together and you're paying my medical bills."

"Nah, she won't say a word." Kane grinned at her. "Doctor–patient privilege and all that." He leaned against the counter. "FYI, people already believe we're involved. I had one old lady ask me when I was going to make an honest woman of you."

Aghast, Jenna gaped at him. "Oh, my God, tell me that didn't happen."

"Sure did. I told her you wouldn't have me if I was the last man on earth and that our relationship was strictly professional." Kane moved to the refrigerator and took out the cream. "She patted my arm and told me not to worry, I would find someone one day."

Jenna giggled, followed by a fit of coughing. "I'd better get back to bed. Give me a call when the coffee is ready."

"What did the doc say is wrong with you?" Kane frowned and caught her arm. "Why did you allow her to take blood? It's risky. You never know who is watching."

Jenna laughed. "Her? I don't think she's a threat to national security somehow."

"Okay." Kane frowned. "Does she think you're contagious?"

Jenna waved him away. "No, it's just a chest infection and I have a prescription for meds that needs picking up. She wanted a blood sample, to look for 'nasties'. I told her to send it to Wolfe. I'll ask him what tests she requested. I'm sure he'll make sure she doesn't do anything untoward." She blew her nose. "I felt like I was

being treated by someone's grandma, she acts like an old woman."
They exchanged looks. "What? I suppose you figured she looked
perfectly normal?"

"She is a little strange." Kane chuckled. "When I noticed your
arm I was worried she might have used a fleam. She looks as if she
stepped out of a time machine."

"It's not funny. You didn't have a needle jabbed in your butt."
Jenna prodded him in the chest in an effort to stop him laughing.
"Next time I'll go see Doc Brown."

"He would be my choice." Kane's teeth flashed white and she
could hear him snickering as she went back to her room.

CHAPTER FIVE

A blast of icy wind cut into Wolfe's face as he stepped from the warmth of the ME's office. Winter had set in and every building had icicles of varying lengths hanging from gutters. Although the snow gave the town a picturesque appearance, the bitter cold temperatures added to the danger of being isolated in the more remote areas. He'd heard some of the older folk often froze to death and vehicles vanished under snowdrifts. He enjoyed living in Black Rock Falls but with the massive drop in temperature this year, he was convinced winter was heading into a new ice age.

As he led the way to his truck, the frozen maple trees surrounding his building creaked and every so often a branch would snap and tumble to the ground, hitting the snow with a soft thud. He took hold of his daughter's arm as Emily slipped and slid along the frozen footpath, her rosy cheeks peeking out from under her hoodie. He had not been able to dissuade her from assisting him today. At least he could be thankful his other two daughters were at home snug and warm.

Last night's blizzard hadn't deterred the townsfolk from going about their business. The snowplows cleared the roads before daybreak and vehicles moved around as normal, many carrying pines from the Christmas tree farm. Kids were everywhere, excited to be on vacation for the holiday season and loving the first snow. As they made their way to his truck a cloud of steam appeared to follow a couple walking by in animated conversation, red noses peeking from scarves and hats covered with snowflakes.

He slid into his vehicle and waited for Emily to fasten her seatbelt. "Are you sure you want to come with me? It's warmer inside."

"I wouldn't miss it." Emily smiled at her father. "This case sounds intriguing. I'm not sure the witness's account is accurate. It seems a bit far-fetched and she would have died out in the blizzard last night. It sounds very suspicious. From the information we have, Miss Tate could have killed her friend and been making up a story to cover the crime."

Wolfe bit back a smile. He had thought much the same thing from the preliminary report. "It's always better to assume the last person to see a person alive is a suspect unless proven otherwise. In cases like this one, we must gather as much evidence as possible. Things may have happened the way she said but as a medical examiner, I need proof either way."

Wolfe had to admit to being proud that Emily had decided to follow in his footsteps and was currently undergoing studies in forensic science. She spent the time between semesters and most weekends working alongside him at the ME's office. Intelligence ran in the family, with all of his daughters exceeding in their studies, but the intelligence came a price. Emily was headstrong and he needed to use every ounce of his considerable patience to keep his girls happy. Too many limitations would curb their inquisitive minds, not enough and they would end up in trouble. After losing his wife to cancer some years previously, finding the right balance had often been more difficult than he would like to admit. It was fortunate that Emily had found a strong friend and older sister figure in Jenna. They had bonded during Kane's recovery in the hospital and having Jenna as a role model could only be a good thing.

"How do we proceed?" Emily glanced at him. "She's nineteen so we don't need her parents' consent to examine her."

He turned to Emily. "We act with caution. The young woman is an unknown quantity. She informed Deputy Rowley she witnessed a

murder but we need to examine the blood spatter on her to determine
if she was involved."

"Do you want me to collect samples or just observe?" Emily
folded her gloved hands in her lap. "Or would you prefer I speak
to her, woman to woman? She's about my age and I might be able
to squeeze information out of her. Remember, to most people you
look intimidating." She gave him a beatific smile. "If I'd just met
you, I'd be running for the hills."

Wolfe pulled out onto the highway and set out for the hospital.
"We're there for a forensic evaluation, so I'll need you to watch her
undress and collect her garments. Say as little as possible to her. I'll
take her statement, then I'm pretty sure Sheriff Alton will want to
question her."

"Jenna is still feeling poorly. I called her before and she mentioned
the doctor giving her a shot of penicillin." Emily frowned. "With
Kane housebound, I believe that makes you the senior officer." Her
jaw became a stubborn line. "You have every right to take charge."

Wolfe wiped a hand down his face and forced his concentration
to remain on the hazardous slippery road. "No need. Jenna is quite
capable of organizing a search from home. She'll have Rowley running
things at the office and right now, he's doing a mighty fine job. I
don't need the extra work, Em. I hardly get time with you and the
girls now." He flicked her a glance. "I just want you to observe the
collection of evidence procedure, okay?"

"I guess." Emily's mouth turned down at the corners "If you
say so."

Wolfe pulled into the space designated for police vehicles and
climbed out. He collected his bag from the back seat and turned to
Emily. "She's on the restricted floor and Rowley should be with her."

He stepped over the pile of gray, frozen snow thrown up from the
snowplow and held out his hand to assist Emily. They made their way

inside the hospital and took the elevator to the restricted floor. The sheriff's department had made a few changes in the last few months to ensure the security of everyone on this level. Scanners were set on every doorway, each room or corridor requiring a card to gain entry. No one could enter without a deputy present and seeing a Blackwater deputy on duty made him smile. Even ill and short-staffed, Jenna had arranged for the girl to have around-the-clock security.

A doctor waiting with Rowley outside an examination room gave Wolfe an exasperated stare.

"Mr. Wolfe, I must protest. My patient has not received care since her arrival." The doctor's face was red with annoyance. "I must maintain duty of care but Deputy Rowley insists that you examine her first. She is alive, not a corpse. You have no right. She could be suffering from exposure."

Wolfe straightened. "In any crime, as the Medical Examiner, I have the right to examine a potential suspect and collect evidence. I'm sure you're aware Deputy Rowley has spoken to Miss Tate and he assured me she doesn't require emergency medical treatment. She was given a hot beverage and a blanket by the truck driver who found her—which, coincidently, has contaminated any trace evidence of a third party in this crime." He gave the doctor his best back-off glare. "It is imperative I examine her clothes in situ. The blood spatter will indicate if she is telling the truth about her friend's abduction and possible murder." He waved a hand toward the door. "This won't take long but I can't risk further contamination. You are welcome to observe."

"I'll wait." The doctor leaned against the wall and folded his arms across his chest.

Wolfe removed his gloves and coat then turned to Rowley. "I can take it from here. Has the sheriff called?"

"I spoke to Kane just before you arrived." Rowley lowered his gaze. "I'm heading over to speak to Sky Paul's parents, then heading back to the office. Kane is doing a background check on Ella Tate. He hasn't found a listing for her family. Can you ask her for a next of kin contact?"

Wolfe nodded. "Sure. Keep me in the loop and I'll make sure everyone gets a copy of my report." He had a thought and stared at Rowley. "Did you Mirandize her?"

"Nope. I figured she's a victim." Rowley's cheeks pinked. "Dang, she is in custody and you're going to question her about a crime."

"Yeah. It's normal procedure. The last person to see a victim alive is the first suspect we look at."

"I know that but she sounded so convincing." Rowley shrugged. "I'll go do it now."

Wolfe sighed. "No, you have enough to do. I'll do it. You'd better be on your way."

"Yes, sir." Rowley turned on his heel and headed for the elevator.

Wolfe turned to Emily. "I'll be taking a statement from Miss Tate after the examination but I'll need you to record our conversation from the moment we enter the room." He opened his bag and handed her his voice recorder.

"Okay." Emily took the device.

Once inside the examination room, Wolfe introduced himself and Emily. He pulled on a pair of latex gloves and donned a mask. "I'm going to take your statement but first, do you mind if I take a few photographs and some samples from your face and clothes?"

"No, do whatever you want if it helps to find Sky."

Wolfe walked around her, taking in the scratches on her face and the blood spatter over her left side, her cheek and her left glove. If she was left-handed, she could be the killer. He pulled a candy bar out of his pocket and handed it to her. She took it with her left hand. "You must be hungry. I am in this weather."

"Thanks." Ella gave him a quizzical stare. "I was hoping the hospital would feed me soon."

Wolfe smiled. "They will as soon as I've finished. Before we start I need to advise you of your rights under the law." He read her her rights then pulled his camera out of his bag. "Do you understand your rights?"

"Yeah, but I'm not under arrest, am I?" Ella gaped at him, wide-eyed. "I didn't do anything wrong and I don't need a lawyer. Why read me my rights? I'm a victim. I don't understand."

"I'm an officer of the law and I'm detaining you until further notice. I'm going to be asking you questions about a crime. A girl is missing presumed murdered and as you're the last person to see her alive, I wouldn't want you to incriminate yourself." Wolfe moved around her, taking photographs of the blood spatter. "Are you left-handed, Miss Tate?"

"Yeah. Why?" Ella peered at him from under the hood of her coat. "I'm warm now. Why can't I remove my coat and gloves?"

Wolfe lifted Ella's arm. "Hold out your arm and turn it from side to side." He clicked away. "I'll need to take a few swabs from your face, then I'll be taking your clothes back to the lab. The hospital has provided you with hospital scrubs and a dressing gown until your family arrives."

"Oh, wonderful. I saved for ages for that coat." Ella's eyes flashed in anger. "My boots were two hundred bucks."

"Do you really want to wear them when they're covered with your friend's blood?" Emily moved closer. "Haven't you realized you're covered in blood?"

"N-no." Ella peered at her arm. "Where?"

"All down your left side." Emily frowned. "I think your clothes are ruined."

Wolfe watched the girl's reactions. "Do you have a number we can call to notify your family where you are?"

"Not right now." Ella lifted her chin. "My brother was deployed a couple of weeks ago. That's why I'm spending my vacation with

Sky. Christmas in Black Rock Falls is supposed to be spectacular but it's freezing."

"It *is* very cold here." Wolfe shrugged. "If necessary I'll be able to get a message to your brother. I'm sure he is allowed to Skype you from time to time."

"If he could I wouldn't tell you." Ella cast him a disapproving glance. "Please don't ask me again."

Fully aware of the security required around military deployment overseas, he nodded. "Sure, I understand." He took a collection kit from his bag. "I'm going to take a few samples from your face and hands. It won't hurt."

"Okay." Ella turned her face to give him access.

"I'll be happy to lend you some of my things." Emily smiled at her. "We look about the same size."

"My bag is in Sky's car. When you locate it, can you bring my things to the hospital?" Ella looked hopeful. "I have just about everything I own in her car. My cellphone should be in there as well. I threw it at the man and it bounced off him and fell on the floor. It's pink and has my name in rhinestones on the cover."

Wolfe moved around her, taking samples of blood from her face and neck. "You mentioned to my deputy that Sky's car vanished overnight. It might be under a snowdrift. If you give me your cellphone number, I'll pass it on to the deputies searching for the car. They might hear it ringing under the snow."

"Sure." Ella repeated it twice to Emily, who entered it into her contacts on her cellphone.

He turned to Emily. "Call Webber and pass on the number."

"Okay." Emily slipped outside into the passageway.

Wolfe bagged and labeled everything, then handed Ella some large plastic bags. "The bathroom is through there." He pointed to a door. "When Emily comes back, I want you to place all your clothes into the plastic bags. You may keep your underwear on. I don't think the blood soaked through everything."

"It wouldn't have gone through all of them. I have layers of clothes under my coat. Two sets of thermals. I couldn't fit everything into my bags, so I wore the rest. If there's no blood on them can I keep them too?"

That explains why she didn't freeze to death. Wolfe rubbed his chin. "If you're okay with Emily examining your clothes first to make a determination, then you can keep anything not bloodstained."

"Sure." Ella dropped her gaze to the floor, then lifted it slowly to look at his face. "Then can I take a shower?"

"Yeah, but before you go, let me see your hands." Wolfe waited for her to remove her gloves then examined her hands for any sign of frostbite or blood. He found none. He met her gaze. "Okay, thanks. When you're done, I'll take your statement."

When Emily returned, he waited for her to collect the clothes then leaving her inside to wait for Ella to shower walked into the hallway and called Jenna. "Rowley is on his way to chat to Sky Paul's parents. I'm waiting to take Ella Tate's statement."

"What has the blood spatter told you?" Jenna cleared her throat. *"Victim or suspect?"*

Wolfe let out a long sigh. "I'm leaning toward suspect. The blood spatter is consistent with her inflicting the damage and her attitude is not what I would expect from someone who has suffered this type of trauma. She is hostile rather than devastated. In fact, she seems to care more about her bloodstained clothes than the fact someone murdered her friend in front of her. Something else. She isn't exhibiting signs of frostbite considering she sheltered in a tree during a blizzard for six hours. Although she is wearing numerous layers of clothes, including two sets of thermals, socks, and had fur-lined boots."

"If she was under a snow canopy she could keep warm." Jenna coughed and wheezed. *"Sorry. Where was I? Ah yes, I know small animals burrow under the snow to survive, it's possible."*

He noticed Emily waving him toward the door. "I have to go, ma'am. I'll call you when I have more information." He disconnected.

CHAPTER SIX

Sky Paul tried to fight her way back to consciousness. Fleeting memories filtered into her mind, of a dark road at night and someone hitting her. Underneath her, warm bedding pressed against her back. Perhaps it was all a bad dream and she was at home and in her own bed. She tried to force open her eyes, but the dream tugged her back down and she dozed in that relaxing place between sleep and wakefulness. A memory nagged at her and she tried to grasp the truth of it. Somewhere in the deep recesses of her mind, a nightmare hovered. Had her mind conjured the man by the side of the road and the blinding headache? She remembered driving with Ella to Black Rock Falls, but not getting home. Some parts of the puzzle dangled just out of reach and she could not escape the daunting feeling of unease. *I have to wake up.*

She fell back into the deep chasm of sleep and woke some time later with a throbbing headache. So the memory of a head injury was real enough. Her tongue stuck to the roof of her mouth and she couldn't remember being so thirsty. She opened her eyes and the first thing she noticed was a bag of fluid hanging from a pole beside her bed and the beep of a machine. *I'm in a hospital.* With care, she turned her throbbing head to stare at the woman in the next bed hooked up to a number of machines. She was about her age with dark hair and one hand with bright pink nail polish rested on the turned down sheet.

She tried to touch her face but could not lift her arms. Fearing the head injury had paralyzed her, she wiggled her fingers and they worked fine. Glancing down, she gaped at the restraints securing both wrists to a bar along each side of the bed. She tried to wriggle free but the bands held her tight. Panic grabbed her. "Nurse, I need help." Her voice came out in a dry squeak.

Footsteps, then a figure dressed in green scrubs, hat and mask came into view. Sky blinked at the man. "I need a drink—and what's happened to me?" She wriggled on the bed. "Why am I restrained?"

"Calm down, Sky. Everything is going to be fine. You were in a car wreck and I can't give you a drink just yet. The straps are for your own safety." He took a syringe from a dish beside the bed and inserted it into the tube running into her arm. "Go back to sleep now."

A warm glow spread through her and she closed her eyes, then the voice from her nightmare shocked her awake.

"I said to keep her in an induced coma and hook up the other machine." Another man wearing the same green hospital scrubs hovered over her. The familiar raspy voice slammed into her, making every hair on her body stand to attention.

The man sounded impatient. "And before you go home today, leave the trash by the back door. I'll dispose of it later."

Confusion and terror shuddered through her. What was happening? No one had explained anything to her. Where was Ella? Sky fought to stay awake, but even her intense fear was no match for the drugs coursing through her veins. The pain slid away and darkness surrounded her.

CHAPTER SEVEN

He absorbed Trudy's terrified expression and smiled as the drugs took hold. Kidnapping and murdering women empowered him to such a degree it had become an insatiable need. He hadn't experienced a normal emotion in any form, not ever, and during his forty-five years had only gained three acquaintances he could trust.

He liked making his victims believe they were safe in a hospital ward, then watching the shock on their faces when the realization hit them that they were under his control. He would kill them and enjoy every slow moment. He wouldn't give them a second thought once they'd died. Having no remorse was a gift he valued and one he'd inherited from his father.

As a cattleman's son, he'd raised orphaned calves by hand but by the time he'd reached ten years old his father had forced him to slaughter them. Rather than upsetting him, it had excited him. His father's words hummed in his ears. *You are like me, son. We don't give a shit.*

He hadn't cared when his father died either.

He attached his surgical mask then pulled the curtain surrounding the bed to one side. His attention lingered on Sky. Her disappearance would be all over the news by now. Finding her friend in the car had spoiled everything. He would have taken her as well if the stupid bitch hadn't run away but Ella Tate had left him all the information he needed on her cellphone.

Young people posted their plans online telling everyone where they were going and what they were doing. By posing as man in his early twenties, he had three thousand friends to choose from and it had been easy to discover when Sky would be leaving college to return home. The selfie posted from the Blackwater Roadhouse at 11.00 p.m. had given him plenty of time to drive to the highway and wait for her. Although, Sky had neglected to mention Ella would be traveling with her to Black Rock Falls.

He walked into the small office adjacent to the ward and scanned his computer. Within a few minutes, he found posts by Ella and friended her too. Soon she would be telling the world—and him—where she was and what she was doing. It had become part of the new culture. Hell, people even posted images of their dinner. He grinned. "Okay, Ella, I'll just wait for you to come to me." He disconnected and strolled out into the ward to look at his new prize. *Life just gets better.*

CHAPTER EIGHT

Jenna's day was getting worse by the second. She had finished reading Ella Tate's statement but Wolfe was not answering his cellphone. How could she conduct an investigation by virtual remote control without his first-hand input? She called his cellphone again and left a message. The only time Wolfe turned off his cellphone was during an autopsy and as no one had reported finding a body, she had no idea what was happening. With his constant worry about his daughters, he would divert his calls to Kane's cellphone as backup and yet Kane's phone had not rung.

She pushed her hair from her face and leaned back into the pillows. With no reports coming in from her deputies, she had no option but to wait. Hearing Kane's footsteps coming along the hallway, she lifted her attention to the door. He had been a remarkably good patient and with the tables turned proved to be a very caring nurse. Although, since losing his memory, he had the same lost look as when he arrived in Black Rock Falls over a year ago. She assumed the memory of his wife's death had hit him hard for a second time and she would try to support him the best way she could by being his friend. She understood grief, after losing everyone she loved in the world, and he would need time to recover in both mind and body. When he appeared at the door with two cups of steaming coffee, she smiled at him. "Thanks. Did you read the statement Wolfe sent through?"

"Yeah, and from the amount of blood on Tate, Sky Paul shouldn't have survived the first attack. If there was a second, as Tate suggested, we're searching for a body. If the man left her on the side of the highway, there's no way she survived a blizzard." Kane sighed. "I ran a background check on Tate." He placed both cups on the bedside table and lowered himself carefully into the seat beside her bed. "Ella Tate was a troubled teenager, mixed with a bad crowd but when her parents died, she went to live with her brother and seems to have straightened out her life. Her brother is a Navy Seal and when deployed she is on her own, no other family. I gather he is away now and assume that's why she planned to spend Christmas with Sky's family. I'd like to interview her and see what's going on in her head. Her story reads more like fiction than fact."

Jenna sighed. "Wolfe is concerned. From the blood spatter on her clothes, she may have hurt her friend but apart from that, we have nothing." She chewed on her bottom lip, thinking. "I've called him four times and he's not picking up. That's not like him and why haven't his calls been diverted to your phone?"

"I guess because they're being diverted to Webber's." Kane shrugged. "I'm not too sure why he isn't getting back to you."

Realization slammed into her. "I *know* why. Webber is out with Walters searching for the victim or her car. There's no signal out that far from town and I guess Rowley has the satellite phone in his truck. I'll try again later. Once they come around the bend and head past the road leading to the meat processing plant, they'll get reception."

"I'll use the radio in your truck to contact them. I doubt they are far from Walter's cruiser." Kane pushed to his feet. "Where are your keys?"

Jenna opened the drawer beside her and pulled out her key fob. "Here. Be careful on the steps."

She waited patiently for him to pull on his coat and pull the hood over his woolen hat before venturing outside with Duke firmly at his heels. Kane was walking easier now but could not hide the serious headaches he suffered the moment he went outside in the cold. After five minutes he returned and she could hear him shaking the snow from his coat and removing his boots. She picked up her coffee and sipped. Moments later, he stepped into her room.

"They haven't found a trace of the missing woman or vehicle. No sightings from the chopper. The chopper searched for miles in all directions and has now returned to base. The snowplow has cleared a few miles in both directions of the coordinates the truck driver gave Rowley." Kane sat down and reached for his coffee. "The snowmobile guys located the woods and the old barn mentioned in the statement as well. They cleared a path to the trees along the fence line but found nothing stuck on the wire."

Jenna sighed. "There should be fibers on the wire if her coat was stuck as she said, unless the snow washed it off."

"Not likely the snow would make a difference. Webber checked it out and I doubt he'd miss evidence." He sighed. "They've been out there for hours, I told them to call it a day and return to the office. The chopper will be out again at first light with the rest of the team to search but the chances of finding anything with it snowing will be impossible."

Jenna nodded. "Thanks. I figure Rowley will be checking in soon. I don't envy him his job."

Moments later Jenna's cellphone pealed. She snatched it up and put it on speaker. "What have you got for me, Rowley?"

"The last time Mrs. Paul had contact with Sky was at 11:00 p.m. She called to say she had reached the Blackwater Roadhouse and was getting gas and something to eat. She was upset."

Jenna exchanged a look with Kane. "Did she say why?"

"Yeah, they had an argument about Sky's brother. She didn't go into details but said it was pretty heated. Sky told her mom she wished she could drive away and leave Ella at the roadhouse."

"We'll need Sky's cellphone number. If it's turned on we might be able to trace it and locate her."

"I have the details in the report. I'm at the office and I'll send the file now. I've gotten a BOLO out on Sky, her car and the description of the man Ella gave me. I'm writing a media report and will call it in now. Any calls will be diverted to your cellphone, ma'am. Someone might have seen something. Is there anything else you need me to do, ma'am?"

Jenna tapped her bottom lip, thinking. "Have you seen Wolfe this afternoon?"

"Yeah." Rowley sucked in a breath. *"He's at the Paul residence, taking blood samples, I believe, to crossmatch the blood found on Ella Tate."*

Jenna heaved a sigh of relief. "Walters and Webber are heading back to the office. Once they've had lunch, send Webber over to the ME's office to assist Wolfe. You can close up. There's another blizzard forecast."

"Do you want me to ask Wolfe to track the cellphones or call the Blackwater Roadhouse and follow up?" Rowley sounded apprehensive.

Jenna glanced at Kane. "No, that's fine. Kane will be able to track the cellphones from here. I'll call the Blackwater Roadhouse and follow up on the argument. If it was bad enough for Sky to mention it to her mom, someone might have heard them." She turned her head away and coughed. "Could I ask you a personal favor?"

"Sure."

"Could you pick up my meds from the pharmacy on the way home?"

"Yes, ma'am." The line went dead.

Her cellphone and Kane's ringtones went off in unison. "That will be the file." She smiled at Kane. "Go work your magic."

"Yes, ma'am."

CHAPTER NINE

It was a nightmare. The heaviness of limbs and the inability to open her eyes had Sky convinced nothing was real. She tried to wake but just as in her childhood night terrors, her eyes refused to open. Somewhere just out of reach she could hear the soft murmur of voices, and bright lights shone red against her eyelids. She tried to speak but her mouth refused to form words. Her ears made a strange buzzing sound and she could hear a slow beep, beep, beep close by.

She tried to rationalize her situation. The memory of the man at the side of the road, the pain in her head, then waking up in the hospital and being told she was going to have an operation. She remembered the headache then the floating sensation after the nurse injected something into the tube in her arm. If she could remember all these things, she sure wasn't dreaming. *Why can't I open my eyes?*

The voices came closer and a familiar smell smashed another memory into her mind—but was it a memory or a bad dream? She remembered the smell of the man who'd hit her and dragged her into his truck. In sheer panic, she used every ounce of strength but she could not as much as flutter her eyelids. Someone touched her face, a gentle touch, almost a caress, her head moved from side to side then she heard a voice.

"I know you can hear me." The man leaned over her. "Isn't this fun? You must be enjoying the drugs, well some of them at least." He chuckled. "I can do whatever I please. I can cut you or pull out every one of your fingernails and you'll just have to lie there and take it. Does that scare you, Sky?"

Inside, Sky was screaming. Terror made her heart race so fast the monitor sounded an alarm. Someone would come, they had to. She heard soft footsteps and from his voice, it was the nurse.

"Is everything okay?" He moved closer and cool fingers pressed against her jugular. "She may be allergic to the drugs."

"Nah." The man's voice seemed closer now. "She's just excited to see me, is all."

Terror gripped Sky and she tried to call out and tell the nurse she was not okay, but she could not move a muscle. What was happening to her? Then she heard a chuckle and hot onion breath brushed her face. She wanted to turn away but every muscle had frozen.

"He can't help you, Sky. I own him." The man bent close and whispered in her ear. "I might keep you for two or three days, or a lifetime, before I kill you. Won't that be fun?"

CHAPTER TEN

Monday

Kane's patience was at an end. He wanted—no, needed—to get back to work. Being holed up inside the house twenty-four seven was driving him crazy. He'd spent all Sunday tracing cellphones and doing whatever else he could to aid the investigation, but he needed to get out for a while. The search for Sky Paul had come up with big fat zero. The search team had checked all the outlying factories and found no signs of life. All had shut down for the holidays. Snowdrifts of well over six feet deep covered both sides of the highway and with more forecast, they had no chance of finding Sky or her car until the melt.

After finishing a punishing weight training session, he aimed a few experimental kicks at the punching bag and his injured knee held up just fine. Although the reconstruction had compromised his flexibility, with a few adjustments to his stance he would still be able to kick hard enough to take someone down. The pivots would be a problem, though. With a reconstructed knee and repaired tendons he would never be one hundred per cent fit again. "I'll just have to punch harder." He smashed his fists into the bag and didn't hear Jenna walk into the gym.

"If you punch any harder the bag will split." She gave him a long considering stare. "You okay?"

"Nope." He grabbed a towel from the bench and wiped the sweat from his face. "I'm going stir crazy. I'd like to get back to work now you're feeling better."

"What about the headaches?" Jenna narrowed her gaze at him. "You haven't been outside for any long period of time to test if you can handle the cold yet."

Kane shrugged and looked at his hands. "I have. I slipped out to help Rowley with the horses this morning." He smiled. "Trust me, it's no worse than before and if I wear a woolen cap under my hoodie it keeps my head warm."

"I can't stop you, Dave, but please take it easy for your first day back and take Duke with you or he'll figure you've left him again." Jenna rubbed the dog's ears. "He's worried about you."

Kane looked at the sad eyes looking up at him and smiled. "Don't worry, Duke. I'll take you with me." He looked back at Jenna. "Anything special you want me to do?"

"Why don't you interview Ella Tate at the hospital? She's being treated for exposure, so we have an excuse to keep her there without charging her." Jenna dropped onto the bench and looked up at him. "The doctor hasn't mentioned releasing her yet, so we have another day at least." She sighed. "Wolfe should have analyzed the blood samples he took from her by now."

Kane hung the towel around his neck and sat down beside her. "It's no secret it's Sky Paul's blood, the Tate girl admitted as much." He mopped at his face. "With nothing coming up on their cellphones, and no reports of anyone seeing Sky or her car, if what she said is true the killer could have destroyed the SIMs and dumped the car in a million places. Apart from the waterholes alongside the river, there are mineshafts all over the area. Search and rescue have checked the industrial buildings, and they'll keep on looking for another couple of days, but they don't hold out much hope. In this weather, if her vehicle is out there we won't locate it until the melt." He rubbed his temples.

"Not with more blizzards forecast, that's for sure." Jenna frowned. "I know you'll hate me saying this but I still think it's too early for you to return to work. Humor me and give it half a day to see how you go. There's more bad weather due this afternoon and you might get stuck in town."

"If that happened, I'd bunk with Rowley." He turned to look at Jenna's worried expression. "Okay, I'll go into the office after breakfast and be back before two."

"That sounds like a plan. Now you're ready to go back to work, I guess you'll be moving back into your cottage?" She pushed her hair behind one ear and raised both eyebrows in question.

Not wanting to ruin their close friendship, Kane stared at the floor, concentrating on the swirls in the polished timber and trying to find the right words. He remembered how close he had gotten to Jenna but it was more like a pleasant memory than the budding relationship they had enjoyed a couple of months ago. The image of his wife, Annie, drifted through his mind and his stomach gave a little twist. The short-term memory loss suffered due to his recent head injury had only involved his time in Black Rock Falls, and the car bombing and watching his wife die was as if it had happened yesterday. *I feel like a married man.*

His memory of the last year had returned but the pain of losing Annie was like a raw patch on his heart. Sure, he enjoyed living in Jenna's house but right now, he needed his own space as well. He wanted time alone to get his head straight. All his recollections had jumbled together and the last thing he wanted was to hurt his best friend. "Yeah, I'll move back to the cottage as soon as you're ready to return to work. Rowley has offered to stay on and help me with the horses for a couple more days."

"Darn." Jenna laughed and gave him a playful punch on the arm. "I was just getting used to washing your smelly socks."

"I don't have smelly socks." Kane frowned at her. "Do I?"

CHAPTER ELEVEN

After breakfast, Kane waved Duke into the back seat of his truck, slid behind the wheel, placed his go cup of coffee in the holder and turned the heater up full blast. His dog was over possessive and leaving him behind wasn't an option. The bloodhound had stuck to him like glue the moment he'd pulled on his coat. Last Saturday, the short trip to his cottage had resulted in Duke howling like the end of the world was coming and tearing at the front door. Jenna was not impressed. He turned in his seat and patted Duke on the head. "I hope you'll be able to cope with the cold weather." He had bundled him up in a thick black doggy coat, one of four Jenna had purchased after seeing Duke's teeth chattering, and had brought along a thick thermal blanket to cover him. "I'll have to leave you in the car when I go into the hospital, so you'd better be good."

The snowplow had driven through over half an hour earlier and should have cleared a path into town by now. He waited for Rowley to drive past then followed—although he was heading straight to the hospital to interview Ella Tate, Jenna had insisted Rowley keep an eye on him. He smiled to himself. She didn't know him as well as she thought. He would never get behind the wheel of a car if he had any doubt of his capabilities and the specialist had given him the green light. His head was fine and the headaches would ease with time. *Unless someone else takes a shot at me.*

*

Ella Tate's expression of horror when Kane walked into her hospital room spoke volumes. He found her sitting by the window and she had frozen, as if suspended in time, at the sight of him. He figured, from her wide-eyed expression and the way she gripped the arms of the chair, she hadn't recognized him as a deputy. Her reaction to him as a potential intruder gave him the impression the story she had given Rowley had been the truth. "Miss Tate, I'm Deputy David Kane. I'd like to have a few words with you, if you don't mind?"

He removed his gloves, unzipped his thick overcoat and eased it off his shoulders, then tossed it onto a chair. The badge on his regulation jacket was now clearly visible and he noticed a subtle change in her posture. Taking his time, for her to relax, he pulled out his notepad and pen, then dragged a chair to the window and sat opposite her. "How are you feeling today?"

"I'm okay." Ella blinked a few times as if she was having a problem focusing.

Kane smiled. "That's good to hear. Did I startle you when I came in just now?"

"Yeah, you look like the man who attacked Sky and chased me. I thought he'd come back to kill me too." She gripped the blanket covering her legs so hard her knuckles whitened. "Have you found her yet?"

Kane shook his head and made his voice as conversational as possible. "Not yet but we have search and rescue out looking for her." He leaned back in his chair. He would ask her about the man who attacked her a bit later when she calmed down. "What can you tell me about the time leading up to the incident? Why were you and Sky driving to Black Rock Falls so late?"

"My brother was deployed and will be away for the holidays, so Sky's family invited me to stay with them for Christmas. I've never had a vacation in Black Rock Falls, so I jumped at the chance." She sighed. "We were going to come down at the weekend but then Sky's mom called and told her a blizzard was forecast, so we left straight away."

"You drove straight through from Billings? That's a six-hour drive. You're both at college there, is that right?"

"Yeah, we're at MSU." Ella shrugged. "We stopped for gas and to grab a burger. We would have made it if Sky hadn't insisted on stopping." She took a deep breath and gave Kane a long hard look. "You sure look like the man who killed Sky."

Kane nodded. "So, he was big like me, six five? Or like me in looks?"

"Same size, dark clothes, wearing a woolen cap with a hoodie over the top like you." She ran her gaze over him, examining him closely. "Big hands like yours and he made the same swishing sound as he walked."

"Okay. That's good." Kane made a few notes, just to act as if everything was routine, then he lifted his gaze. "In case you're wondering, it wasn't me. Today is my first day out for six weeks. I've been holed up at the sheriff's house recuperating. I smashed my knee and had to have it repaired and I think you would have noticed the limp."

"That's good to hear." Ella went beet red. "Oh, not about your knee. I'm sorry. I meant about it not being you."

Kane shrugged. "That's okay. Let's get back to the night Sky went missing. When was the last stop for gas?"

"Blackwater." Ella picked at her fingernails. "We had a stupid argument about her brother." She glared at him in a flash of anger. "She told me not to get involved with him. I couldn't believe she would ban me from seeing him. We've been roomies since we started at MSU." She looked away. "It was as if an army brat wasn't good enough for her family."

So you killed her. Kane rubbed his chin. The mood swings worried him and she had exhibited the same behavior during the interview with Wolfe, yet her reaction to him had seemed real enough. *Unless she is a very good actor.* "I gather you resolved the problem before you'd gotten back on the road?'

"Yeah. What could I do? I told her I'd stay away." She sighed. "Don't you want to know what happened?"

Kane shook his head. "No, I've read your statement. I just need a few more details. You can't remember his vehicle at all?"

"Not really." She stared at the floor.

Aware people often blocked out terrifying events or accidents, he tried to jog her memory. "Close your eyes and try to remember driving toward the vehicle."

"It was dark. He had flashers going. It was difficult to see his vehicle."

Kane smiled at her. "That's great. You said he was a big man, so how did he appear beside his vehicle? Taller or the same?"

"I'm not sure." Ella frowned. "He was sort of bent over so his hood fell over his face. "

"Was he leaning against the door?"

"No, he was leaning against—it was a pickup." Her eyes popped open and she smiled at him. "A big light-colored pickup."

Kane nodded. She appeared genuinely surprised she had remembered. "Okay. You said he was carrying an ax and laid it on the seat." He frowned. "An ax is pretty big and so was he, and yet he managed to lean into the car between the steering wheel and seat with an ax in one hand, is that right?"

"He had an ax." Ella closed her eyes again then opened them. "It was a small ax. Like about this long." She held her hands about one foot apart.

Kane nodded. "Was it just a blade or was it a different shape, like a hammer on one side for instance?"

"I only saw it for a split second but I know it was metal." Her expression became solemn. "It went like this: we stopped, Sky opened her window and he hit her with the ax, opened the door, dragged her out, dropped the ax on the seat then tried to grab me. He was big and couldn't fit all the way into the car. I had time to open the door and run."

"Okay. It was probably a hatchet from what you're describing. An ax has a long handle." Kane made notes. "So you don't really know if Sky is dead, do you? She called to you later, didn't she? How do you know he'd killed her?"

"I don't, not for sure, but I heard her scream." Ella's eyes filled with tears. "It was terrible, like he was killing her. I couldn't help her, could I? I was terrified. He threatened to hurt me too."

"Not many people would take on a man of my size carrying a weapon." Kane wanted to be sympathetic, but visions of Jenna luring a killer away from him to save his life slid into his memory. Friends performed heroic acts when necessary and the missing girl was Ella's best friend. He needed to push a little and see if a dark side was hiding beneath her devastated façade. "Did you think to maybe follow him back to the road and see for yourself? It was pitch black, as you mentioned in your statement, and the brush is thick along the side of the road. It would have been easy to hide in the ditch beside the road."

"Really? Are you some kind of jerk?" Ella's eyes flashed with anger. "Do you honestly believe anyone would put themselves knowingly in danger like that? He had an ax, or hatchet or whatever. I'm just not that brave, sorry."

Concerned the woman was suffering from PTSD, he nodded. "That's fine. You mentioned planning to stay with Sky's parents. If they are still willing to have you, are you willing to remain with them until we find Sky? Right now, we would prefer you to stay in town. We'll need you to identify the man who attacked her."

"Yeah, I know Sky's family and I'd like to be here to find out what happened to her." She sighed. " don't really want to stay alone in my brother's apartment."

Kane folded his notebook and pushed it with his pen into his pocket. "Okay, I'll speak to the doctor and call in on Mrs. Paul. Thank you for your help."

"Find Sky." Ella lifted her chin.

Kane opened the door and glanced at her. "I'll do my best."

In the hallway, he nodded to the deputy on duty outside Ella's door and made his way out through the security doors. He ran into an angry man, who introduced himself as Sky's father.

"What are you doing about my daughter and why can't I see Ella?" Mr. Paul's face turned a nasty shade of purple. "What the hell is going on here?"

Kane dropped his voice to just above a whisper. He'd discovered long ago that people tended to quieten down to listen if he spoke softly. "The sheriff has search and rescue out looking for her and we have a BOLO out on her and her vehicle. We are waiting for people to call in sightings. At this moment, we don't have any suspects but the sheriff has every resource working on the case. Ella is currently in protective custody but as soon as I speak to the sheriff, I'll see if we can make arrangements with the doctor to have her released into your care, if you like?"

"Damn sure, I'd like." Mr. Paul glared at him. "It's bad enough my daughter is missing, maybe murdered, but believing Ella is involved is crazy."

Kane pulled out his cellphone and waved it at him. "Just give me five."

He walked out of earshot and called Jenna. "I've spoken to Ella Tate. She's a strange one and displayed mood swings but that could be due to PTSD. She is defensive and angry. That's not the usual behavior I'd expect to see in a person who has just murdered their best friend and I can't imagine how she managed to hide both body and vehicle without a trace." He sighed. "I pushed her buttons but her story didn't change from her statement and I asked questions from all angles. I doubt she's involved. I believe it happened like she said and I don't figure she is a flight risk."

"I'm not sure we should cut her entirely loose just yet. She is the only witness." Jenna's voice sounded husky from her cold. *"Sky's mother called and I gave her an update on the search for Sky. She is anxious to speak to Ella. She can't understand why we're keeping her at the hospital without visitors. I guess if you're convinced Ella is telling the truth, we can let her go on the proviso she stays with the Pauls."*

"Sky's father is here now and willing to take her." Kane leaned against the cold wall and stared into space. "Do you want me to speak to the doctor and see if she's okay to leave?"

"No, that's okay, Wolfe spoke to him already. Ella is physically good to go but from what Wolfe said about her, he suggested she should see a shrink." Jenna cleared her throat. *"He's already arranged for her discharge from the hospital. All you need to do is send the Blackwater deputies home and explain the terms of release to Mr. Paul."*

"Roger that." He rubbed his chin. "Did you ask Wolfe what tests the doc wanted done on you?"

"Not yet. If you're dropping by his office maybe, you can ask him. Tell him I said it was okay. Then I think you should head home. Rowley and Walters have everything covered at the office. Nothing is happening in town, everyone is inside waiting for the next blizzard. Rowley diverted the media and BOLO hotline calls to my cellphone." She sighed. *"If Rowley gets stuck in town he can get to his home from the office and we can handle the horses tonight."*

Kane smiled. It was as if she was reading his mind. A persistent pain throbbed in his head and his knee ached after the long walk—not that he would admit it. "I can manage alone. I'll grab some comfort food on the way home from Aunt Betty's Café; the cold weather makes me hungry."

"I can hear your stomach rumbling from here." Jenna chuckled. *"See you later."*

CHAPTER TWELVE

Somewhere in the darkness, Sky could hear someone humming. The return to consciousness was immediate and she recognized the hiss and beep of machines. Fear and sheer panic grabbed her as she remembered the man who'd kidnapped her. Hopelessness surrounded her. She had to tell someone and staying conscious was her only hope. Sensing someone close by, she did not attempt to move and until she discovered who it was, playing possum was her only advantage.

She lifted her eyelids a crack and could see a male nurse in theatre scrubs bending over her. He lifted one of her arms and washed it. After drying it, he placed it back down before continuing to bathe her in a professional manner. *Okay, I can deal with a sponge bath.* With infinite care not to cause attention, she moved her gaze down her body, surprised to see the sides of the bed missing and the restraints from her wrists.

Her heart picked up a beat and she could hear the monitor beeps increasing in speed. The nurse would notice she had woken and give her more zombie drugs. She forced her muscles to relax and the beeps slowed a little. Too late: he stopped humming and examined her face. Panic gripped her as he moved along the side of the bed, wiping a warm cloth over her chest. It took every ounce of her willpower but she managed to keep her breathing slow and steady.

The nurse dried her, pulled down her hospital gown and covered her with a blanket. He picked up his things and headed for the door.

The room fell into darkness with only the glow from the machines lighting the room. Trembling with the thought of enduring the taunting of her kidnapper again, she waited until the nurse's footsteps faded and turned her head to look at the bed beside her. It was empty, stripped down to the mattress. The young woman with the pink fingernails had gone. She eased up onto one elbow, then sat up slowly. Her head ached and she touched her face, running her fingers over the lump on her cheek. Her nose hurt and she recalled the blast of pain in the car. The memory of that night slammed into her. The man they'd stopped to help had hit her then thrown her onto the side of the highway. She recalled crawling along the frozen grass calling out for Ella. *Where is Ella?*

A wave of dizziness rolled over her and the monitors made strange sounds. What if she set off an alarm and alerted the nurse? *I have to get to a phone and call my mom.* She slid off the bed onto wobbly legs and scanned the room. The machines would be easy to silence; all she had to do was turn them off at the wall. Then she noticed the machine attached to the needle in her arm. She had seen one of those before, when her grandma was ill. Without a second thought, she dragged the needle out of her arm. The sticky connectors went next. Free to move around, she found a tiny flashlight used for examinations and made her way to the door using the wall for support.

After peering into the shadowy hallway and listening for a moment, she eased outside. The place was as silent as a tomb and so cold. Using the flashlight, she crept along the hallway and came to a room. Terrified of finding someone inside, she pressed her ear to the door. No sound came from within and no light shone under the door. She took a deep breath, gripped the door handle and turned.

The door swung open to reveal a small kitchenette. Metal cupboards, like lockers, along one wall and a table and chairs in the center. A clock on the wall told her it was a little after five. She turned and made her way back to the hallway. Shadows seemed to loom up around the small beam of light as she made her way slowly into the unknown. Anyone could be there in the blackness, watching her and waiting to drag her back to her room.

With her heart pounding as if it might burst, she moved slowly, step by step, through the gloomy building. The small flashlight slid along the hallway, turning shadows into imaginary men trying to grab her. She hated the dark and the complete lack of windows made the passageway close in on her. A rush of panic hit her in a nauseous wave and she leaned against the cold wall, breathing out great puffs of steam. The idea of being underground without escape terrified her.

At the end of the hall, she stumbled through the open door of a small office but no phone sat on the desk. Disbelief and dismay twisted her gut with every step. Nothing resembled a hospital. No windows, no wards and the only thing the same was the antiseptic smell. There was no way out, no stairs or doors, and her only choice was to keep moving along the hallway. An icy chill underfoot made her shiver and her feet ached with the cold. Her footsteps seemed to echo off the walls and anyone close by would hear her. The pulse beating loud in her ears throbbed in time with the pain in her head but she kept going.

The flashlight hit two large aluminum swing doors and the sight of her reflection made her jump back. With no other exit in sight, surely the way out had to be through there. She pushed on the doors and peered into the gloom. The room had a peculiar smell. She eased inside and allowed the doors to swing shut behind her then lifted the flashlight.

The beam moved over a gurney covered with a lumpy white sheet. She took a few steps closer—and froze. Terror gripped her by the throat. She couldn't breathe. From one side of the gurney hung a thin pale arm. Unable to move, Sky trembled as she moved the flashlight down the arm, over a limp hand… to the bright pink fingernails.

CHAPTER THIRTEEN

After speaking with the manager of the Blackwater Roadhouse, Jenna discovered the argument between Sky and Ella had been so loud they'd been asked to leave. The thought of Sky driving when she was mad worried her. Perhaps the argument had clouded the young woman's judgement when she'd decided to stop to help the man who had apparently broken down. In Ella's statement, she had begged her not to stop but to call a tow truck. She scanned her notes on the case for a moment then followed the smell of freshly brewed coffee into the kitchen. To her delight, Kane had set up the coffee maker before he left to tend the horses with Rowley.

She opened the refrigerator door and caught sight of a number of plastic containers with the Aunt Betty's Café logo on the tops and each marked with their contents. It would seem Kane had overruled her decision to cook dinner and collected enough takeout to feed the three of them for a few days. The sound of a vehicle approaching caught her attention and she closed the door and made her way to the front of the house. Under the floodlights, she recognized the ME's truck. *What's Wolfe doing here?*

When Emily jumped from the vehicle and scooted off toward the stable, Jenna pulled open the front door and waited for Wolfe to climb the steps onto the porch. "Emily is in a hurry, what's wrong?"

"Nothing's wrong, she wanted to ask Kane something, is all." Wolfe stamped away the snow, wiped his feet, stepped inside and removed his boots. "I spoke to him before. He said it would be okay." He shrugged out of his coat.

Jenna took it and hung it on a peg. "Come into the kitchen. The coffee is just about ready." She led the way.

"Great. I needed to discuss a few things with you in private." Wolfe dropped into a chair facing the door and leaned on the kitchen table. "I'll cut to the chase before the others arrive. You asked me to give Kane the details of the tests the doctor ordered but as they are very specific and personal, I figured I should speak to you personally."

Perplexed, Jenna poured the coffee, added the fixings for both cups and placed them on the table. She dropped into a chair and looked at him. "The doc said she was looking for 'nasties' so I gather she wanted to eliminate anything unusual."

"Like HIV, hepatitis, syphilis and herpes?" Wolfe turned his coffee cup in circles and met her gaze. "She did an HLA test as well, and blood group." He sighed. "I would expect a full blood count, iron levels, vitamin B12 maybe, but not the others."

Jenna leaned back in her chair. "Maybe she thinks I'm promiscuous."

"You have the opposite reputation, Jenna." Wolfe frowned. "The HLA test is at genetic level, which set my alarm bells ringing. You may have a different face and name but nothing changes your DNA. And the people you were involved with have a sample of it." He looked at her. "I know it was Viktor Carlos. I worked with the team hacking his organization. We took you out of play when we discovered he had one of his people hacking databases searching for you and they included a DNA profile."

A wave of nausea hit Jenna. After so long could there really be someone left alive in Viktor Carlos's cartel searching for her? As DEA Undercover Agent Avril Parker, she had exposed his racket and sent him to jail. A couple of years later a rival underworld organization had wiped out his entire gang. She gaped at Wolfe in disbelief. "You knew all this and didn't tell me?"

"My information was that every member of his cartel was dead." Wolfe sipped his coffee but his gray eyes never left her face. "Problem is, when something like this happens, we have to figure his family has started up again. A son or maybe a cousin and you know they'll carry a vendetta against someone for many years. You went deep into their organization, didn't you? They trusted you."

Memories like bad dreams flooded into her mind. She had given everything and almost lost her soul bringing down a monster. How would she ever forget? She nodded. "Yeah, they trusted me like one of the family."

"I know how difficult that must have been, Jenna." He cleared his throat. "I know you married his brother and had blood tests done, right?"

"Yeah, did you have to remind me? I only survived because I knew it wasn't real. They treated their wives like property, or brood mares. If he'd found my stash of contraceptive pills, he would have killed me." Realization hit her like a sledgehammer. "Oh, Jesus, their family doctor did blood tests."

"And has your DNA profile." Wolfe placed his cup on the table. "I'll give Doctor Mavis Weaver's name to my contact and have her checked out. Do you remember the name of the doctor you went to see back then?"

"No. I don't remember him telling me his name." Jenna chewed on her fingers. "Can you hide the DNA results from her?"

"Yeah, I plan to but if this is who we think it is I wouldn't have gotten all the blood." Wolfe frowned at her. "She would have sent it away for a second test and right now I can't find out where she sent it. From now on, Jenna, no blood tests unless I do them, okay?"

"Sure. I didn't think. I've slipped into this life so well, I forgot about my past." The front door opened and she could hear voices. "Does Kane know the details of my mission?"

"No, and he won't hear them from me, although he has clearance." He reached across the table and squeezed her hand. "He's a good man and you know by now you can trust him with your life. It wouldn't hurt to explain the potential threat without going into details. Maybe beef up the security around here. Leave it with me; I'll get someone from HQ to come out." He withdrew his hand. "I'll keep you advised."

"Hi, Jenna." Emily strolled into the room, cheeks rosy from the cold. "How are you feeling? You still look pale."

Jenna forced a smile. "I'm fine. I'm going back to work on Wednesday."

She noticed Kane's concerned expression and sighed. *There is no way I can keep all this from him. He knows, just by looking at me, that something is wrong.*

CHAPTER FOURTEEN

Shocked, Sky gaped at the gurney, unable to move. Her chest tightened, making it difficult to breathe. A faint whistling some distance away snapped her back into action. She turned and moved the flashlight along the wall, searching for a place to hide. An exit close to the gurney had a card scanner fixed to the wall to one side of it. Her legs shook with fear. The whistling was coming from behind that door. The beam slid over a huge aluminum refrigerator, then a glass-topped entrance came into view. She crept across the floor and pushed into the room. A strong smell of antiseptic hit her and, terrified at what she might find inside, she sucked in a trembling breath then scanned the area with the flashlight.

The room contained a sink and, on one side, a floor-to-ceiling cupboard with a sliding door took up the entire wall. It opened silently and she peered inside. Blankets and sheets filled the shelves alongside containers of different sizes. She grabbed a blanket and wrapped it around herself, then wedged herself into a small space beside a broom. After turning off the flashlight, she shut herself inside.

The whistling had gotten louder by the second. Panic gripped her, twisting her belly into knots. If her kidnapper had come to kill her, he would find her bed empty and start searching. Her knees trembled so hard, she had to squeeze them together to stop them rattling against the door. The whistling was closer now. She peeked through a crack in the cupboard and stopped breathing. From her position, she could see the red light on the front of the refrigerator in the other room.

A beam of light burst through the exit and the next moment the lights came on. She recognized the big man at once as the man who had kidnapped her. He wore the same black hoodie covering his face. The whistling stopped for a few seconds as he pinned the door back and went to collect the gurney. He pushed the woman's body through the exit and into the hallway. As he moved away, the whistling started again and Sky could hear his footsteps and the squeak of the gurney's wheels echoing in the distance.

The open door was a way out and her one chance to escape. Moving as quietly as possible, she left her hiding place and crept across the room and out into the hallway. Ahead, the passageway went straight for a few yards then made a sharp turn to the left. Icy coldness seeped through the blanket and her short panting breaths sent clouds of steam into the air. Panic-stricken that the man would be back soon, she slid the flashlight into the pocket of the scrubs and pulled the blanket over her head. The way out had to be close by but she figured if she could hear him, the moment he stopped whistling, he would be able to hear her as well. She clenched her jaw and followed him.

Reaching the corner, she edged her way along the wall and took a quick peek. The man was nowhere in sight but she could see an open door to the outside and snow piled up on each side. Rather than the crisp clean air she expected, a heavy odor hung in the air.

A loud whirring sound followed by the unmistakable noise of heavy machinery blasted her ears. Not caring if she made a noise, she sprinted for the open door, then flattened her body against the wall and looked outside. Snow had lightly dusted a cleared walkway lit by a row of lights. She could make out footprints and the imprint from the wheels of the gurney. On one side was a high brick wall that ended some yards ahead. She had no choice but to see where the pathway came out. With her heartbeat thrashing in her ears, she ran slipping and sliding along the path, using one hand on the wall for support.

The grinding noise had gotten louder and a stench like death wafted toward her. She reached the end of the wall and froze on the spot. Not ten yards away the man was hoisting the naked body of a young woman onto a conveyer belt. The wide belt carried the woman to an opening in a huge machine with whirring blades like a wood chipper.

Horrified, Sky pushed her knuckles against her mouth to stop a scream of protest. Black spots danced before her eyes and she blinked, not believing what she was seeing. As the body moved slowly into the gaping maw of the machine, she gagged at the terrible noise and vomited bile.

Trembling with fear and disgust, she backed into the cover of shadows and took in her surroundings. She had to get away. On the left, walls rose out of the shadows, dark like a prison. Ahead, a frosty path led to a parking lot not twenty yards away. A white pickup with the windshield thick with ice sat all alone, and beyond it the safety of darkness. Could she make it there before the man had finished his ghoulish task?

After taking one, quick look at him, she took off at a run. Great clouds of steam escaped her lips as she gasped in freezing air. Unable to get traction on the ice, she made it a few yards before the sound of heavy footsteps thundered behind her.

He had seen her.

She screamed and, lungs bursting, ran for her life. The parking lot had a low fence, snow piled on poles connected with loops of ice-covered chain. The footsteps crunched behind her and she screamed again, the frigid air burning her throat. He grabbed at her, tearing the blanket from her shoulders.

"Give up. You can't get away from me." She recognized the voice of the man who'd kidnapped her. "Come easy or I'll finish you right now."

Sky glanced over one shoulder and glared at him. "Get away from me. I saw what you did." She ran at the fence, leaping over the chain.

She landed hard on her knees, sliding across the ice, but scrambled up again and tried to run. He was on her in seconds. Pain slammed into her head and the metallic taste of blood spilled over her tongue. The ground came up fast and her face landed in a pile of fresh snow. Cold seeped through her thin clothes and she tried to speak but her mouth refused to work. A snowflake landed on her outstretched arm, lacy and perfect. The frozen landscape slipped into oblivion and the light around her faded. *I'm going to die.*

CHAPTER FIFTEEN

Tuesday

A cold crisp morning greeted Jenna and she woke feeling surprisingly well. Since she had fallen ill, Kane would tend the horses, work out and shower before knocking on her door to deliver a steaming cup of coffee. She sat up in bed, pushed the hair from her eyes and smiled at him. "You're spoiling me. I used to wake up at five every morning and now I lounge around until it's almost seven. It's going to be a struggle to get up in time for work tomorrow."

"You'll soon drop back into your old routine." He placed the cup on her bedside table. "Right now, you can't work out and I have Rowley helping me tend the horses, so you don't need to come outside in the cold and dark." He turned to head for the door. "I'll have breakfast ready in ten."

"Dave." Jenna reached for her coffee. "I didn't get a chance to speak with you last night, with Rowley here, but a problem has come up. Wolfe gave me some info you need to know. Can you hang back after he leaves this morning so I can bring you up to date?"

"About the Sky Paul case?" Kane paused in the doorway.

Jenna shook her head. "No, this is personal."

"You're not ill, are you?" Concern etched Kane's expression. "If so, I have time now. He's at the cottage."

"I'm fine. This is something from before we met." Jenna gave him what she hoped was a meaningful look. "I'll explain later."

"Roger that." Kane strolled out the door.

During breakfast, Jenna discussed the daily running of the office. Apart from the Sky Paul case, her deputies had to cope with the usual day-to-day problems in town. Rowley reported a large number of vehicle collisions due to the bad weather, and the usual complaints. She eyed him over the rim of her cup, then placed the cup on the table. "Contact the Department of Transport and see if they can spray more brine on the roads in town. They invested in more snowplows this year and are concentrating on keeping the highway clear, so maybe they need to be advised of the situation."

"Yes, ma'am, I'll get on to it right away." Rowley rose from the table, rinsed his plate and cup and placed them in the dishwasher. "We have people coming home for the holidays and I figured a public announcement to make sure they have chains or all-weather tires fitted to their vehicles would be beneficial."

Jenna nodded in agreement. "Yeah, and maybe add to stay indoors during a blizzard and keep off the roads unless necessary." She shook her head. "I can't imagine why people come here in winter. I would be taking a vacation somewhere warmer, if I had an option."

"Me too." Rowley smiled.

Jenna glanced at her notebook. Working away from the office was a pain, like dealing with problems second-hand. "Another thing, with the Sky Paul case, I'm thinking 'what if' as we have nothing to go on. What if the man Ella Tate saw wasn't alone?"

"Possible but if there was another man in the car wouldn't he have helped try and catch her?" Kane scooped eggs into his mouth. "Why do you figure there are two men involved?"

Jenna sighed. "Because Sky's vehicle vanished from sight and the man who attacked her had the keys."

"Most vehicles around this way carry some type of towing device." Rowley frowned. "It would be easy to hitch it to the back of his truck and tow it anywhere. It could be in another state by now."

Jenna sighed. "Yeah, search and rescue said much the same. The time between the incident and getting on scene was far too long." She looked at her deputies and shrugged. "It was just a thought."

"We could make a visit to the local recycling yards but they were told to be on the lookout for the missing vehicle." Kane cleared his throat. "Most have shut down over the holidays as well."

Jenna nodded. "It's worth a drive-by. If they're closed, the car could have been abandoned outside."

"I'll go take a look." Kane stood and refilled his cup. "But I figure search and rescue or the snowmobile team would have found it, even with the blizzard."

"I'll head into the office and open up." Rowley shrugged into his coat and looked at Kane expectantly. "The snowplow should have cleared the roads by now."

"I'll be in later. I have to drop into the ME's office to speak to Emily." Kane sat back in his chair, making it groan under his weight. "I promised to take her some information on profiling."

"Okay." Rowley nodded at Jenna and headed for the front door, stopping to pull on his boots.

Once the door closed, Jenna explained the blood test situation to Kane. "Wolfe is concerned about security and is contacting HQ."

"Don't be surprised if a chopper lands here with a specialist crew on board." Kane frowned. "They tend to move swiftly. I'll call Rowley and tell him I'm staying home today."

"It's no big deal, Dave." Jenna lifted her chin. "I managed just fine before you arrived. I'm armed and aware of a potential threat. I'm sure I'll make it until you come home at two." She sighed. "I can't see anyone risking an attack in daylight."

"That would depend on the threat." Kane's expression of concern spoke volumes. "Did Wolfe mention anything about hacking the doctor's computer?"

Jenna shook her head. "No, and I would say to do that legally would be difficult with the patient privilege laws."

"I doubt HQ will be waiting for a court order, somehow." Kane drummed his fingers on the table and smiled. "Wolfe told me you have information that's even above my pay grade, so they'll do one of two things—hack the doctor's computer to see who she is contacting, or come and take you out of the equation."

The thought of leaving her home, Kane, Wolfe, Rowley, Emily and her sisters hit her hard in the pit of the stomach. "I'm not leaving Black Rock Falls. You and the others are the only family I have now." She stared at him in disbelief. "I'll refuse to go. I nearly lost you once and I'm not losing you again."

"You won't have any choice."

CHAPTER SIXTEEN

It was with some reluctance Kane left the house with Duke on his heels. With a possible threat hanging over Jenna, the last thing he wanted to do was leave her alone at an isolated ranch. Her insistence she would carry her Glock in a shoulder holster did little to ease his worry. If an assassin got through her inadequate security system, she wouldn't have time to get to the safe room in the barn. Her ring when activated alerted his cellphone but he would be too far away to lend assistance in an emergency, yet she insisted on staying alone, giving the excuse that she would need to be available if Wolfe organized a team from HQ to update her security. Unconvinced his trip to the recycling yards was a priority he stood on the stoop for a few moments staring out across the landscape.

The overnight snow had flattened the view and the early morning rays of watery sun glistened like streaks of gold across the ice-covered grasslands. Winter in Black Rock Falls was a cruel beauty, turning the trees surrounding the perimeter of the house to black creaking menaces. The frozen snapping branches sounded like gunshots in the stillness. "A blanket of snow" well described the scene before him. The silence was as if nature had turned down the volume.

His boots crunched in the snow on his way to the garage. He started his truck, allowing the engine to idle, then strolled back to his snow-covered cottage. Icicles hung down from the gutters and frost covered the windows in swirling patterns. It reminded him of a gingerbread house. He turned over the keys in his palm then decided not to go inside, feeling as if it was an invasion of Rowley's privacy.

Later this afternoon, he would start to move his belongings out of Jenna's house. Rowley had already taken his horse from the stable and was making noises about being anxious to return home. Not that he blamed him. With his family returning home for the holidays, he would want to spend time with them, and then there was his dog. The plan had been for Rowley and the dog to move into the cottage, but they soon discovered Duke was a territorial creature and refused to allow another male dog inside.

Kane made his way back to his truck and backed out of the garage. He heard the whirr of chopper blades then a bird set down beside the corral, sending out more snow than a snowplow. Unsure of the identities of the occupants spilling out the door, he drove to the front of Jenna's house, slid from the seat and pulled out his weapon. One of the four men headed toward him and the other three hauled equipment out of the chopper. As the man approached, Kane aimed his pistol at the man's head. "Stop where you are."

"We're under orders, Deputy." The man lifted his hands.

Kane held his Glock steady. "Hold your cred packs out where I can see them."

"Sure." The man pulled out his military-issue cred pack and issued an order for the others to do the same. "Wolfe organized a security update for a Jane Doe. We can handle it from here, Deputy."

Kane scrutinized each man's credentials, and satisfied they were legit, holstered his weapon. "I don't think so. Wait here. I'll go speak with her."

He headed back up the steps and slipped inside to find Jenna, face ashen. "It's the guys from HQ here to install a new security system. I suggest you disguise yourself a bit, maybe cover your hair, put on sunglasses. They don't know who we are and referred to you as Jane Doe." He squeezed her shoulder. "I'll stay until they leave. I suggest you head over to the safe room. I'll come get you when they're done."

"Thank you. I'll slip out the back door. I'll call Rowley and tell him you'll be late. I don't want him figuring you've wrecked your truck and be heading back here." Jenna gave him a small smile, then jogged to her bedroom.

Kane opened the front door and gazed at the four men. "Okay, where do you want to start?"

"We'll need access to all rooms, to alarm the windows, and we'll be setting up a new perimeter silent alarm system."

Kane rubbed his chin. "That will take hours."

"Nah, one at most. We use wireless laser technology now, no wires and impervious to all weather conditions. Easy to use, fast to install. I'm told she has a CCTV screen array." He waved a little box. "This baby collects the data, sends an alert to as many cellphones as you like. We'll update the CCTV and be gone before you know it."

After hearing the back door open and shut, Kane waved him inside. "Okay, you're good to go."

Like him, Jenna had no photographs and in fact nothing personal on show in her house to identify her. Fortunately, the previous evening he'd moved her cruiser into the barn and fitted the chains, ready for her to drive to work on Wednesday morning.

The men moved with swift efficiency and, after explaining the system to Kane, left in a cloud of disturbed snow. He collected Jenna from the safe room. "That didn't take long."

"How do you know they haven't fitted cameras in every room or listening devices? I don't trust anyone." She dragged off her coat and tossed it onto a kitchen chair.

Kane shrugged. "I watched them, but we can do a sweep of the place if you like?"

"Oh yeah, I forgot you have all the gizmos." Jenna pulled a face. "I remember the day you arrived."

Kane chuckled. "So do I." He headed to his room and pulled out a suitcase. "Do you know how to use one of these?" He held up the headphones and scanner.

"Yeah, I remember." Jenna heaved a long sigh. "It seems like a lifetime ago. I can manage. Rowley will be waiting for you."

Kane handed her the equipment. "I'll explain the security system before I go. It's much easier than before and we can set it or deactivate it via our cellphones. I've added three numbers to the alarm, yours, Wolfe's and mine, just in case. They gave me three remotes to carry in our rigs. They'll recognize us when we drive in and won't trip the alarm. If there is a false alarm, you can send an automatic message to notify both of us." He led the way into the office with the array of screens. "Now you can pan the entire ranch and zoom in. I'm amazed they got all this done so quickly."

"It's great." She listened as he went over the details. "Okay, that's easy to understand. So you can activate the alarm again when you drive out?"

"Yep." Kane headed for the door. "If you do find any bugs, don't nuke them until Wolfe has looked at them. We need to know what or who we're dealing with." He turned at the door. "I'll call with an update on the recycling yards at lunchtime."

"Okay." She followed him out. "Drive safe."

CHAPTER SEVENTEEN

The hiss of the life support system filled the quiet room as he peered down at Sky. His need to silence her had ruined his plans. He should have been more careful; one punch had come close to killing her and had been no fun at all. After carrying her back inside and removing all evidence of her escape, he'd called the nurse back to work and explained how it was his fault she had fallen out of bed and hit her head. The well-trained and overpaid man had not said a word but set about making sure Sky would be okay.

Annoyed, he went back to his office and sat in front of his computer. His visit with his girlfriend on Saturday night had been adequate but she hardly filled his insatiable need. She was a means to an end and he could control her by telling her what she wanted to hear. He had become so skilled over the years he could charm anyone into believing anything he said. His life had become a web of skillfully told lies. Most of the time people were gullible and if he told them he could walk on water they would believe him.

If his current occupation hadn't been so lucrative in both money and satisfaction, he could have followed a different path. People believed him no matter what crimes he committed or lies he told. He had charm in spades and could talk his way out of trouble. After his father's death, he convinced his partner to sign over his business and bank account to him the week before he died. The idiot actually believed he would look after his family for him. Hell, he would rather cut their throats.

The thought made him chuckle but he quickly sobered. The urge to kidnap was getting strong again; the adrenaline rush was long gone from Sky's abduction. Now all he had to do was to find someone in the middle of winter in a blizzard. He logged in to his social media sites, scrolled through his many profiles and smiled. Several young people had made plans to return to Black Rock Falls for the holidays. He made a list and decided to take as many as possible; it was a long time until the spring break and he needed his hospital ward full.

Out of interest, he went to Sky's Facebook page and read the posts. At last, Ella Tate was online and trying to get a group together to search for her friend but had gotten no response. He went to her page to search through her images. He found she was staying with Sky's parents in Black Rock Falls and responded at once when he friended her. He went on to search for other suitable people to kidnap and the computer buzzed a message. Ella wanted his help to find Sky. He read it and smiled at his good fortune. *Oh yes, of course I will help you find your friend.*

CHAPTER EIGHTEEN

Frost crystals coated Kane's truck by the time he led the way from the recycler's yard in Black Rock Falls with Rowley close behind him. He inhaled, clearing his lungs of the smell of oil, grease and body odor. Winter had its own smell, crisp and clean. As he exhaled, a plume of steam surrounded him. He slid behind the wheel and started the engine. After a brief look around the yard, he'd examined both the crusher and shredder then had a chat to the proprietor, Chuck Burns. It had been a waste of time and their search had found no evidence. He glanced at Rowley, whose chapped lips and bright red cheeks mirrored most of the people in town. He idled the engine, and turned on the heater to defrost the windshield. At least the snow had stopped for a while but a voice of doom on the news had forecast another blizzard for later in the day.

Even with the bitter cold and with the constant threat of headaches, he hadn't regretted returning to Black Rock Falls. He'd found a home in this strange town and the people accepted him. Nothing seemed to dampen the spirits of the townsfolk and he admired them for their strength. They rarely complained and bundled against the weather in brightly covered clothes, hats and scarves made a colorful display. As he drove back to town, he waved back at people clearing their driveways. To most, snow or sunshine, it was just another day. He turned the truck onto the main street and headed to the office.

The town had turned into a Christmas card overnight. Trees hung heavy with snow and every house had a white roof and a line of icicles hanging along the front like lacy bunting. Kids with red runny noses built snowmen in front yards, laughing and throwing snowballs as if they hadn't noticed the freezing temperature.

Christmas trees with lights blinking adorned many front windows and decorations proclaiming the holiday season filled the town. He turned to Rowley. "I guess we should drive up to the industrial area and check out the other junkyard."

"Not much point." Rowley rubbed his hands together. They shut down for four weeks at least over winter." He glanced at Kane. "The snowmobile team went up there looking for Sky Paul and said the gate was chained up."

Kane frowned. "But they weren't looking for signs of a crushed car." He took the road out of town, glad the brine spreader had cleared the highway. "In cases like this, we have to play the 'what if' game. We have no clues, zip, and in truth, we don't know if we have a victim. We have blood evidence and a sketchy report from a woman who could be involved in a murder."

"So, what if she killed her, you mean? Well, she was the last person to see her alive and that kinda makes her an automatic suspect." Rowley unzipped his jacket and removed his gloves as the heater kicked in. "Do you figure she drove the car to the recycler's, had it crushed with the body inside then walked back to the road?"

"Nope because that 'what if' is missing a vital piece of information." Kane flicked him a glance then kept his eyes on the frozen landscape. "The chance of Ella Tate knowing the guy or watchman or whoever is involved with the junkyard would be remote. Someone had to be there to crush Sky's vehicle. It's not something she could do alone."

"So what is your 'what if'?" Rowley looked at him interested.

"What if the incident played out as Tate said and the killer owns the junkyard?"

"Killed the girl, towed the car here and crushed the evidence?" Rowley smiled. "Makes sense."

Kane took in the beauty of the brilliant white countryside, flattened by the snow. He remembered his first drive into Black Rock Falls along the same highway, in the snow at night. The isolation and eerie quiet, the blackened trees standing along the road like a battalion of soldiers' guns held at attention. He could not imagine a young woman choosing to spend a night up a tree or walking miles in the snow. Her survival had been close to a miracle. "So now we have two possible scenarios."

"I guess we could cross-check her phone records with the owner and see if she knows him." Rowley pulled out his cellphone and scanned files on the case.

Kane nodded. "Yeah and if she does know him, she could have contacted him from the Blackwater Roadhouse to tell him they were on their way."

"Why kill her best friend?" Rowley turned in his seat. "It seems a bit extreme just because she argued with her over Sky's brother."

"Yeah, the motive is a sticking point with me too." Kane glanced at his GPS. "Are we close to the place Tate said they were attacked?"

"Yeah, see those trees over there? That's where Tate said she spent the night." Rowley pointed out the window. "Going on her statement the attack must have happened opposite."

Kane slowed his truck to a crawl. No vehicles moved in either direction and the place was as silent as a tomb. He scanned the area, seeing the recent grooves from the snowmobiles along the partially cleared path. The group of pines where Tate had sheltered were heavy with snow, their branches bending under the weight. High in the tree beneath snow-covered branches would be the safest place to survive a night in these conditions. Out of the wind, the snow-laden branches would form an igloo of sorts around her.

He turned to Rowley. "How far is the junkyard?"

Straight ahead, first turn on the right, there is a bright orange sign. The road was cleared so we should get through okay." Rowley pulled on his gloves and peered out at the sky. "I'm not sure how long the blizzard will hold off, the sky looks fit to burst."

Glad of the snow tires, Kane eased his truck along an ice-covered blacktop that wound its way past a field of rusty old cars dating back fifty years or more. Each had a liberal coating of white and crazed frost patterns across the windows. He pulled up in front of the huge iron gates and blasted his horn. The place looked deserted and he slipped from the car, dragging down his hat firmly over his ears then pulling up his hoodie. He opened the door and Duke jumped down beside him and sniffed the frozen ground then sneezed.

Kane did a visual scan of the area then turned to Rowley. "We need to find out when they shut down. The heavy machinery used to lift the vehicles into the crusher and the crusher itself doesn't appear to have the same amount of snow piled up on them as the surrounding buildings." He took out his cellphone and took a few photographs. "See here, where the gate opens the snow is only a few inches deep."

"Yeah, but they use a lot of salt up here in the driveways." Rowley kicked the snow from his boots on a tree stump. "And I would say someone would drop by from time to time to keep an eye on the place."

Kane pushed the phone back inside his coat. "Maybe, but there's not much to steal, is there? I'm not sure many would try to scale this fence in winter." He sighed. "I'll look out the snow gauge measurements for this area. Right now if the owner shut down before the first blizzard the amount of snow doesn't tally. If he shut down after then he would have been open the day after the attack. If so, why wasn't he here during the search?"

"The snowmobile group said the gates were locked when they came by and they've been by three or four times searching the area." Rowley stared into space. "What next?"

Kane headed back to his truck and pulled open the back door for Duke to jump onto his blanket. "We find out when they shut down and ask them to allow us to look around. If they don't allow us inside to search the place, I think we have enough for a search warrant."

CHAPTER NINETEEN

The issuing of a media statement was a double-edged sword. Unlike a BOLO, the "be on the lookout" order issued by law enforcement to find or apprehend lost people or suspects, the media release hotline opened up a Pandora's box of useless information, all of which had to be sifted through just on the off-chance someone had actually seen something useful. After a couple of hours' searching, Jenna had discovered one small lead but it could wait until she refilled her coffee cup. The persistent cough had eased but her head still ached and the illness had weakened her more than she would care to admit. She pushed to her feet and, hands on hips, leaned back stretching her back.

The snow brought with it an eerie silence and although the sky was heavy with cloud cover, a bright white light streamed through the windows. The condensation from the heating had frozen in a leafy design on the windowpanes and she rubbed a hole in the frost to peer outside. Across the driveway, Kane's cottage appeared surreal, coated with snow and decorated with foot-long icicles hanging from the gutters and windowsills. The boughs of surrounding pines hung down under the burden of snow appearing strangely green amidst the barren black sticks of the maple trees and brown and gray brush. Cold seeped through the windows cooling her skin. The ranch house was over one hundred years old and every winter she promised to finish the double glazing to keep out the bitter wind but something always came up to stop her. Time it seemed was her enemy, she rarely had enough time to go to the beauty parlor for a haircut let alone make improvements on the place.

The silent alarm flashed on the wall panel and her cellphone vibrated. As if she had waited for this moment, a calm descended on her. She might be alone but she could defend her home. In three strides, she went to the gun safe and moments later had a rifle loaded and within easy reach. She strapped her backup weapon to her ankle. The ringtone on her cellphone informed her Kane had received the same alert. She scanned the array of screens and the vehicle heading toward the house then accepted his call. "I have a visitor driving an old Dodge Durango maybe a 2000 model, could be silver, it has a deal of snow on it."

"Doctor Weaver was driving a silver truck, most likely it's her." She could hear the roar of Kane's vehicle. *"I'm out at the industrial area a mile or so past where Sky was abducted. Rowley is with me. Wolfe can be there in twenty. I'll call him."*

Jenna chewed on her bottom lip, watching the vehicle make steady progress down her driveway. "No, don't bother him just yet. If she came alone, I'll be able to handle her. I'd pretend I'm not home, although the smoke coming from the chimney is a dead giveaway." She sighed. "I'll be fine. The alarm just spooked me after what Wolfe told me about the blood tests Doctor Weaver ordered. It makes her an unknown threat."

"Roger that. I'm on my way back to the office. Don't hang up. I'll hand you over to Rowley in a minute and put you on speaker. Just don't allow her to jab you with a needle."

"No way. I'm not sure how we'll explain this situation to him." Jenna pressed her back to the wall and watched the bundled up figure climb from the vehicle and head for the front porch. "We can't tell him the truth." She grabbed her coat from the peg and shrugged it on. No way was she allowing the woman inside.

"I'll figure something out." Kane's voice sounded serious. *"Is she alone?"*

Jenna peered inside the frosted windows of the doctor's car. "Unless someone is lying down inside her truck, she seems to be. Radio silence now, I'm opening the door." She slipped the cellphone into her pocket and turned the handle. "What brings you out in the cold, Doctor?"

"I was passing and thought I'd drop by to see how you're recovering." Dr. Weaver looked up at her from the bottom of the steps.

"I'm much better, thank you." Jenna stepped out onto the porch but kept her distance.

A tingle of worry lifted the hairs on the back of her neck at the way the doctor kept her hands in her pockets. As the woman moved closer, Jenna caught an unnerving expression crossing the woman's face. Apprehension, or was it indecision she caught in her small beady eyes? She couldn't put her finger on it but when a nerve in the doctor's cheek twitched, it alarmed her. She didn't trust this woman and wanted her off her ranch.

"You still look very pale." Dr. Weaver's expression was determined now. "I'll check you over, no charge."

"No need. I'm fine." Jenna allowed her coat to fall open just long enough for the doctor to notice the weapon, sitting snug in its shoulder holster.

"You should be inside out of the cold." Dr. Weaver's attention moved to the pistol. She frowned and the foot she'd raised as if to mount the steps fell back to the packed snow at the foot of the stairs. "Your blood tests came back and apart from a slightly elevated white cell count you are fine. The higher white blood count is most likely due to the infection. You should take another blood test in a few weeks just to be sure."

Jenna forced a smile. "That's great news. Wolfe will do one for me. You shouldn't have come all the way out here to tell me. You could have called me. It's dangerous on the roads at this time of year." She glanced behind her and cleared her throat. "I have to go, I have a visitor."

"Oh." The doctor gave her a confused stare. "I thought you were alone. I drove past Deputies Kane and Rowley out on the back highway."

"I'm not sure I remember how being alone feels anymore." Jenna laughed and hoped she didn't sound hysterical. "Since I've been ill, I've had streams of visitors daily. I'll get more rest when I've gotten back to work." Shivering dramatically, she pushed open the door. "It's cold out here. I'd better let you get back to work." She gave her a wave. "Thanks for dropping by."

Jenna shut the door and turned the lock but Dr. Weaver just stood there staring at her with the same expression. The sight of her just standing there unnerved her. She pulled out her cellphone. "Rowley put Kane on."

"She gone?"

A shiver went up Jenna's spine. "Nope, she's just standing there staring at the door." She walked onto the family room and wiped a hole in the frosted window to look outside. "She has a strange expression on her face and said she thought I was alone."

"That's not good. I'm dropping Rowley at the office and coming home." Kane cleared his throat. *"What's she doing now?"*

Jenna had not taken her eyes off the doctor. "She's leaning on her truck and talking on her cellphone. Do you know if Wolfe has gotten any information on her yet?"

"Nope. I'm sure he'll let you know when the FBI have finished looking into her background."

Heart pounding, Jenna gaped at the woman in disbelief. "Holy crap she is heading back to the house." She swapped the cellphone into her left hand and pulled her weapon, surprised at the shake in her grip. "What does this woman want with me?"

"Old memories are hard to shift, Jenna. It's normal to go on alert if you feel threatened." As usual, Kane's voice was calm. *"Look, if she believes someone is in the house with you she would be stupid to try anything. If she comes to the door again, speak to her through the window."*

Jenna holstered her weapon with some reluctance, pushed open the family room window and looked at the doctor. "Is anything wrong?"

"I think I dropped my keys." Dr. Weaver moved her boot through the snow at the foot of the steps and stared at the frozen ground.

Jenna kept the cellphone to her ear. "You had your hands in your pockets the entire time you spoke to me. I don't think you dropped them here. Maybe try looking closer to your truck." She sighed. "I would come out and help you but I have to take this call. Kane is only a few minutes away and will give you a hand when he arrives."

"It's okay, here they are." The doctor held up the keys. "They were in my pocket. Silly me. Sorry to have troubled you." She trudged back to her truck, started the motor and drove away.

"Has she gone?" The sound of Kane's engine had stopped.

Surprised the woman had unnerved her to such an extent, Jenna heaved a long sigh of relief. "Yeah, where are you?"

"Outside the office. I'm heading home now."

"Good." Jenna peered out the window. "I'm not sure who she was calling, so I'll be in the safe room just in case. Come get me." The sound of a powerful motor filled Jenna's ear as Kane headed his truck back out onto the highway. *"I'll stay on the line until you arrive. Drive safe."*

"Roger that."

CHAPTER TWENTY

Ella paced up and down before the roaring fire in Doug Paul's man cave. She wished Sky's family would listen to her and stop treating her as if she'd lost her mind. None of them seemed to be doing anything to find Sky. They all sat around waiting to hear news from the sheriff. The waiting was driving her nuts. She glared at Doug. Unlike his small sister, he was well built and athletic, but they had the same hair and eyes. "I figure I've waited long enough for search and rescue to find Sky. They have to be searching in the wrong place. I want to borrow your truck and look for her myself."

"I'm not allowing you near my truck." Doug glared at her. "Mom will have a fit if you go out there alone."

Ella lifted her chin. "I won't be alone. I met a guy online, a medical student, who says he will help me look for Sky. I'm meeting him later."

"Do you honestly believe we could find her if search and rescue failed? Didn't you watch the news? The sheriff had everyone available out looking and the news chopper was doing updates—they had fifty or more people on the ground. The deputies were on scene directing the search. Trust me, the sheriff is moving heaven and earth to find her." Doug snorted. "You're nuts if you figure you and some med student will find her in the middle of the night."

"Well, at least I tried. Not like you sitting all cozy in front of the fire while Sky is out there freezing to death." Ella walked across the room and pointed to a framed map of Black Rock Falls hanging on the wall. "How old is this map?"

"I'm not sure but it's not a map, it's one of my dad's aerial shots." He turned in the chair, making the leather upholstery moan, and stared at it. He gave it to me for my last birthday, so it's not too old at all. Why?"

Ella peered at the image, then traced her finger along the highway. She pointed to a number of buildings scattered all over one side of the image. "What are all these buildings used for? Are they cattle ranches?"

"Nope. The place you said Sky disappeared is a mile from the industrial area of Black Rock Falls. The grasslands out that way are a honeycomb of abandoned goldmines and not many people use it for grazing. The buildings there are potteries, ironworks, a recycling yard and industrial machinery mostly." He pointed to a group of six or eight buildings. "The only place up that way with any cattle is the meat processing plant. The cattle are trucked in then held in those fenced areas before processing." He moved his finger to a huge building. "That's the meat processing plant and here"—he slid his finger along the map—"is the fertilizer factory." He turned and looked at her. "Why?"

Ella nodded. "Why hasn't anyone mentioned searching the factories for Sky? All they mention is searching the highway, but I can see all these places are only a mile or so away from the highway. What if someone works night shifts at one of these places and he is the man who took Sky?"

"That's unlikely at this time of year. All the factories are in shutdown over the holidays and they would have alarm systems. If Sky made it that far and I doubt it, she would have frozen to death. And anyway, someone would have found her by now." He shook his head. "The news said the search and rescue chopper searched the entire area, and the team on the snowmobiles checked out all the factories."

Ella gripped his arm. "She has to be in the area."

"What makes you say that?" Doug leaned one shoulder against the wall. "He could have tossed her into his trunk and driven anywhere before you reported her missing. He had about nine hours' start at least."

Ella shook her head and gripped his arm tighter. "Then where is her car?" She lifted her chin and glared at him, trying to make him understand. "I saw one man. How did he move her car? One man can't move two vehicles."

"Yeah they can." Doug strolled to the door to the garage. "Come here, I'll show you." He led the way through a door into a huge garage. "See this?" He pointed to a piece of machinery. "It's called a towing frame or an A-frame. It attaches to the back of my truck and hooks up to the front of another vehicle or trailer. No driver required. It doesn't take up much room in the trunk. Many people use them."

"Okay." Ella rubbed her arms against the chill. "But I think it was an ambush. Somehow he knew we would be there."

"Out at midnight with a blizzard coming? No way." Doug shook his head. "We didn't know what time Sky would arrive until she called Mom from the Blackwater Roadhouse so how could the man who attacked her possibly find out?"

Ella shook her head. "I don't know but I have this feeling she's out there somewhere. We have to go find her." She led the way back into his man cave and peered into the dancing flames in the hearth. "If I'm right, that man might have a place close by. He could be out waiting for another person to kill." She turned to look at him. "I figure if we get there at the same time as he took Sky we might catch him. We'll outnumber him and this time, you can take that." She pointed to a shotgun in a rack on the wall. "He won't be expecting us to fight back."

"You're in Montana." Doug shook his head. "Most people carry weapons in their vehicles out here. If he is doing as you say, chances are he'd be dead by now."

She glared at him. "Well, he was alive and well the last time I saw him. Take the shotgun." She frowned. "And I have arranged to meet a guy named Jim. I can't leave him out there to freeze his ass off waiting for me to arrive or turn on the news to discover the killer murdered him too."

"Okay, I'll take the gun. That area is a black hole for phone reception and you would be surprised how many people break down or are involved in a wreck within that one mile stretch. It's like it's cursed." He stared down at her with a determined expression. "But if you must go, bundle up and meet me back here. I'll grab some blankets in case we get stuck out there."

Ella winced. "Do you figure we'll get caught in a blizzard?"

"Maybe. I said it was a stupid idea but if you insist, we'll do it my way and turn back if the weather gets bad. We have the shotgun and my truck's GPS has a satellite tracker. If anything happens, someone will come out and find us as soon as they know we're missing." He waved her away. "I'm not hanging around waiting for you all night to get ready. It's freezing out there, and I want to grab some coffee to go from Aunt Betty's Café before we head out of town, and they close the store at eleven thirty."

Ella stared at him, wondering if he believed her story or the threat they faced if they came across the same man. "Sure, but bring plenty of ammunition. I'm not taking any chances."

CHAPTER TWENTY-ONE

He took one last look at Sky's face without one shred of regret at the sight of her lifeless staring eyes. No one understood how he felt when the women eventually died. To him, once they'd screamed their last breath they had the same value as an empty candy wrapper he needed to toss away in the trash. He would be happy to leave her alongside a road but then the cops would have a body and this way was nice and tidy.

After hoisting her onto the conveyer belt, he pulled off the blanket covering her then hit the switch. He waited for a few moments as she slipped inside the chute. The machine groaned and trembled with the effort; then, as her fair hair vanished from view, he turned away and pushed the gurney back inside.

His luck was changing. From the media reports, the sheriff suspected Ella Tate was involved in Sky's disappearance. He chuckled as he entered his office, sat down at the desk and deleted his phony social media profile to make sure no one could connect him to his victims. The sheriff would be the same as most people in law enforcement and have a profiler trying to get inside his brain, but he could easily outsmart most people. Right now, the sheriff's focus would be on Tate, so she would be looking at her if anyone else came up missing. Hell, they were already convinced she murdered Sky. The profiler would write her up as a confused, violent college student and it would be case closed. *Until they arrest her, I'm free to do as I damn well please.*

CHAPTER TWENTY-TWO

Trepidation gripped Ella as she looked out the window of Doug's truck. The forecast blizzard had not arrived and although the sky had a foreboding heaviness, the night was crisp and the roads clear. Black Rock Falls was like a movie set, with Christmas lights strung out between the lampposts flashing bright colors on the snow-laden storefronts. Out the front of Aunt Betty's Café sat a waving snowman with a blinking red nose. Inside, a festive tree shimmered with garlands and glass balls. A sign on the window offered a list of tempting seasonal dishes to keep out the cold.

As they drove out of town, past the park with the gigantic Christmas tree and nativity scene, she looked back on her life since her parents died. She had become a military brat, dragged from post to post by her brother, but in a year or so she would be out on her own, looking for a job and a place to call home. She just needed to find Sky then she could make plans to move to Black Rock Falls. The Paul family had been caring toward her and she liked Doug. Having people she knew in town would make all the difference. She dragged her gaze away from the vast, empty white landscape and glanced at Doug. He drove hunched forward over the wheel, peering through the icy windshield. Snowflakes were already building white lines on the wiper blades. She cleared her throat. "I'd like to live here after college. It's been a long time since I could call a place home."

"It's a growing area. I'm not moving away—there's plenty of work here." Doug lifted his chin as if to indicate ahead. "What's going on there? Is that the same vehicle you saw the night Sky went missing?"

The headlights of Doug's truck picked up a light-colored pickup on the side of the road with its flashers on. A wave of morbid apprehension washed over her. She gripped the side of the seat, trying to keep calm. "Yeah it could be him. I'm pretty sure it was a white truck, or maybe silver." She glanced at him. "I can't stop shaking, it's like déjà vu."

"Yeah, but this time, you're with me and we have a shotgun." Doug's face was grim. "Let's do this."

A person bundled up against the cold climbed from the cab, slapped a cowboy hat over the top of a black woolen hat and wrapped a scarf around his face, then strode around his truck. As they drove closer, the headlights moved across deep gouges in the snow. Ella gasped at the sight of another vehicle nose down in the ditch beside the road. Although partially buried in the pile of gray snow, she could make out the red taillights. Clouds of steam poured from the crumpled hood and one door hung open. "Oh, my God, it's a wreck."

"The roads are covered with ice and it wouldn't take too much to lose control." Doug slowed then shot her a glance. "What about him? Does he look like the man who attacked you?"

"He was wearing black and had a hood pulled down over his face, so I didn't get a look at him. He was big like him… but the cowboy hat makes him look taller, I guess." She shook her head. "No, I don't think that's him. That's probably Jim, the guy I met online."

"You didn't think to ask this Jim guy what he looks like?" Doug gaped at her. "Or what vehicle he drives?"

Ella dragged her attention away from the wreck. "I *know* what he looks like. I've seen his profile picture online and he said he drives a white pickup." She waved a hand at the parked car ahead.

"I can't see his face or the color of his vehicle from here—I guess it could be white."

"Okay." Doug pulled his truck to the side of the highway, leaving the engine running. "Stay here with the shotgun. I'll go see what I can do to help." He gave her a long concerned look. "You do know how to use one, don't you?"

Anxiety gripped her. Her parents had died in a wreck and seeing the car all bent out of shape brought back too many bad memories. "Yeah. Now go, someone could be dying out there. I won't lock the doors in case you have to run back." She held out her hand. "Give me your cellphone and I'll see if I can get any bars and call 911."

She took the phone and peered at the screen, then pressed 911, but there was no signal. As Doug had mentioned, the mile-long black hole for phone reception seemed to attract trouble. Seemed it was fast becoming the Bermuda Triangle of Black Rock Falls.

CHAPTER TWENTY-THREE

It was past midnight and sleep would not come for Jenna. The doctor's visit had shattered her nerves, bringing back horrific memories of another life and the threats of being on someone's hit list. Since Kane's arrival, he had become her safety net and she believed the threat of her past life emerging was close to impossible with most of the players dead. The problem was the men involved had families and there was always someone willing to carry out a vendetta. Now with one stupid blood test she could be back on the cartel's hit list.

She stared at the ceiling and allowed her mind to wander over the last few months. Apart from spending a good deal of time assisting Kane's rehabilitation, she had fulfilled her duties at the office. She'd worked long hours then returned home to relieve the nurse Wolfe had arranged for him. Kane was different since the shooting and, although he'd been as kind and considerate as always, had avoided her attempts at closeness between them, much like when he'd first arrived. Something had changed but she couldn't quite figure out what was wrong. She sighed. Wolfe would know, but it would be easier to walk into Fort Knox and pick up a couple of gold bars than to get information on Kane out of him.

Jenna threw back the blankets, dragged on her dressing gown, pushed her feet into her slippers and walked into the kitchen. After taking out the fixings to make hot chocolate, she heard footsteps behind her. Heart pounding, she spun around to find Kane coming through the doorway. "You scared the hell out of me."

"Sorry." He peered over her shoulder at the counter. "Can you make a cup for me too? I can't sleep tonight."

Jenna took in his tousled appearance and strained expression. "Sure. I can't sleep either. There are so many things going around in my head." She made the hot chocolate and handed him a cup, then sat down at the table. "Where is Sky Paul and is Ella Tate involved?"

"I wish I knew." Kane eased down into a chair and winced. "From what I can see the pair have been friends since they became roomies at college. I've spoken to a few of their friends from the campus and they all say the same thing, that they argue all the time but they are best friends." He examined her face, then sighed. "That's not all that's worrying you, is it? You must feel like you have a bullseye on your back again and trust me, I know how that feels."

Jenna sipped her beverage, peering at him over the rim of the cup. She shrugged. "Well, yes, there is that, but I've lived with that problem before and with you and Wolfe on the case, we'll be able to stop them getting close." She sucked in a deep breath. "I'm more worried about you."

"Me?" Kane looked astonished. "I'm fine and getting better by the day." He placed both hands around the cup, dwarfing it in his palms. "Oh, you mean about the memory loss?"

Relieved, Jenna nodded. "Yeah, you've been distant, almost like a stranger at times."

"I'm sorry, Jenna." Kane looked wounded. "My memories are all jumbled. The time since I arrived here is as if it happened five years ago and the car bombing feels like a couple of months ago. When I saw you in the gulley after the shooting, I didn't recognize you, I didn't know where I was and the last thing I remembered was seeing my wife die."

Understanding flooded over her. No wonder he had been so distant. She reached across the table and squeezed his arm. "I'm so sorry, Dave. You did mention that at the time, but I thought you had all your memories back now." She sighed. "So they are all there but not in chronological order? Oh, now I understand. Don't stress about it, just take it one day at a time. I can wait, Dave. I did before and I can do it again."

"This is why I need to move back into the cottage." Kane stretched out his leg and rubbed his knee. "I need the normality, the old routine we had before to get my head straight." He lifted his gaze to her. "I value our friendship, Jenna, and I want to be closer. If you get shipped out, I'll go right to POTUS if necessary to be reassigned with you."

Jenna chuckled. "Now that's the kind of BFF I need. Can we take Wolfe and the girls with us? I'd like to keep the family together."

"Me too."

CHAPTER TWENTY-FOUR

The temperature had dropped by the time he turned onto the highway. He'd driven slowly, intending to pull into a side road and wait for Ella Tate and her companion to drive by in his black truck. He'd planned to get up behind them and give them a blast of his horn. Seeing a sedan flying down the highway doing at least sixty was a surprise and more so when the driver lost control on the sweeping bend and slammed into the ditch alongside the road. He stopped and put on his flashers, then grabbed a flashlight. He made his way through the snowdrifts using the track the car had cut as it left the road. When he reached the steaming vehicle, the driver, a woman in her late forties, was gushing blood from a neck wound and would be dead soon but a young woman lay unconscious in the passenger seat, her head cradled in the airbag. Not able to believe his luck, he grinned into the darkness. "Well, some days are diamonds."

His excitement had turned sour when he spotted headlight beams cutting through the darkness toward him. The vehicle slowed as if the occupants were examining him. The freezing cold cut into his cheeks as he picked his way back to his vehicle. The truck approached with caution and not wanting anyone to identify him, he wrapped a scarf around his face and pulled down his cowboy hat. He hoped the approaching vehicle would be carrying Ella Tate but if not, no one would recognize him. As the car slowed, he gave the driver a wave but stood his ground. A young man stepped out of the truck and headed in his direction.

"Are you Jim?"

A buzz of excitement shivered through him. *Oh, this is gonna be so easy.* "Yeah. I gather you're Doug. Is Ella here?"

"She's in my truck." Doug glanced at the steaming car. "Any survivors?"

He touched the syringes in his pockets, left hand for Doug and right hand for Ella. "Yeah, one—the driver didn't make it." He shrugged. "No use trying to call for help out here. If you lend a hand to carry her, I'll lay her on the back seat of my pickup and drive her straight to the ER. I would have lifted her myself but I was worried she might have a back injury. We'll need to keep her as straight as possible and support her head."

"Yeah, I'll help." Doug looked apprehensive. "She might sue us for moving her. You sure we shouldn't drive up the road until we get some bars and call an ambulance?"

Smart guy but I'm smarter. "She'll freeze to death before the paramedics arrive. Coming with me is the best chance she has right now, but I'll need your help. You'll need to hold her to protect her neck. Can you do that?"

"Okay." Doug didn't look totally convinced, but gave a curt nod. "Ella will follow us in my truck."

With effort, they eased the young woman from the car, taking care to support her head. He made Doug hold the young woman's shoulders and it was easy to convince him to slide into his back seat with the woman's head on his lap. "There's a blanket in her car. I'll grab it and her purse. The hospital will need to know her identity."

He used the time to retrieve the syringe from his pocket. Gathered the purses and cellphones from the vehicle and returned to the car. Anticipation shook his hands as he opened the door closest to Doug and handed him the blanket. "I'll go and tell Ella to follow us."

"Sure, the keys are in the car." Doug smiled. "Be careful; she has a loaded shotgun with her."

The moment Doug turned to cover the young woman with the blanket, he plunged the needle into his jugular, followed by a second into his thigh. Doug went out in seconds without a murmur. *One down.* After shutting the door, he slipped and slid his way along the ice-covered blacktop to Doug's truck. He paused at the back of the truck in the darkness to make sure the scarf covered his face then slipped the syringe out of his pocket and uncapped it. He moved slowly around the truck then shone the flashlight through the window. There she was, not holding a shotgun but just staring at him with a half-smile on her lips. *There is one idiot born every minute.* "Hey there, Ella. Remember me?"

CHAPTER TWENTY-FIVE

Wednesday

So cold. Ella fumbled for the blanket covering her and pulled it up to her ears. Her neck ached and a strange numbness gripped her legs. Her teeth chattered like castanets, sounding horribly loud in the complete silence. Heavens above, the cold had seeped into her bones. She blinked, staring at the brilliant white wall in front of her. Startled, she gazed around her. She was inside a car and the white wall was a windshield covered with snow. *How the hell did I get here?*

Condensation dripped down the windows and she lifted her gloved hand to wipe it away, then thought better of it and searched around the car. She found a hamburger wrapper and used it to wipe a hole in the mist. Outside, the snow-dusted highway stretched in both directions. She searched her memory, remembering speaking to Doug about searching for Sky. They had climbed into his truck with a shotgun and headed out of town. *Then what happened?*

She searched the cabin. The shotgun lay across the back seat just as she remembered. Two empty go cups sat in the console along with a variety of candy. Perhaps she had fallen asleep and Doug had decided to search alone. What the hell was the time? She was desperate for a pee. From the daylight, she figured it must be way past nine. She eased open the door and winced as a blast of arctic air hit her face. If she came here with Doug, he must be close by. Her numb legs hit the blacktop and she turned and gaped in horror at the wrecked sedan a few yards away. *Have we been in a wreck?*

Sickened, she edged forward, not believing her eyes. The door to the wrecked sedan hung open and the interior light showed a woman with long hair covered in blood hanging half out of the smashed windshield. An ugly gash across her throat left her in no doubt that the poor woman was dead. Ella gaped in disbelief. The woman's blood had frozen as it dripped off the hood and hung in grotesque red popsicles. She bit back a rush of nausea and waded through the thick snow to the vehicle. She had to look inside in case someone else was inside injured.

Shivering with cold and fear, she reached the wreck and steeled herself, then peered inside. Apart from the driver, the car was empty. She kept her eyes averted from the woman's horrific injuries and, gripping the side of the vehicle, eased her way around the car, searching the immediate area for any survivors. She turned to examine Doug's truck. It appeared to be undamaged. Perhaps he'd come across the car wreck and stopped to lend assistance, but if so where had he gone? She scanned the frozen tundra.

"Doug, are you out here?" Her voice seemed dampened by the snow. The eerie quiet closed in around her. She called many times but no reply came and a trickle of fear raised the hairs on the back of her neck. Alone in the middle of nowhere and her friend was missing. *Not again. This can't happen twice in one week.*

Slipping and sliding perilously along the edge of the ditch, she reached Doug's SUV. Snow dusted the black truck and by the thick coating of frost crazing the paintwork, they must have been here all night. If she couldn't find Doug, she would drive into town and get help. She had the GPS to get her back to Black Rock Falls. She wrenched open the door and her gaze fixed on the ignition. She let out a sob of desperation. No keys. A chill shivered through her to the bone. What had happened to Doug? Why would he leave her and his truck on the side of the road? Nothing made sense. He had to be close by somewhere. Maybe he had wandered off into the bushes. She leaned against the truck and cupped her mouth. "Doug, Doug, answer me. Stop messing around."

Silence. In fact, there was no noise at all. No birds, no traffic not one sound. It was as if she was completely alone in the world. Alone in the middle of nowhere with a corpse.

CHAPTER TWENTY-SIX

A commotion at the front counter at the sheriff's department drew Jenna's attention away from the computer screen. She had spent the last hour or two since arriving updating her files, collecting reports from the local search and rescue teams and keeping the media informed about the status of Sky Paul's disappearance. Nothing seemed to add up in this case and finding no body or trace of the young woman had left her grasping at straws. She had her deputies searching for anyone who may have been passing through the local area at the time of Sky's disappearance. The thought had occurred to her to check the whereabouts of men living in town fitting the description Ella Tate had offered of the attacker, then her deputies walked through the main entrance to the office, all shaking the snow off black hoodies. The description "tall with broad shoulders" resembled at least half the men in town.

A knock came on the door and the receptionist, Maggie, stuck her head inside the room.

"I have Mr. and Mrs. Paul in the waiting area. They insist on speaking to you right away."

Jenna pushed to her feet and smiled at Maggie. "That's fine, send them through."

A tall middle-aged man dusted with snowflakes guided a distraught woman wearing a bright red winter jacket and matching knitted hat into the office. Jenna moved around the table and pulled out a chair for Mrs. Paul. "Have you gotten news about Sky?"

"Not a word." Mr. Paul's eyes narrowed and his mouth turned down. "You?"

Surprised by his harsh tone, Jenna moved back around her desk to make a space between her and the angry man. "As you are aware, we have involved the media and sent out BOLOs to all other counties." She met his gaze full on. "My deputies are working around the clock to find her."

"That's not why we're here." Mrs. Paul shot to her feet and leaned across the desk, putting her face not six inches away from Jenna. "My son went out last night to search for Sky and now he's gone missin' too."

It was fortunate Jenna had dealt with a number of irate people in her time and this kind of display no longer intimidated her. She dropped her voice to just above a whisper. "When did you last see your son?" She sat down and folded her hands on the desk.

"Last night at supper." Mrs. Paul sank back into her chair and swallowed hard. "Doug left a note to say he and Ella had gone for a ride out toward Blackwater. The pair of them haven't returned and he's not answerin' his cellphone."

"I figured they might have stayed over at the Blackwater Motel seein' the weather has been so bad, but they're not there." Mr. Paul stood behind his wife rubbing her shoulders. "It's not like him not to contact us."

"Are you aware an eighteen-wheeler rolled over on the highway a mile out of Blackwater last night around eleven? It spilled a load of toxic chemicals, blocking the highway in both directions." Jenna sighed. "It's been on the news all morning and the Department of Transport would have erected a flashing sign on the highway just outside of town."

"You sayin' that if Doug wrecked his truck last night in the cellphone dead zone, no one would have been by and he wouldn't have been able to call for help?" Mr. Paul frowned. "We'll head out now and go look for him ourselves."

Jenna shook her head. "That's not necessary. We're better equipped to handle the situation. I'll bring in my deputies and we'll go over the details." She lifted the phone and called Kane. "Grab Rowley and come to my office. We have a situation."

Moments later Kane led Rowley through the door. He looked at her and raised one eyebrow in question. She lifted her chin and explained. "When we've finished here, Deputy Rowley will make out a missing person's report. I'll get a search organized immediately. I'll need details of your son's vehicle."

She made notes and looked back at the couple. "What time did they leave?"

"We don't know. Late." Mr. Paul glanced at Kane. "My son's vehicle has a GPS with a tracking device. Do you know the kind? He can find his car using his cellphone."

"Ah, that's useful. We should be able to trace the vehicle." Kane took out his notebook and pen. "If you give me your son's plate and cellphone number, I'll get someone onto it straight away."

"I don't have his license plate number." Mr. Paul's expression was grim.

Jenna pushed a lock of hair out of her eyes. "Is his car insured by Barker's here in town?"

"Yeah, we all are." Mr. Paul brightened. "They'll have the details."

"Would you call them, please? It will be quicker." Jenna went through the contacts on her cellphone and read out the number. She glanced up at Kane. "When we have the information, I'll ask Wolfe to locate the vehicle, but we won't wait; we'll head out toward Blackwater in case they've had car trouble and Wolfe will call when he has the coordinates. It is a cellphone dead zone, as you know, so grab your satellite phone and anything else we might need. We'll take your truck."

"Yes, ma'am." Kane headed out of the office.

Jenna waited patiently for Mr. Paul to obtain the plate number of his son's truck, then called Wolfe. After disconnecting, she met the worried couple's eyes. "Usually when an adult comes up missing we wait a while in case they show, but as he went looking for Sky, we can't be sure he hasn't gotten into trouble. The first thing is to find his vehicle. If we don't have any luck locating him in the next hour, I'll put out a BOLO." She stood and waved the couple toward the door. "I want you to file a missing person's report so we have all Doug's details on file. If you go with Deputy Rowley, he'll start the paperwork. I'll call you when we find him."

"Thanks." Mr. Paul led his wife from the office.

She pulled open the bottom drawer to her desk, took out her backup weapon and secured it to her ankle. Her Kevlar vest went on next, then she pulled her overcoat from the peg and shrugged it over the top. She glanced up as Kane's form blocked the doorway. "Wear your vest; I could be a target and we don't know who we're dealing with at the moment."

"Great minds think alike, they say." Kane opened his jacket to reveal his vest. "I was going to suggest the same to you. At first, I figured Sky's vanishing act followed by Ella's and Doug's could have been contrived to get you alone in a black spot." Kane narrowed his gaze. "Although the timeline doesn't fit."

Not wanting to discuss the matter in the office, Jenna frowned. "We'll talk in the car." She looked him up and down. "Phone? Gear?"

"In my truck with a Thermos of coffee, soup and a stack of sandwiches I picked up at Aunt Betty's earlier." Kane smiled at her. "I figured we'd be eating on the run today."

Jenna pulled on her thick woolen hat and gloves, then followed him out the main entrance. The bitter cold hit her face in a stinging rush. Snow fell, dusting her coat with white flakes and making the sidewalk slippery. Winter had its own special smell, a combination of snow, wood-fire smoke and pine. A blanket of snow covered the town but it was awash with color, from the decorations hanging between the streetlamps and across the main street to the red-cheeked townsfolk, most wearing brightly colored scarves and hats. Kids darted everywhere, puffing out great clouds of steam as they built snowmen or threw snowballs. The pure white snow was fun for the children, but she figured after three months or more they, like everyone else, would look forward to the melt.

She glanced at Kane's truck—"the beast", as he called his modified unmarked black Dodge, was fitted with winter tires, for safety. She heard an excited bark and smiled at Duke peering out the window. She climbed into the passenger seat and leaned over the back to rub the dog's ears. "Hey, Duke, nice harness."

"Yeah, he has a fear of cages, so a harness was the next best thing to keep him safe." Kane smiled at her. "I can attach his leash to it as well." He slid behind the wheel and started the engine.

Jenna waited until they reached the highway before starting a conversation, busying herself with filling two go cups with coffee from the thermos. She figured Kane needed all his attention on negotiating the icy roads and idiot drivers through town and the suburbs. The highway into Black Rock Falls, although blanketed each side by endless white, had been cleared and brined since the last blizzard. A bright yellow flashing sign informed motorists: *Highway closed between Peak Crossing and Blackwater.*

She turned in her seat, cup in hand. "You mentioned something about the timeline?" She handed him a coffee.

"Yeah." Kane took the go cup, sipped then placed it in the console. "Sky went missing Friday night but the doctor didn't take blood from you until Saturday. If you're a target, it would make more sense for her to be involved in Doug Paul's disappearance. I figure she would know you'd run the investigation from home and wouldn't be out looking for her." He sighed. "As a sniper, I wouldn't risk taking down a target with a chopper overhead and a team on the ground. Out here in the snow, I'd be a sitting duck."

Jenna considered his words and nodded. "Yeah, but she knew I was returning to work today."

"Exactly." Kane glanced at her, then his attention went back to the road. "No vehicles on the highway and no search and rescue around to spot a sniper."

Fear skittered up Jenna's spine, raising the hairs on her body. "Yeah, if she has a match on my DNA and knew I was alone yesterday, she might have tried to subdue me. She was desperate to get inside the house." She shuddered. "Why else would she come by when she could have called me? I don't trust her. I should never have allowed her to take blood."

"I don't either and we have people checking her out. If she as much as jaywalked we'll know by tonight." Kane's lips twitched up at the corners. "She may be working with the cartel to get a positive ID on you but because of the timeline, I can't tie her in with Sky's disappearance. How could she possibly know Sky and Ella would be on the highway at that particular time?" He sighed. "I wish I knew what prompted Doug and Ella to suddenly go searching for Sky in the middle of the night."

The satellite phone rang and Jenna picked it up. "Alton."

"It's Wolfe. I've located Doug Paul's truck. I'll give you the coordinates."

Jenna uploaded the information into the GPS. "Thanks. Anything on Doc Weaver yet?"

"Not yet. I'm expecting an update soon, I'll let you know."

"Thanks." Jenna disconnected and looked at the GPS screen. "The truck is about a half-mile ahead on the highway."

The truck came into sight as they rounded a bend. Someone leapt from the cab, ran into the middle of the road and waved their arms. She could see her mouth working but could not hear her. "Is that Ella Tate?"

"I figure it's a possibility." Kane grimaced. "If so, where's Doug Paul?"

"Maybe he's injured." As Kane slowed his vehicle, Jenna's attention went to a line of deep grooves leaving the road and cutting through the frozen bank of snow. "That doesn't look good."

"Nope." Kane sucked in a breath. "Looks like someone ran off the road and into the ditch."

They pulled up behind Doug Paul's truck and Jenna spotted the faded red taillights of a crumpled wreck through a coating of snow. The vehicle sat at an odd angle. The driver's side wheels had cleared the ditch but the other side hadn't been so lucky. She turned to Kane, pulling up her hood. "I'll take a look, and you'd better get Ella out of the cold."

She jumped from the truck and gasped at the icy chill seeping through her thick clothes. Breathing out great clouds of steam, she made her way toward the wreck then stopped mid stride at the horrific scene before her. A body stuck half out the windshield and a sparking trail of blood had frozen to the white paintwork. "Oh, my God."

CHAPTER TWENTY-SEVEN

The sharp smell of antiseptic drew Doug out of a deep sleep. Voices, low and mumbling, drifted through the miasma in his foggy brain. He dragged open his eyelids but, finding the effort too much and the light far too bright, closed them again. His mom usually threw open the drapes and cleaned his bathroom when she wanted him to do some chores. He opened his mouth to call out and remind her he was on vacation but his tongue had stuck to the roof of his mouth. Where had he ended up last night? His mind wandered back to his day and he remembered leaving the house with Ella and hunting for Sky. A stark image of a woman thrust through a windshield flashed into his mind and he opened his eyes. Above, a bright light shone down on him. Heavy drapes surrounded his bed. There was an unnerving familiarity to the beeps and sucking sounds of the machinery. The same noises he remembered from visiting his grandpa in the hospital in the days before the old man died.

Am I dying? What the hell had happened to him? He turned his head to call out to the distant voices and the room tilted then a tidal wave of nausea hit him. *Oh, that can't be good.* He closed his eyes and took a few deep breaths until the feeling passed. Under him, crisp, smooth sheets pressed against his flesh, so he was not suffering from paralysis. Yet he felt strangely unattached to his body and checked to make sure he had all his body parts. He wiggled his toes and moved his fingers, but the effort to lift an arm sent pain searing through his left side. Agony had awoken like a sleeping tiger to gnaw at his flesh. Dear Lord, had someone shot him? He trembled, panting in torment. Sweat coated his brow and salty rivulets stung his eyes. He tried to force words from his dry throat. "Help me." His voice came out in a raspy whisper, but someone heard.

The curtain swished open. A man dressed in hospital scrubs and wearing a mask peered at him. Then he turned away and moments later turned back, holding a syringe.

Doug lifted his chin and had to force out the words. "What... happened... to me?"

"You've been in a car wreck. Don't you remember?"

Doug shook his head. "No, what happened?"

"I don't know but you're going to be fine." The man's dark eyes carried no compassion. "Don't fight the drugs, it's better if you sleep right now." He pushed the needle of the syringe into a tube running into Doug's arm. "This won't take long to work. I'll be back later to set up the machine, then you'll get regular doses. I won't allow you to suffer." He pulled the drapes around the bed, leaving a large space, and hurried away.

The memory of having to have his old cancer-riddled dog euthanized flashed across his consciousness. *I won't allow you to suffer.* They were the exact words the vet had said to his dog. Perplexed, Doug peered through the gap in the curtains and met the terrified gaze of a young woman in the next bed. She had a bruise on her forehead and pulled feebly against the restraints attached to her wrists. He blinked. She seemed strangely familiar. Another doctor, or maybe a nurse, dressed in hospital scrubs but larger than the first man, came into view. The man had his back to him as he bent over the young woman.

"Hello, Olivia." He gave a low chuckle. "You owe me, you know. I found you in a car wreck. We're gonna have so much fun together." He pressed the tip of a scalpel under one of her terrified eyes, then removed it and held it before her. "Not now, but I'll be back soon."

Doug recognized the man's voice and, terrified for the young woman's safety, fought against the drug. It was Jim, Ella's friend. He wanted to say something but his throat was parched and his words came out in a sigh. Jim straightened and stepped away. *What the hell is going on here?*

Memories of the car wreck and helping a young woman flooded into his mind. Jim had insisted he helped him to take her to the ER. The moment the injured woman was in his arms, Jim had moved like lightning and plunged a needle into his neck. The next thing he remembered was waking up in the hospital in agony. Had another vehicle slammed into them to injure him or was he involved in some twisted game? He stared at Jim in disbelief. Holy cow, the medical student was threatening a helpless patient. Cold chills ran through his bones but he could not move. His body seemed to be floating away and as the medication took hold, his vision blurred but his hearing was working just fine.

"Do you like the drugs, Olivia? I call them zombie drugs. It means you see and feel everything. Won't that be fun?" Jim chuckled deep in his chest. "Over the next few days, we're gonna be seeing a lot of each other."

CHAPTER TWENTY-EIGHT

A blast of freezing air blasted Kane as he slid from his truck, sending a stab of agony through his temple. He pulled his woolen cap over his ears and tugged up his hoodie, pulling the strings tight around his face. He grabbed the first aid kit, pushed the satellite phone into one pocket and rounded the hood of his truck. Ella Tate was slipping and sliding in his direction, babbling so fast he couldn't catch a word of what she was saying. He looked at her wild expression. "Are you injured?"

"No, just cold."

Kane frowned. "What happened? Is Doug inside the truck?"

"No, he's vanished." Ella's teeth chattered like castanets. "I woke up in the truck not long ago."

He took her by the arm and led her back to Doug's truck. "Can't you drive?"

"Yeah but he took the keys." Ella shivered beside him, hugging her chest.

As Kane crunched his way along the ice-covered blacktop, the smell of brine burned his nostrils. He bent and examined the surface of the road and frowned. The ice wasn't as thick as he'd imagined which meant the snowplow had cleared this road and spread brine in the last twenty-four hours. He straightened and peered inside Doug Paul's truck and spotted the shotgun. There was no sign of the owner and nothing to indicate the pair of them had been drinking. He took in Ella's distraught expression. "Come with me and you can tell the sheriff what happened. There's coffee and soup in my truck."

Kane lifted the shotgun from the front seat, unloaded it and carried it back to his truck, securing it in a box in the back. He moved to Ella's side and patted her down, then, satisfied she carried no weapons, opened the door and waved her inside. "Jump in. Wrap a blanket around you. I'll be back in a second."

After giving Duke a pat on the head, he headed back toward Jenna, following the car tracks through the pile of snow. He scanned the carnage then moved his attention back at Jenna. "Any survivors?"

"Nope." Jenna grimaced. "Let's get out of the cold and see what she has to say."

Kane touched her arm. "There was a loaded shotgun in the truck but she's clean."

"Okay." Jenna brushed snow from her coat, then led the way back to his truck and climbed inside.

Kane followed and slid back into the warm. He turned to look at Ella. "Did you witness the accident?"

"I don't even remember getting here. Last thing I remembered I was talking to Doug around eleven last night. I woke here and Doug went missing." Ella's teeth chattered as she spoke. "I don't know what's happening to me. I feel like I'm going crazy."

He took in her wild appearance. "No six-five man chasing you with an ax this time?"

"No, and no one has been by." Ella snuggled in the blanket. "Where is everyone?"

"The road is closed at Blackwater." Kane turned to Jenna. "Do you want me to drive her to the hospital and have the paramedics check her out?"

"No, I want to stay on scene. Call the paramedics on the satellite phone and notify Wolfe, then go over the vehicle. Give Rowley a call to run the plate; you won't have bars on your cellphone out here." Jenna sniffed and swiped at her nose. "I'll take her statement."

Kane glanced at Ella, then back at Jenna. His gut told him something didn't sit right. "Do you mind if I ask her something first?"

"Go right ahead." Jenna poured coffee into a cup and handed it to Ella.

Kane turned in his seat and took in Ella's appearance. She looked small and frightened wrapped in a blanket; but psychopaths came in a variety of types. "Two of your friends are missing and you're out in the middle of nowhere carrying a weapon. You say you don't remember how you got here. Do you often suffer blackouts?"

"Not until this morning. Look, I didn't *do* anything to Doug or Sky." Ella glared at him. "You can tell if someone fired the gun recently, can't you? I haven't hurt anyone."

"We didn't say you did but we have to ask questions to piece together what happened." Jenna gave Ella a smile. "Drink the coffee. It will keep you going until the paramedics arrive." She gave Kane a frown. "I can take it from here."

"Okay." Kane slid back out into the biting wind and made his way to the wreck. He leaned in the open door of the sedan and pulled the keys out the ignition, then dropped them into his pocket. He took out the satellite phone and called the paramedics for Ella Tate. The hospital informed him unless it was life or death situation, it would be a wait of more than two hours due to the amount of minor accidents around town. When he informed Wolfe of the situation, he agreed to transport Ella to the hospital if necessary and collect the car wreck victim.

After disconnecting, Kane scanned the interior of the vehicle and frowned. No purse or cellphone and, after examining the empty bag of takeout from the Blackwater Roadhouse, he had to assume more than one person was inside the vehicle at the time of the accident. Perturbed, he searched around and under the vehicle, climbing up packed snow piled up by the snowplow to peer beyond the car. Sleet cut into his face as he unlocked the trunk and peered inside. Three suitcases met his gaze, all with airline tags in the name of Olivia Palmer.

He called Rowley on the satellite phone to run the plates and discovered the vehicle belonged to Mrs. Ruby Palmer, a widow from Black Rock Falls. As usual, Maggie the Black Rock Falls Sheriff's Department receptionist was acquainted with the family. Olivia was a third-year student, who came home for Christmas every year. Her mother would have picked her up at Sweet Water Creek airport outside of Blackwater due to the temporary closure of the Black Rock Falls runway after the blizzard.

After asking Maggie to check the ER on the chance someone had come by and taken Olivia to the hospital, he disconnected and continued his search of the wreck. If the door had opened, it was possible the impact had thrown Olivia clear, but he found no signs of blood or a body imprint anywhere in the snow. Where was she and where was Doug Paul? Right now, with no clues to three people's disappearance, if someone suggested aliens had abducted them he might add it to his list of possibilities.

He pulled out his cellphone and took images of everything including the position of the body, the contents of the takeout bag and trunk, then went back to record the path the car had traveled from the road. He walked up and down the highway peering for any sign of braking and found none. The packed ice on the highway was marked with chains but he would expect that from the local traffic. He frowned and concluded the vehicle had taken the bend in the highway too fast, lost control in the icy conditions and slid across the road. The airbags likely deployed when the car hit the wall of compacted snow, blocking the driver's view and denying her any chance to steer the vehicle out of trouble. Without a seatbelt to protect her, when the car slammed into the wall of the ditch Mrs. Palmer smashed through the windshield.

With feet and fingers numb with cold, he headed back to his truck and climbed inside. A wave of heat and the smell of hot soup surrounded him. He gave Jenna a rundown of his conclusions, then glanced at Ella in the back seat, sipping from a cup. His attention slid back to Jenna. "What do we have?"

"Practically nothing." She filled a cup with soup from the Thermos and handed it to him, then pushed a bag of sandwiches within reach. "We'll talk outside."

Kane placed the cup in the console, grabbed a sandwich and reluctantly opened the car door and got back out into the bitterly cold wind. "Let's make this quick, my brain is freezing."

"Sure." Jenna examined his face and frowned. "She recalls making plans to meet a friend out here around eleven last night and they were going to search for Sky. The shotgun was for protection in case they met up with the man with the ax. She remembers planning to leave but not getting into Doug's vehicle." She sighed. "That's it. She has no memory until she woke up freezing cold in Doug's truck. He took his keys and cellphone."

"So we have to assume they met her friend." Kane glanced at Ella. "It's more than likely Doug found Olivia alive in the wreck and they took her to the hospital."

"Maybe, but why leave Ella here to freeze to death? She could have followed in Doug's truck." She glanced at the wreck. "It's not as if poor Mrs. Palmer is going anywhere. No, I don't figure that's what happened. The hospital would have notified us of the wreck last night." She pushed a lock of hair inside her cap and frowned. "I'll call Rowley to chase it down just in case someone forgot to call us."

"Already on it. Maggie is checking now." Kane rubbed his temple to relieve the ache. "Wolfe is on his way with Webber and as soon as he gives the all-clear, I'll have a tow truck come out to collect the wreck."

"Okay, I'll give Maggie a call and see what she's found." Jenna took the satellite phone he offered and shivered. "If this is another axman attack, why do you figure he left Ella behind unscathed both times? He had to have a reason."

Kane's mind went into overdrive at the implications. "Only one I can think of: to throw us off his scent and have us chasing our tails. It doesn't take a genius to know in any crime of this kind the last person to see a victim alive is the prime suspect until proven otherwise and the main focus of the investigation."

"Yeah, any TV cop show would tell him that, so he figures if we believe Ella is involved it will give him time to clean up his trail." Jenna wrinkled her nose. "Too bad for him we've dealt with enough psychopaths in the last couple of years not to fall into that trap."

"I figure he probably drugged her. Having her not remembering how she arrived here would add to her apparent instability." Kane rubbed his chin. "We'll run it past Wolfe; it could be a reason why she is acting so disorientated."

"That sounds like a plan. We'd better get back in the truck before we die of exposure." Jenna offered him a small smile and reached for the passenger door. "I'll speak to him when he's finished with his preliminary examination of the scene."

Kane climbed back behind the wheel, ate sandwiches and sipped soup, feeding bits of bread to Duke, while he waited for Jenna to finish her call. The shake of her head and worried expression said it all. Two more young people had disappeared along this road and they didn't have one single clue. If Ella was telling the truth and a hatchet-wielding crazy was stalking the backroads, they needed to find him and fast. It seemed each new season in Black Rock Falls brought with it a new brand of twisted psychopath. *What type of lunatic are we dealing with this time?*

CHAPTER TWENTY-NINE

As snowflakes landed on her eyelashes and ran over her cheeks, Jenna waited patiently for Wolfe to extract the grotesquely frozen body of Mrs. Palmer from the wreckage and load it into the back of the coroner's van. The ME had taken a great deal of time examining the body in situ and had gotten Webber to measure the distance from the road to the crash site. He had painstakingly walked the blacktop with Webber and his daughter Emily to determine where Mrs. Palmer lost control of her vehicle. His detailed examination of the interior of the vehicle, and most particularly the passenger-side door, had Jenna intrigued, but it wasn't his report she was waiting on. It was obvious that Mrs. Palmer died in a car wreck.

After speaking with Ella Tate, she couldn't make up her mind if the confused young woman was a good liar, a psychopath or suffering memory loss. She had left her in Kane's capable hands for further questioning, with Emily to listen in for experience. Having a young woman of the same age as support would be beneficial; Emily had incredible insight and had the ability to look at things from a different angle. As Wolfe shut the doors to his van, Jenna went to his side. "Find anything interesting?"

"Not conclusive but I'm with Kane on this one, I'm convinced someone else was in the vehicle. There are long blond hairs on the headrest and seat. The passenger-side carpet has marks on it consistent with someone sitting there recently wearing snow-covered boots, and I'm not convinced the door opened on impact." He brushed snowflakes from his face. "This is a late model vehicle and the doors lock automatically once the car reaches ten miles per hour. The chances of them flying open during impact would be minimal. The seatbelt is across the seat as if someone lifted her from the car and there is a small spot of blood on the airbag. I'll test it against a sample from Mrs. Palmer but it will be three days or so before I get a result."

Three people missing in similar circumstances in less than a week spelled serial killer. Jenna winced at the implications. "So, another kidnapping or worse?"

"It's a possibility." Wolfe pulled his hat down over his ears. "More so as the wreck wasn't reported. My concern is, if this is an unfortunate accident, why leave Ella out here? She had no food, no car keys. It seems a very irresponsible thing to do." He motioned to the van. "I'll get the body back to the morgue and thaw her out. We are only assuming the wreck was responsible for her death. Until I examine her, the cause is undetermined. She could have been shot for all we know." He sighed in a cloud of steam. "The vehicle is ready to be taken back to the inspection lot. I'll call the tow truck and make the arrangements. I have a satellite phone with me."

"Thanks. Before you go, I need to ask you something." She rubbed her hands together in an effort to prevent her fingers from freezing.

"Ask away." Wolfe indicated with his chin toward Emily sitting inside Kane's truck. "She isn't making a nuisance of herself, is she?"

Jenna smiled at his concerned expression. "Not at all, she is an asset. Be careful or I'll convince her to join the sheriff's department."

"That might not be as far-fetched as you think. She's planning to talk you into allowing her to ride along with you during her vacation to learn more about police procedure. She is a born profiler and I believe once she finishes her studies, she might well want to combine her talents."

"Like you?" Jenna chuckled. "Why am I not surprised? If she was a boy, I would have thought you'd cloned her."

"I'll take that as a compliment, ma'am." Wolfe looked suitably proud. "Was there something else on your mind?"

"Yeah. I've interviewed Ella Tate and she insists she can't remember anything since she decided to look for Sky Paul last night." She huffed out a puff of steam. "I've seen this before, this sudden memory loss, and it's usually in people who have been given date rape drugs. How long does it stay in the system and can we test her for it?"

"It depends which one they used, there are a few. As you know, she would have to ingest the drug, which is unlikely unless they used ketamine—that drug is used as an anesthetic on animals most times but would have the same effect." Wolfe's pale eyes narrowed. "We'll have about twenty-four hours to test for it and it might be an idea to look for a needle prick wound. If the perpetrator stuck her, he'd act fast so she couldn't fight back. He wouldn't be careful and as she is rugged up, I'd be looking for an exposed area, maybe neck or face."

"I'll ask her if she has any sore spots." Jenna chewed on her ice-cold bottom lip. "If she agrees to a blood test now, do you have your medical kit with you?"

"I never leave home without it." Wolfe turned back to his van. "I'll grab what I need and you can talk her into giving me a sample of her blood."

Jenna made her way over the slippery blacktop to Kane's truck and opened the door. "Emily, would you mind waiting with Webber? I need to speak to Ella."

"Sure. Thanks for allowing me to sit in." Emily wrapped a scarf around her face and dropped from the front seat, then skated precariously toward her father's van.

Jenna exchanged a meaningful look with Kane and turned in her seat. "Ella, I'm concerned your memory loss might be due to a drug."

"I don't take drugs." Ella gave her an indignant look. "Neither does Doug."

"I didn't say you did but the memory loss you're describing is consistent with a date rape drug." Jenna met the young woman's bewildered gaze. "Do you remember anyone sticking you with a needle or do you have a sore spot anywhere?"

"I don't remember but I do have a sore neck, right here." Ella pointed to her neck.

Jenna leaned over the back seat and peered at the small mark right at the jugular. "That could be a needle mark. If we take blood we can discover if someone drugged you."

"Okay, if it makes you believe me." Ella sighed. "How much longer do I have to sit here?"

"Five more minutes." Jenna looked at Kane. "Get a photo of that needle mark. Wolfe is heading over to take her blood." She smiled at Ella. "You'll be riding back to town with the ME. I'd like to have the paramedics check you over then you can go stay at the Pauls' house."

"No hospital." Ella glared at her. "I'm not hurt, I'm just cold and I need a pee."

"Okay, as long as you stay home until we discover what happened to your friends." Jenna watched Kane take a few images of the needle mark, then looked back at Ella. "Agreed?"

"Sure." Ella shrugged. "I don't know anyone else in Black Rock Falls to visit anyway."

After Wolfe took the blood and Ella accompanied him back to his van, Jenna leaned back in the seat and sighed. "Wolfe figures someone, possibly injured, was carried from the wreck to a waiting vehicle."

"It looks that way but from the variety of car tracks on the highway it's impossible to confirm another vehicle was involved." Kane waved a hand toward the road. "I found chain marks all along the ice opposite the wreck, but at this time of the year this road is often busy with people coming home for the holidays. Someone could have stopped here anytime between the first snow and the freeze but there's no conclusive evidence to suggest a vehicle stopped there last night." He stared out the windshield as if thinking over their impossible situation. "There is no evidence to suggest a kidnapping, no vehicles, or blood evidence apart from the small spot on the airbag, which could easily be blood spatter from Mrs. Palmer. We have zip." He sighed. "I doubt we'll find anything wrong with Doug Paul's truck either and he would be aware of the weather conditions and had a perfectly good vehicle to shelter inside until help came. Only a fool would set out on foot and where would they head? There's nothing for miles out here. I figure it's pointless calling out search and rescue again in the hope they find two people walking in the snow. If they'd kept to the highway like any sensible person, we would have seen them and at the speed I was driving I wouldn't have missed them."

Jenna nodded. "I'll give the media an update and put out another BOLO in case someone gave them a ride, and get search and rescue out again. It's all we can do for now. Ella recalls the time she spoke to Doug last night being around eleven. The road sign would have already been erected or soon after. I'll find out the exact time they erected the sign." She met his gaze. "This would mean if anyone picked up Doug and Olivia they would have been traveling from Blackwater to Black Rock Falls before eleven when the truck blocked the highway. There is only one way they could have traveled and that's into Black Rock Falls or beyond." She looked at him. "We need to be looking for them closer to town or in town."

"Another thing to consider. From all accounts Doug is a sensible guy." Kane's eyebrows bunched together in concentration. "If he'd found Olivia alive, he would have driven her straight to the hospital and called us to attend the wreck. So, something else happened here and it's obvious to me Ella isn't involved. I figure she's a patsy." His wide shoulders lifted in a shrug. "There is only one conclusion. This isn't a coincidence and whoever kidnapped them took Sky as well. I'm with you; in this weather, they have to be close to Black Rock Falls. It's the only logical conclusion."

Jenna poured more coffee from the Thermos and sipped, warming her hands on the cup. "Yeah, and if we hadn't found Ella alone in Doug's truck, we would have written this up as a nasty accident."

"Maybe not." Kane sipped his coffee. "You would have checked the trunk and found the bags belonging to Olivia. One of them had a Montana State tag on it as well, so we'd assume her mother collected her from the airport, which is what Maggie suggested."

Jenna frowned. "I'll tell Rowley to call the airport and find out when she arrived. We know it was before eleven last night because the overturned truck has blocked the highway since then." She finished her coffee and turned to Kane. "We'll head back to the office."

"I'm getting low on gas, so we'll have to stop in town." Kane turned his truck around and headed back down the highway. "What bothers me is why kidnap Doug? If this is some weirdo on a killing spree, they usually stick to the same gender. What is the motive?"

"Both sexes, young, good-looking, says sex slaves to me." Jenna wrinkled her nose in disgust. "They get them hooked on drugs then use the addiction to control them. I've seen young men, women and kids sold overseas. It's a growing problem and something we need to consider."

"You look as if you have a plan." Kane raised one eyebrow.

Jenna nodded. "I'm considering potential suspects. Maybe our suspect is a truck driver who passes through on a regular haul. He could have made it through earlier, seen the women alone in their car and nudged them off the road. It happened to me easily enough, remember."

"Scared her off the highway maybe." Kane stared straight ahead, his brow wrinkled in concentration. "I checked the vehicle all over and found no scrapes or paint transfer from another vehicle."

Jenna shook her head. "That doesn't mean a thing. A fourteen wheeler bearing down on a driver, especially on a bend in these conditions, could make anyone panic and right now it's all I have to go on." She sighed. "I'll contact the local business council and get a list of the factories in the area open for short periods during the shutdown for deliveries." She shrugged. "I figure it's a place to start because I'm running out of ideas." She glanced at him. "One thing for certain, if this kidnapper is an opportunist, he is the luckiest man I know."

CHAPTER THIRTY

Thursday

He walked into her office and, shutting the door behind him, clicked the lock. His visits thrilled her, especially knowing there were people outside and they risked discovery. When she stood to greet him with a hungry look on her face, he dutifully moved around the desk to embrace her, as any lover would do. "I've missed you. I should come by more often."

Oh yeah, he could play the part. Hell, he'd been playacting his entire life. It amused him that people actually believed him. Not that he cared about anyone's opinion of him, but he often wondered what caring for someone would actually feel like. Perhaps it came close to what he expected to receive from someone.

As his pa had taught him, value was what a person expected to receive. He smiled at his girlfriend and noticed the way her eyes changed when she gazed up at him. Many women looked at him that way and he figured he could have any of them. Most who wanted him had outstanding beauty, wealth and likely figured him husband material, but no woman would hog-tie him into marriage.

His girlfriend was not pretty, in fact, she was somewhat plain, but to him she was a commodity. Her use to him was twofold. He needed her expertise and loyalty. Making her believe he cared for her had been easy but his genius had prevailed when he convinced her to go along with his plans. He smiled down at her; he had her wrapped around his little finger. In fact, if everything went to hell, he wouldn't need to kill her to guarantee her silence: she would willingly protect him and pay the price.

No one could implicate him in any wrongdoing because he had outsmarted everyone, with the exception of Sheriff Alton. She hadn't taken the bait and had allowed Ella Tate to walk, so now he would throw her another curveball and kill someone at random. He would go out for a drive later and cave in the head of the first unsuspecting gullible fool who stopped to help him, then leave the blood-soaked body on the side of the road. The sheriff would be scratching her head, wondering how many killers she had lurking along the same stretch of highway. He bit back a chuckle. Oh, yeah, just the thought of hearing a skull crushing and watching blood seep across the snow would soothe his urge to kill for long enough to act the part of a devoted boyfriend.

CHAPTER THIRTY-ONE

At her desk, Jenna allowed the previous day's events to percolate in her mind. Frantic for the safety of the missing people, she had ordered search and rescue out at dawn again. They had been searching the highway south of the wreck and truck-spill for stranded motorists but a sweeping yet thorough search had again yielded nothing. At least now she had a timeframe; the Department of Transport had blocked the highway and erected the road closure signs at midnight in both Black Rock Falls and Blackwater. This would put the time of the car wreck and the abduction of Doug and Olivia between eleven and midnight. She had updated the media release, and hoped someone would call in with a lead. After working through the day making calls and gathering information, she stared at the notes. Somewhere in the pile of information had to be a clue to where someone had taken the missing people.

A few of the factories opened during the shutdown on a limited basis, as she had surmised. The local meat processing plant opened up one day the week prior to Christmas to ensure fresh meat was available before the holidays. It ran a skeleton staff, processed no more than ten steers and had been in shutdown for two weeks. The local recyclers remained open on various times depending on the need to crush or shred waste. Kane and Rowley had checked them out and not found a trace of Sky's vehicle.

Jenna stared at her notes then back to Rowley's case files. As meticulous as usual, Rowley had run down a list of anyone who regularly visited Black Rock Falls. The list included truck drivers bringing supplies from other towns or interstate, real estate brokers and the mail delivery trucks, including FedEx and UPS. She added a reminder to speak to the snowplow drivers; they moved up and down the highway more frequently than most, but she figured kidnapping two people in a snowplow would be near impossible. *But they might have seen something I can use.*

There was a knock on her door and she dragged her attention away from her computer screen and looked up to see Kane. "Come in. Have you found anything useful?"

"Yeah, I have a list of the drivers who regularly come through town on the days the people went missing. But that's not why I'm here." Kane took a step forward, then stopped. "It's way past seven and Maggie is anxious to get home to her family." He cleared his throat and his expression was serious. "Rowley's stomach is growling so loud it's making Duke jumpy. Can we make tracks for home soon?"

Jenna glanced out the window into inky blackness. The day had slipped by in what seemed like a couple of hours. "Oh Lord, I didn't notice how late it had gotten. I'm sorry, this case is time-consuming. I've worked all afternoon and have next to no leads at all." She leaned back in her chair. "Please give Maggie my apologies and send her on home. What is Rowley doing, is he staying in the cottage tonight?"

"Nope, he moved all his things out this morning." Kane smiled. "He's happy to be back in his own home."

Jenna stretched and smiled. "I guess you'd better send him home too and we'll head down to Aunt Betty's for a meal, my treat." She pushed her hair from her face. "While we're eating we can work out what to do next. Do you mind if we both go in your truck? I don't really want to drive home alone tonight."

"Me either. I've fed Duke and he'll sleep in my truck while we're eating. He'll be cozy enough wearing his coat and covered with a thick blanket for half an hour." Kane placed the folder on the desk and smiled. "I'll tell everyone the good news."

They dashed into Aunt Betty's Café to avoid the flurry of snow soaking their clothes combined with a cruel wind. Warmth and the wonderful aromas of cooking and strong fresh coffee surrounded Jenna the moment she stepped inside the door. She loved the atmosphere of this place; it was like stepping into a warm hug. It surprised her that a café in a relatively small town stayed open until eleven and later each night. The place was never empty and during the day people lined up to be served. One thing for sure, here nobody ever walked away disappointed.

She smiled at Rowley as he turned away from the counter hugging a large takeout bag. "Have you tried the pumpkin soup?"

"Yeah, I've picked up enough for lunch tomorrow as well in case we're busy." Rowley tipped his hat. "Goodnight, ma'am." He headed for the door.

"Night." She took a quick glance at the daily specials board and her stomach growled in appreciation. Then she made her way through the tables to one against the wall at the back.

The management had a permanent "Reserved for the sheriff's department" card displayed beside the menu. With her deputies dashing in for quick meals, they didn't have time to line up and the staff at Aunt Betty's gave them priority. They all appreciated the kind gesture. Jenna removed her coat and gloves then took her seat. Opposite her, Kane draped his coat over the back of the chair and sat with his back to the wall as usual, his eagle eyes scanning the customers for any strangers in town.

They ordered and within minutes Jenna was humming with contentment over a large bowl of pumpkin soup. She had ordered steak with all the trimmings as well and Kane followed suit. "Oh, this is so good."

"I'm glad to see you have your appetite back." Kane looked at her, spoon hovering over the plate. "While you were working this afternoon, I checked out the database for similar cases. Six people have vanished over the last few months, and all reportedly traveled on the highway from Blackwater to here and were heading for local towns in both directions."

Jenna swallowed a mouthful of soup and sighed. "Why didn't we receive a BOLO or missing person notification?"

"We did." Kane leaned back in his chair as the waitress cleared the plates and replaced them with their main meals. "They were logged and handled by Rowley and Walters."

Surprised Rowley hadn't brought the incidents to her attention, Jenna frowned. "Rowley never fails to update me and Walters is the same."

"Yeah but you had a few things on your mind at the time." Kane cut into his steak. "The first few were reported when you were in Washington DC visiting me in the hospital, the others during the week you took off work to care for me, and the last one came through when you were too ill to speak to anyone. Rowley was in charge and he dealt with it." He lifted his fork and paused it at his mouth. "All the paperwork is in order. The last person to go missing was Trudy Simmons, twenty years old, out of Glass Ridge. She was heading from Blackwater to a school reunion in her hometown. All the reports came from different counties. Rowley checked with the hospital, hotel and gas station in town and found no trace of her. He followed protocol and convinced Wolfe to use his new facial recognition software on the CCTV footage he collected from town, and came up with a big fat zero. Rowley handled all the cases in the same way, did the usual checks and found no trace of them. It's just like Sky and Doug Paul. They seem to have vanished without a trace."

Jenna sipped her coffee and eyed him over the rim of her cup. "So Rowley filed the reports, sent copies to the relevant counties and didn't bother me with them. I can see why in the circumstances—they didn't concern our department." She frowned. "But he should have brought them to my attention now."

"He chased them down again today and you have all the details in your files." Kane smiled. "As you spent the entire afternoon locked in your office on the phone, he informed me."

Intrigued, Jenna considered the information. "What about the ages? There has to be something that ties these cases together."

"All are between nineteen and twenty-two." Kane went back to his meal and they sat in silence for a few minutes.

In an effort to come up with a suspect, Jenna allowed the information she had gathered earlier to percolate through her mind. She finished her meal and waited for the waitress to refill her coffee cup. "I've been going over a list of possible suspects." She leaned back in her chair. "It has to be someone who uses that highway regularly and I have a list of people. Delivery drivers mostly, but I can't help thinking the postal service van would be up and down that road daily. Mail comes into the post office, is sorted and then the local mailman delivers it, right?"

"Uh-huh." Kane nodded and chewed slowly, then swallowed. "We would have to find out what time the usual delivery arrives. It could be overnight."

Excitement thrummed through her. "Okay, we have at least one person to talk to." She leaned forward in her seat. "Who else would come through overnight?"

"Milk maybe?" Kane pushed his plate to one side and reached for his coffee. "I'm not sure what perishables are delivered daily. I do know when I dropped by for the soup and sandwiches earlier today the waitresses were worried about supplies getting through from Blackwater."

Jenna took out her notepad and looked up at Kane. "FedEx deliveries would be easy to hunt down but there must be other deliveries or truck drivers who pass through town on a regular basis."

"Most will have logbooks but all these places will be closed now." Kane smothered a yawn. "It's been a long day and I still have to tend the horses."

After so long at home, Jenna did not feel the least bit tired. "Oh, I'll help with the horses. I have more to tell you. We'll chat on the way home." She paid the bill by credit card, stood, dragged on her coat and headed for the door.

As they made their way home, snow built up on the windshield wipers and, once they turned off the main highway onto the road leading to her ranch, the way became treacherous. She had faith in Kane's driving but was aware of how slowly he was moving along the ice-covered road. She cleared her throat. "The other thing I wanted to mention is not all the factories shut down for the entire holiday season. Some of them open one day a week to keep supply available to the local stores."

"Now that's interesting because I patrolled the area and found no sign of anyone being there for at least a week." He leaned forward, peering ahead as the snow pelted his truck. "The junkyard gave me the impression the gate could have been opened since the first blizzard but that place wouldn't need to supply local stores."

The back wheels of the truck slid sideways and Jenna's heart picked up a beat. She gripped the seat and looked at Kane. His face was a mask of concentration. He turned and smiled. "It's okay; we hit a patch of ice. Worst case we'll slide into the ditch and at this speed we'll be able to drive right out."

Jenna barked out a laugh. "Oh, you're filling me with confidence."

"Trust the beast and the new snow tires." He chuckled. "Not far now."

Jenna breathed a sigh of relief. "Okay, so we have a few things to hunt down tomorrow. I'll get Rowley and Walters to start looking for people we can interview. I figure we should check out the factories I know are open during the shutdown and see if there's anyone we can speak to."

"Okay." Kane maneuvered his vehicle through the gate and floodlights lit up the property.

A beep sounded as the remote in Kane's vehicle connected with the alarm system and he slowed at the house. She turned to him. "Give me five to change. I'll meet you at the stables." She grabbed her things and slipped from the car.

"I'll come inside and make sure it's safe." Kane opened his door and stepped outside.

Jenna waved him away. "I'll be fine." She pulled out her weapon. "The new security system would have alerted me if anyone had stepped foot inside my gate but I'll check anyway."

"Then I'll wait here until you give me the all-clear." Kane leaned against his truck and watched her climb the steps.

Jenna went inside, dropped her belongings on the hall table and did a sweep of the house, then went to the door and waved at Kane. "All clear."

She headed for the bedroom. At least she had a few leads to hunt down. Agreed, it was not many, but it was a start and if the man with the ax existed in her town, she would find him and discover what had happened to Sky and Doug Paul and Olivia Palmer.

CHAPTER THIRTY-TWO

Thursday night

It was late when Levi Holt passed through Black Rock Falls on his way to spend his vacation with his folks in Blackwater. The road report on the radio told him the highway was clear and rather than risking another blizzard blowing in, which would mean being stuck in Black Rock Falls for days while the snowplows did their job, he decided to drive through the night if necessary to get home.

The dark road wound ahead of him like a frosty black snake, cutting through the snow-covered landscape. The world had turned gray and black the moment the sun set. Trees and the odd buildings became murky and foreboding. His mother had warned him about the dangers of traveling at night and he'd heard the reports of people going missing, so he took his time, searching ahead for any sudden changes in road conditions. The sky was patchy with clouds and once in a while the full moon popped its head out between the heavy clouds. He turned up the radio and sang along to the tunes, or munched on a bag of beef jerky he'd placed within easy reach on the seat beside him.

The idea of seeing his friends again made him smile. The selfies they had posted on Facebook, wearing Santa hats and urging him to come straight away after his final shift at Tire and Mechanical, had made up his mind to drive all night.

He slowed to round a sweeping bend sparkling with small patches of ice, and noticed ahead a vehicle with its hood up and flashers blinking orange in the dark. *Dammit, I guess I'll have to stop.*

After coming alongside the pickup, he buzzed down his window. "Hey. Need any help?"

"Yeah, engine just stopped. It's got plenty of gas." A man slid out from behind the wheel. "I've been hopin' a truck driver would come on by and radio a tow truck for me. I can't get no bars out here to call anyone."

Levi frowned. "Can't help you call anyone but I know engines. I'll take a look," He closed the window, found his flashlight and slid out into the bitter cold, leaving his engine running.

"Thank you kindly." The man walked to the front of the vehicle. "I have a wrench if that's any help?" He waved the tool.

"I have tools in my truck." Levi turned on the flashlight and approached the front of the pickup.

It was fortunate at that moment that the moon slipped out from behind a cloud or he wouldn't have seen the shadow of the man's arm raised above his head. Levi ducked to one side as the wrench chimed against the radiator. Fear gripped him by the throat. He spun around, striking out with his torch and catching the man hard across his right arm. When the stranger gasped in pain and staggered backward, Levi didn't wait for an explanation, he slipped and slid in the snow at the edge of the blacktop. "What the hell?"

The man came fast, swinging wildly at him and missing by inches. All Levi had was his flashlight. He shone it into the man's eyes, hoping the high-powered halogen beam had blinded him for a second, then took off at a run and slid across the road. He dived back into his truck, his hands trembling as he locked the doors. He reached for the shifter just as the maniac came at him again. The wrench shattered the side window, showering him with glass. He slammed his foot on the accelerator, spinning the wheels on ice and fishtailing down the highway.

Heart racing so fast he could hear it thumping in his ears, he stared out the broken window at the man running after him. "That must be the guy the news said has been kidnappin' people."

Terrified, he slammed down on the gas. The powerful engine roared but the back wheels lost traction. He fought for control but slid across the highway, coming to rest in the deep-packed snow beside the blacktop. Without warning, the engine spluttered and died. Every muscle trembling, he gaped into the side mirror at the dark shadow of the stranger hurrying purposefully toward him. Sheer panic gripped him. "Oh, Jesus."

He sucked in a freezing breath and turned the key. The engine turned—nothing. He tried again. "Come on, come on."

Grasping desperately at his knowledge of engines, he pushed down hard on the gas and turned the key again with trembling fingers. He let out a sob as the perfectly tuned motor burst into life, but the crazy man had gained on him and was little more than twenty yards away. He squeezed the gas pedal down gently and his truck moved forward. "That's it, nice and slow, you can do it, girl. Get me the hell out of here."

At last the tires' chains dug into the ice, giving him traction, and he aimed the truck back onto the highway. As he drove away the man vanished into the darkness behind him, but he kept one eye on his mirror, not sure what to do if the maniac followed him. The icy wind buffeted him through the broken window but he dared not stop to cover it. A half-hour later, he entered Blackwater. Five more minutes and he would be home. Once safe inside, he would call 911.

CHAPTER THIRTY-THREE

Friday Morning

The heating in the office was failing miserably and Jenna stuffed a few tissues into the gap at the bottom of the rattling window. The weather had been acting strange of late. Blizzards blanketed the town with snowdrifts so high, people had to dig out their vehicles, and the next moment a howling wind came through town as if the devil himself was chasing it. This had to be the coldest winter she had spent in Black Rock Falls. When Rowley knocked on her door with a somber expression she had some idea the news about the furnace was not good. "What did Mr. Jeffries say?"

"We need a new furnace, he don't figure they make parts for ours anymore." Rowley had abandoned his regulation Stetson and opted for the same thick woolen hat Kane preferred and had it pulled down over his ears. "Problem is, if you want to buy a new one, getting it here at this time of the year will be difficult." He handed her an invoice from the plumber. "He said he could do something to keep it running but it might only last a day or two. At the bottom of the invoice is a quote for a replacement."

Jenna glanced at the paperwork and nodded. "I'd normally have to get the mayor to approve an expense that big but we have enough in the budget. Thank him for me and tell him to go ahead with the repairs. I'll see if we can find a furnace. Wolfe seems to have connections everywhere. Maggie will pay the plumber what he is owed for today." She inhaled the smell of cinnamon and hot chocolate. "If that's Kane with the food for our meeting, grab Walters and come back as soon as possible."

"Yes, ma'am." Rowley headed out the door.

A few moments later Kane walked through the door, his cheeks reddened by the wind and carrying bags of takeout from Aunt Betty's Café. "Ah, just in time." Jenna took a bag from him and peered inside. "I thought I smelled cinnamon buns."

"Yeah, and I had the Thermoses filled with hot chocolate as well." He smiled at her. "There's enough cake and cookies to keep us going until lunch." He turned back to the door. "I'll shuck my coat and grab some cups."

When she had her deputies settled, she pulled down the white-board covered with names she had gathered of people of interest. She turned to her deputies. "I called our contact at the FBI and his response to our current spate of missing people was that we're pretty much on our own with this case. We've no solid evidence to suggest a man kidnapped the missing people apart from Ella Tate's statement. Normally she'd be a person of interest but we can't jump to conclusions. Although we did find her at the scene of two or more people's disappearance, we believe her to be an unreliable witness, due to the influence of drugs or mental capacity. We're still waiting for the toxicology report from Wolfe about the involvement of date rape drugs. If this is the case, she will slowly regain her memory and we'll interview her again." She pointed to a list of names. "In the meantime, we have two people missing and likely a third. We haven't been able to contact any of Rose Palmer's relatives but we do know she arrived at the airport at nine to pick up Olivia Palmer. Rowley is hunting down Olivia's friends via social media in the hope they may be of assistance." She turned to Rowley. "Have you found anyone?"

"Yeah." Rowley stared down at his iPad. "I've added them to the file."

"Good." She smiled at Walters. "I'll leave that part of the investigation in your capable hands. Call me if you find any leads."

"Sure thing, ma'am." Walters looked happy to be remaining inside today. "I'll see if I can put a firecracker under the plumber fixin' the furnace too."

"That would help." She met Kane's gaze. "What have you got for me, Kane?"

"I've been scanning the database for any similar incidents to add to what Rowley discovered yesterday and found more unsubstantiated reports about people vanishing without a trace throughout the state. They're all aged between eighteen and twenty-five, all but one was traveling alone and their vehicles have never been located." He poured a cup of hot chocolate from the Thermos, then leaned back in his chair, cup in hand. "One thing that joined the dots for me was that they all traveled though Black Rock Falls. I figure they're connected."

The hairs on the back of Jenna's neck prickled. It was obvious they had another killer in town. "So if the kidnapper, let's call him Axman, has been doing this for some time, how do you figure he's disposing of the vehicles and bodies?" She glanced at her deputies.

"We're only assuming Axman killed these people. The slave trade we discussed is always an option." Kane's eyebrows knitted together in a frown. "Has Wolfe given a cause of death for Mrs. Palmer?"

"Not yet." Jenna leaned on the desk, palms flat, and stared at Kane. "Sure, we might find bodies of people who died of natural causes after the melt but Ella Tate's statement and the amount of blood we found gives me cause to believe at least Sky suffered considerable injury by an ax-wielding man." She straightened. "So yes, until one of these people walks into my office, alive and well, we're looking for bodies." She went back to the whiteboard. "Rowley, what would be the best place to dispose of a vehicle in the immediate area of the kidnapping?"

"The area he seems to be stalking is mainly industrial." Rowley filled his cup and his brow wrinkled in concentration. "There are masses of old shafts left from goldmines. They could be dumping grounds for both bodies and vehicles. Some shafts go down miles." He took a cinnamon bun from the bag. "We already checked out the local junkyard. It was deserted."

"It was on that day." Kane gave Jenna a direct stare. "I'm convinced someone's opened the gate since the night Sky disappeared. We can't rule out the chance the Axman had an accomplice to dispose of her vehicle."

Jenna made notes on the whiteboard. "That is a possibility but it's easy enough to tow a car without a driver. The Axman would only need access to the yard and the knowledge to use the necessary machinery. Did you see a crusher at the recycling yard?"

"Yeah and a shredder, but he would need more than the key to the gate, we're talking heavy-duty machinery here." Kane reached into the bag for a cookie. "He would need keys and the skills to move the vehicle into the compactor using the electromagnet crane." He shrugged. "Placing a body in the trunk of a car and crushing it is not new. It used to be quite popular body disposal back in the day."

Jenna's stomach clenched at the thought of using a crusher to dispose of a body. "Well, there's no way he towed Sky's truck out to a goldmine in a blizzard without leaving a trace. The snow was four foot deep in places. The recycling yard is a logical option and one of them is in the location of the kidnappings."

After scanning the board, Jenna sat down. Now convinced they had a lunatic in the backcountry, she needed to step up the investigation before he struck again, but without evidence, she might as well be chasing her tail. She needed one simple clue to get the ball rolling. "Okay. I have a list of factories in the area on file. Rowley, chase down the owners and get me their numbers. Get me the names of anyone who might work during the shutdown." She wrote on the board. "We'll start with the junkyard. I'll organize a search warrant, notify the owner to meet us on site and head out with Kane." She moved her attention to Kane. "Call Wolfe. I want him along to search for trace evidence just in case the Axman crushed the bodies as well. We'll use your truck, Kane; it's safer in the snow. Can you get our gear together?"

"Sure." Kane went to rise.

"Just a minute." She chewed on her pen, thinking, for a few seconds. "If we assume the Axman is kidnapping and killing these people and then crushing them in their vehicles, what type of crazy are we up against?"

"Without a body and cause of death, I can't give you an accurate profile." Kane shrugged. "I mean, there are the opportunistic killers. They murder because they like the adrenaline rush but the majority of them walk away from the kill site. A dead person is no more use to them than a soda can. Most of them don't fully comprehend they're doing anything wrong. In fact, in a few interviews I've listened to the murderers figured everyone kills—that it's normal." He leaned back and looked at her. "If this man is hiding his kills and their belongings, he plans the murders and chooses the victims for a reason. He likely a sociopath, fully aware of what he's doing and the consequences, but likely believes he's so smart we'll never catch him."

CHAPTER THIRTY-FOUR

The next time Doug opened his eyes and stared at the stark white ceiling. he realized with a jolt his situation was not a terrible dream. He swiped his tongue over dry, cracked lips and wiggled his toes. Although the burning sensation of a red-hot poker stabbed into his side, the heavy feeling in his limbs had eased. He lifted his arms, pushing the covers to one side, and attempted to rise. Agony seared through him on the right side as if a spear had gone through his body and was still sticking out his back. He looked down his bare chest and gingerly ran his fingers over the thick wad of dressing. *What happened to me?*

In a rush, his mind filled with the image of the hopeless expression of the young woman in the next bed. The doctor must have given her the same stupefying drug as they had given him. He would never forget how terrified Jim had made her. He punched the mattress in a fit of anger. No wonder her face was familiar! She was the one in the wreck. He had cradled her head in his lap in the back of Jim's pickup. Jim had called the girl "Olivia" yet hadn't mentioned knowing her at the time.

With care, he rolled to one side and tried to sit on the side of the bed. Agony flamed through him but he managed to drop both legs over the edge. He tugged out the catheter attached to him with disgust. The drip in his arm no doubt carried pain meds. Whatever drugs they had used on him before had gone way past pain relief; they'd turned him into a zombie.

The room moved in and out of focus and threatened to fold in at the edges. Long moments of nausea followed and he gripped the edge of the bed like a life preserver until the ebb and flow of his balance subsided. He wanted to speak to Olivia, then glanced down at his nakedness. The last thing she needed was to see a naked man approaching her bed. Gritting his teeth against the pain, he tugged at the blanket and fashioned a toga, then eased his feet onto the cold floor. Sweat covered his skin and dripped down his nose with the effort of taking one single step. The pain in his side seemed to crush his lungs, preventing an intake of breath.

He reached for the curtains around his bed and they opened with a swish of metal runners. The girl was staring at him and he placed one finger over his mouth to signal her to be quiet. He scanned the room, searching for any CCTV cameras, then dropped his voice to just above a whisper. It came out husky from his dry throat. "I'm sorry I couldn't help you. They had me on some strange drug, I couldn't move."

"I know. They pump that shit into us all the time." She blinked at him. "I couldn't do anything to stop him either." Her bottom lip quivered and tears welled in her eyes. "It was terrible. I thought he was going to cut out my eye."

Not sure what to say, Doug nodded. "I'm so sorry." He swallowed the lump in his throat. "We have to tell someone what's happened."

"Doctors can't just drug people, tie them down and frighten them like that." Olivia sniffed. "I hope we're not in a psychiatric ward by mistake. I've heard of nurses doing all sorts of terrible things in those places."

"I have no reason to be in one." Doug eyed her cautiously. "Have you?"

"No." Olivia blinked away tears. "I was driving home for the holidays with my mom and she wrecked the car. When I woke up,

I thought I'd been hurt. Then he showed up and… well, you know the rest." She let out a little sob.

The poor woman was terrified. "Nothing here makes sense. I can't remember anything happening to me, yet I have a dressing on my side that hurts like hell." Doug waved a hand toward the door. "How often do the doctors come by?"

"I'm pretty sure they've left for the day." She indicated toward the beeping machine beside his bed. "Turn off your machine in case your increased heartbeat signals an alarm and get that needle out of your arm. The machine drugs us every four hours. I know because I heard them talking." She looked at him wild-eyed. "They give me a different drug when that awful man comes to visit and I can't move. He is a sick SOB and insists I'm tied to the bed and drugged." Tears streamed down her cheeks. "I never know what he's going to do next. It's like he gets off on scaring me."

"We have to go get help." Horrified by her words, Doug turned and shuffled to the monitors and disabled all of them, then pulled off the wires attached to his chest. He removed his drip, then released Olivia from the restraints, noticing the way she shrank away from him. "Hey, I'm not going to hurt you. I just want to get the hell out of here." He stared at the door. "They don't just leave us alone all night, do they?"

"I don't think they care if we die." She rubbed her wrists, then, as if making a decision, held out one trembling arm. "Can you take my needle out?"

He detached her drip and made her press down on the wound. "Have you told anyone what Jim is doing to you? That's his name, isn't it? I met him when we pulled you out the car wreck but I don't know why I ended up in here."

"Did you see the accident?" Her eyes became wide and fearful. "Is my mom okay?"

Doug swallowed hard, not sure what to tell her. He was only taking Jim's word the woman had died. Rather than make the situation worse, he shrugged. "She went through the windshield. We had gotten you out the car, then I'm pretty darn sure Jim stuck me with a needle." He looked at her tragic expression. "I don't know for sure but my friend was there. She had my cellphone and my truck."

"Okay." Olivia visibly pulled herself together. "So my mom could be here too?"

"Maybe." He glanced at the door. "We need to find out. How many people work in this ward?"

"Only two but they talk about someone else. The nurse knows what Jim is doing to me. He jokes about it." She bit her bottom lip. "I'm not hurt apart from a bump on the head, so why do you figure they're keeping me here?"

From the quantity of drugs the nurse had pumped into them, he figured the hospital could be part of the sex-slave industry. Once hooked and under control they would be sold overseas to work as prostitutes. He glanced at Olivia's frightened, ashen expression and shook his head. Right now, she didn't need to know. "I'm not sure what's going on but we need to get out of here." He dashed a hand through his hair. "I know Jim is a medical student and I guess the other one is a nurse."

"Yeah. He's the one who administers the drugs and cares for us." She avoided his gaze. "He does what Jim tells him to do. Jim is the creepy one. He has dead eyes. I'm terrified he's going to kill me." Olivia pushed into a sitting position and used the sheet to wipe away her tears. "I heard them talking but I don't know why you're here or how you came by that injury."

Doug touched the dressing on his side. "I don't remember being hurt at all."

"I don't know either but they mentioned you were here because of someone called Sky."

CHAPTER THIRTY-FIVE

Friday Afternoon

Jenna slid the search warrant for the recycling yard into the pocket of her coat, collected her satellite phone and met up with Kane at the front counter. She could see Wolfe and Webber leaning against Wolfe's new SUV in deep conversation and headed outside. The town resembled a frozen tundra, icicles as long as swords hung dangerously from the gutters and snowdrifts in some places came up to her waist. A blast of freezing wind filled with ice blasted her cheeks and she heard Kane's moan of displeasure. The cold would be causing havoc with his head injury but if she suggested he should remain in the office, he would give her one of his disgruntled looks and shake his head. She flicked a glance over him, glad he had taken every precaution to keep warm. Not even the tip of his nose was showing under his sunglasses.

Snow fell in a constant relentless curtain, covering everything in minutes. The frozen trees creaked, threatening to snap in two and shed mini avalanches of snow onto the footpath and any unsuspecting people walking under them. The snowplows and brine-spreaders had been by during the day in their never-ending effort to keep the roads clear. She wrapped her scarf around her head but the woolen cap and hooded jacket did little to protect her face. After sliding her sunglasses on, she moved with caution over the ice-coated sidewalk to speak to Wolfe. "We're meeting the owner, Bill Sawyer, at the yard. He did say no one has been there since the shutdown two weeks ago."

"How did you manage to get a search warrant?" Wolfe straightened and indicated to Webber to get into the car. "We don't have much in the way of probable cause."

Jenna lifted her chin to look at him. "We do. Kane visited the yard on Tuesday and noticed someone had opened the gate after the blizzard. The owner states no one has been there, so I went with what we had, a witness saying an axman attacked Sky. Her car is missing and we have reason to believe the vehicle could be at that location. We need to find evidence Sky or her car was there."

"One good thing about winter. The cold preserves DNA." Wolfe pulled open the door to his truck and slid inside. "We'll follow you."

Jenna climbed into Kane's black truck and noticed his usual supply of hot drinks and snacks piled into the center console but the bloodhound was missing. She waited for him to slide behind the wheel. "Where's Duke?"

"Believe it or not, he's behind the front counter in his basket, with Maggie. She has a heater near her feet and feeds him treats all day long. I guess the clingy stage is over at last." Kane pulled down his scarf and smiled at her. "I asked him to come with me and he pretended to be asleep."

Jenna chuckled and unwound her scarf. "I don't blame him; I'd rather be inside in this weather too."

They headed downtown past the park, surprisingly filled with rosy-faced children playing around the gigantic decorated tree while others created snow angels in the new drifts. The giggling kids were such a contrast to the huddle of parents, hunched against the cold with their hands pushed deep in their pockets. The noise of laughter and screeches of delight as a small group pelted each other with snowballs filled her mind with fond memories of her own childhood. The holidays had been special, filled with warm hugs. She swallowed hard, at that moment realizing having her own kids was an empty dream. The day she'd walked away from being Agent Avril Parker and become Sheriff Jenna Alton, she'd given up everything. *In truth, I don't exist.*

"It's harder in the holidays." Kane glanced at her as if he'd just read her mind. "The memories are a bitch. They blindside me at the strangest moments."

"Me too." She turned in her seat. "I think deep down I wanted to have kids but after my folks died I shut off my emotions. I didn't really consider the future and what it meant to be an agent."

"I knew the risks but I figured they'd be overseas, not here." Kane slowed to take a bend and then, once on the interstate, increased speed. "Worse still was not being able to speak about it to anyone, or being able to do anything." He wiped his hand down his face, then turned to smile at her. "Wolfe wants us to spend Christmas Day with him and the girls."

Filling with a warm glow, Jenna grinned. "Really? I'd love that."

"Me too." Kane chuckled. "The girls told him it wouldn't be Christmas without all the family. They wanted Rowley too, and Webber, but Rowley is spending the holidays with his folks and I hear Webber has a girlfriend."

Jenna gaped at him. "Really? I thought he was interested in Emily and Wolfe was concerned because he was too old for her."

"Long story." Kane shrugged. "I gather Wolfe told him to keep his distance until Emily finished college and since she came home, it seems her crush on Webber is over."

The radio crackled and Wolfe gave his call sign. Jenna picked it up. "Go to our safe channel. Over."

Not that she considered any channel on the radio safe but she switched to channel two and waited for Wolfe to speak.

"As you are waiting on my findings for Mrs. Palmer's cause of death, I checked her rate of thawing before I left and I should be able to conduct

an autopsy on Sunday morning. Problem is our housekeeper likes to attend church and morning tea with her friends. Would you be able to watch my girls for a couple of hours? Emily could stay home with them but I would like her to observe the procedure if possible. Over.

Jenna smiled and glanced at Kane's grinning face. Wolfe had never asked a favor and she welcomed the chance to get closer to his family. "We'd love to. We'll come pick them up first thing. What time is good for you? Over."

"Eight-thirty." Wolfe cleared his throat. *"Julie is keen to see the horses. Over."*

"We'll take them for a ride." Jenna stared ahead into the blanket of white, trying to recognize her surroundings. "It will be a nice break from searching for potential murder victims. Over."

"Are you assuming the Axman disposed of the bodies of the potential victims by using the crusher? Over."

Jenna exchanged a glance with Kane. "Yeah, is there a problem? Over."

"It would be like trying to find a needle in a haystack. If the killer is smart enough to do that, he wouldn't leave the crushed remains close by but add them to a pile. Usually there are stacks of cubes of flattened piles of metal waiting for pickup by the recyclers. I figure it will be best to look at the ones that have the least amount of snow on them. I'll do them first then scan the office for trace evidence. Over."

"Sure. Over and out." She hung up the radio. "The truck ahead of us made the turn to the junkyard. I figure that's the owner, Mr. Sawyer."

They followed the vehicle along the snow-covered road but, surprisingly, the going wasn't as bad as Jenna had expected. In fact, she could see the tracks of a number of vehicles in the hard-packed snow. "This road has been in use during the shutdown."

"It was clear like this when I came by on Tuesday. I figured the snowplows kept it open for the plants." Kane swung the truck around a sweeping bend, then pulled up beside a red pickup. "I'll call them when we get back to the office and get their schedule."

Jenna turned to look at him. "I'll speak to the owner while Wolfe and Webber are hunting down the crushed vehicles and conducting a sweep for trace evidence." She glanced at the many rows of snow-covered cars. "Check out the cars at the front and see if Sky's car is there."

"Okay. My truck will fit down those rows." Kane rubbed his chin. "If it's not in the first few vehicles, I'll take a drive around the yard." He gave her a long look. "I did a background check on Bill Sawyer and he came up clean, but take a look at him. He fits the description Ella gave us of the Axman."

Jenna's attention moved to the man getting out of his vehicle. "So I notice."

CHAPTER THIRTY-SIX

Jenna climbed out the truck and, wrapping her scarf around her face, crunched through the snow to the burly man standing beside the gate to the recycling yard. "Bill Sawyer?"

"The one and only." Sawyer's ruddy face creased into a good-natured grin. "Now what's all this about illegal use of my crusher?"

Jenna pulled the search warrant from her pocket and handed it to him. "We have a warrant to search your premises; we believe there may be evidence to support a missing person's case we are investigating."

"Okay." Sawyer stuffed the warrant inside his pocket without glancing at it, pulled out a set of keys and unlocked the gate. He waved them inside. "Knock yourselves out."

"I'd like you to explain the system to me." Jenna waited for him to walk inside the yard then followed him, with Kane and the others close behind.

"When the vehicles arrive, my crew strips them of all working parts and pulls out anythin' that can be resold. Hazardous materials are removed, the battery and the air conditioning drained. What's left is crushed or shredded."

Jenna nodded. "How many people have keys to this yard?"

"Me and my cousin Wyatt. He's holdin' a backup set in case of an emergency. I hold his spare set too." Sawyer indicated past Jenna with his chin. "He owns the meat processing plant up yonder but that's on shutdown right now too."

Making a mental note to get his cousin's full name, Jenna glanced behind her. Wolfe and Webber were busy brushing snow away from stacks of crushed metal and Kane had climbed up to peer inside the open mouth of the crusher. She turned back to Sawyer. "Do you have many vehicles waiting to be crushed?"

"That line there will be next." He waved toward the rows and rows of vehicles piled up at the back of the lot. "The ones at the back we use for parts mostly, and when they are just shells, we crush them."

"Do many people come by and ask you to crush their vehicles without removing anything?" Jenna watched his face but there was no change in his expression.

"Some do." He shrugged. "I've had a few where the wife has argued with her husband, got his car in the divorce settlement then crushed it out of spite, but if they insist on crushin' the entire vehicle, we still remove the battery and hazardous waste but we charge a higher price. Our profit comes from recyclin' parts."

Jenna nodded. "I gather you check the title before you crush the vehicles?"

"In most cases, yeah I do."

"So you believe it's not always necessary? That would be illegal." Jenna stared hard at him, but the man did not miss a beat.

"Nope. If they are abandoned and not valued at more'n five hundred, I crush them; and I get shipments via insurance companies, burned-out wrecks, abandoned cars with no identification numbers or plates. They are logged and then crushed." He gave her a long look. "I check inside and the trunks before I crush anythin'. I don't want no dead bodies stinkin' up my place."

Jenna's neck prickled. He had just voiced her exact suspicions. "That's a strange thing to say."

"I've seen movies where bodies are crushed in cars." He gave an indignant huff. "It's not happening in my yard."

Jenna turned at the roar of Kane's truck as he drove between the rows of stacked vehicles, obviously searching for Sky's yellow sedan. She looked at Sawyer. "What happens to the waste metal?"

"I sell it." Sawyer smiled. "A scrap metal recycler collects it and ships it to a place where it's shredded, melted down and reused."

Jenna pulled out her notepad and pen. "I'll need the name and contact details of everyone with keys to the yard and I'd like to inspect the logbook for the crusher for the past two weeks."

"Sure thing. They're in the office." Sawyer led the way to a small brick building heavy with snow and icicles. He opened the door with a key from his bunch. "Let me get the light."

Jenna noticed the lack of snow in front of the office door and the crunching under her boots. "Is this sand and salt?"

"Yeah, we drop a couple of bags here before the snow so we don't have to dig out the office." Sawyer kicked the snow from his boots and walked inside. "We shut down for three weeks is all. I drop in from time to time to add more salt."

Jenna examined the books and took copies with her cellphone. The pages for the time of Sky's disappearance and since were blank. She turned her attention to a cabinet filled with lines of keys, some with labels. "What are those used for?"

"Machinery, toolboxes, the lunchroom and the john."

She walked over and stared at them. "So the crane and the crusher keys are here too?"

"Yeah." Sawyer gave her a long, patronizing look. "I can't leave the keys in the machinery. It's against health and safety."

"I see. And I guess it would be difficult for one man to operate the crane and crusher at the same time?" Jenna met the man's gaze. "I figure a person would have to be highly trained to use it as well?"

"Around here? I would say there would be at least twenty or so NCCCO qualified men working in this area who could drive a crane.

It only takes one man, Sheriff." Sawyer lifted his brows and sighed. "The crusher has a crane attached and an automatic push-button set-up so one man can operate it. Same with the shredder, just one red button."

"NCCCO?" Jenna made a note. "What does that stand for?"

"That would be the National Commission for the Certification of Crane Operators." Sawyer leaned casually against his desk. "This is an industrial area and no boss in his right mind would hire anyone without the right credentials. Heavy machinery is in use all over. If you believe someone broke in here and used my crusher, you'll have a pile of people to talk to."

Jenna tapped her pen against her bottom lip, running the information through her mind. She came up with a pile of "what ifs" but often they were the triggers to solve a crime. What if the Axman used the crusher to dispose of cars and bodies and had done for some time? Kane had mentioned people and their vehicles vanish daily. Surmising the Axman worked in this location, had a key to the yard, and the skillset to operate the crusher, time would still be a factor. In Sky's case, the Axman had to tow the car and her body here to crush them, then hightail it out of the area to give the snow time to cover his tracks. He wouldn't have risked the chance Ella had made it back to the highway and waved down a passing truck to get help.

Her mind went to Doug and Olivia's disappearance. The Axman could have used one of the wrecked vehicles in the lot to conceal the bodies. She glanced at the shells of rusty vehicles well within reach of the crane, then at the stack of metal cubes, and a shiver of dread crawled up her spine. The Axman killed at night and could have disposed of the bodies in this deserted junkyard. If he could get in and out again fast enough without someone seeing him, it would be the perfect crime.

The sound of Sawyer's voice dragged her back to the now.

"Is there anythin' else I can help you with, Sheriff?" He pulled out a tin of chewing tobacco and stuffed a wad into his mouth.

"Just one more question and then the ME will do a sweep of your office and other buildings." She cleared her throat. "How long does it take to crush a car?"

"Forty-five seconds."

CHAPTER THIRTY-SEVEN

The walls of the hospital room wavered in Doug's vision and he gripped the side of the bed, not quite believing what Olivia had said. A rush of euphoria hit him at the possibility of finding Sky alive. He swallowed hard. "Sky is my sister. Is she here?"

"I don't know but we can ask someone when we look for my mom." Olivia pulled off the electrodes to her monitoring machine and dragged out all her encumbrances, then slid to her feet. "First we need water. They haven't given me anything to eat or drink since I arrived. Everything we need to survive is apparently fed through the drip." Using the wall for support, she staggered toward the sink, took two paper cups from a dispenser and filled them. She drank thirstily, then filled a cup and returned to him. "Here. Take it slow."

After upending the cup, Doug looked down at his blanket and her paper nightgown. "We'll need something to wear."

"I figure our clothes are in those bags by the door." She pointed at two bulging plastic bags leaning against the wall. "Jim asked the other guy to incinerate them and I guess he forgot, then they argued and stormed out. They haven't been back since." She smiled at him. "I guess the nurse forgot to set up the drug-administer machines and that's why we're awake now." She made her way to the bags and peered inside. "Yeah, these are mine and I figure the others are yours."

"So how come you were awake during their argument and not me?"

She dragged the bags toward him and her. "Jim was visiting me. Even drugged, I can hear and feel everything, like I said before. He enjoys frightening me and threatening to cut out my eyes, it's like he's a sadist or something." She handed him a bag. "Usually the meds in the drug machine knock me out after he leaves."

Aware of time passing and fighting waves of excruciating pain and nausea, Doug went behind the curtain and struggled into his clothes. He went through the pockets of his jeans and found them empty. "Dammit, I left my cellphone in my truck with Ella." He blinked a few times. *Oh my God, Ella.*

"Who is Ella?" Olivia's voice came through the curtain. "You decent?"

"Yeah." Doug slid back the curtain with trembling fingers. The pain had increased with the effort of dressing. He swiped at the sweat leaking from his brow. "A friend of my sister. I was with her looking for Sky when we came across the wreck. She's smart, and she had a shotgun, and if she saw Jim do anything to me she would have gone for help."

"I hope so." Olivia glanced around. "We gotta get out of here right now while we have the chance." She shrugged into her coat and stared in the direction of the doorway, absently picking at the dried blood on her sleeve. "You do know Jim could be just outside that door."

"There's only one way to find out." As Doug struggled into his coat, a cold sweat dampened his skin. He took a few steps across the floor and staggered. Flames of pain washed over him and he leaned heavily against the wall. "Just give me a few seconds to catch my breath."

"You need pain meds."

"No thanks." He slid his hands into the coat pockets and his fingers met the familiar cold metal of his key fob. He distinctly remembered leaving the engine of his truck running to keep Ella warm. "Shit."

Olivia stared at him, wide-eyed. "What's wrong?"

"My keys are in my pocket, which means Ella is here too."

He edged along the wall, then pushed open the swinging doors an inch. He stared both ways in astonishment; he was looking at a dim corridor lit only by a few tiny downlights. His heart raced with the implications of the scene before him; it was as if the hospital room was part of a movie set. Nothing outside fit with any hospital he'd seen before; in fact the place resembled a prison. Alarm bells went off in his head and the adrenaline pumping through him sped up his heart. He allowed the door to shut silently and slumped against the wall. "I'm convinced Jim is involved with the sex-slave industry. We're not in a real hospital. I figure he's keeping us here until he can sell us off to the highest bidder."

"What are we going to do?" Olivia gripped his arm.

He scanned the room. "Open the drawers and search for anything we can use as a weapon."

Olivia complied and came back with two scalpels. Doug took one of them from her, then looked at her pale worried expression. "If anything happens, go for the neck. You can do a lot of damage with one of these blades."

"My brother taught me how to defend myself and he told me the only way to win when the odds are stacked against me is to fight dirty." She held the scalpel in her palm and practiced an upward thrust.

Doug nodded. "Ready?"

"Yeah." Olivia moved closer to him.

They eased out into the hallway and, keeping their backs to the wall, edged along, peering into the shadows, Doug led the way. The temperature had dropped considerably and cold seeped through his clothes. The lack of windows worried him and with each step he took into the narrow dim passageway, his senses insisted they were underground. He led the way, checking the rooms as they went and finding only a locker room and a small office with no phone. A cloud of worry settled over him, the place looked deserted and they found no sign of any other wards let alone patients. Ahead, the hall ended in the glint of metal on a pair of double doors. He turned to Olivia. "That might be another ward. Keep behind me."

She nodded, her eyes appearing dark in her ashen face. "Okay."

Out of breath and fighting waves of incredible agony, Doug peered through the glass panel in the door then slumped against the wall. Despair caught him by the throat. "It's not a ward. Looks like we're alone."

"So where is the exit?" Olivia gripped his arm with trembling fingers. "We've checked everywhere; there has to be a way out."

Lightheaded, Doug indicated the room. "It has to be in there but I'm not sure if I have the strength to push the darn door open."

"Come on." Olivia leaned against the door and it opened with a whine. "Look over there. I can see a door."

They'd made it halfway across the floor when a rumbling noise echoed through the room, along with the sound of someone whistling. Doug's heart raced so fast he thought it might burst through his chest. He looked around for somewhere to hide, but it was too late; he stared in horror as the door opened slowly and a gurney slipped inside, with Jim at the helm. The slow smile crossing Jim's face made Doug take a step back. It was like looking into the face of pure evil.

"Well, look what we have here." Jim slammed the gurney into him with a maniacal grin.

Red-hot pain seared through Doug and he buckled, falling to his knees. He saw Olivia dart forward, scalpel in hand, and the next moment she flew across the room and hit the wall landing like a rag doll on the floor. Doug tried to get up but failed. "Leave her alone, you asshole!"

He winced as Jim lifted a wrench from the gurney and advanced toward him, swinging it casually in one hand.

"You plannin' on goin' somewhere, Doug?"

CHAPTER THIRTY-EIGHT

Saturday, week two

Kane's day seemed to be going from bad to worse. After completing his workout with Jenna, the first since she had gotten ill, he'd headed out to his garage and discovered his truck had a flat tire. On closer inspection, he found a sharp piece of metal wedged deep in the tread, no doubt picked up during the search of the junk yard. That investigation had been a complete waste of time, they had found nothing of interest and although Wolfe had climbed all over the compactor and any suspicious crushed vehicles collecting samples he'd found no evidence of blood.

Changing the tire and heading into George's Garage for a replacement had taken time and after calling Jenna to explain the situation he'd avoided going into the office and headed out to chase down two delivery drivers and the mail truck driver.

After finishing night shifts in sub-zero temperatures the men were none too pleased to see him on their doorsteps early on a Saturday morning. It was the same at each house. The men answered each question with a curt "No." It was as if they had turned into the three wise monkeys—see no evil, hear no evil and speak no evil—just to annoy him. By the time he left the postal worker's house, he wondered if they all had something to hide.

He slid behind the wheel of his truck, glad to be inside in the warm, and checked his notes. His head hurt like a bitch but he decided to chase down one more lead before returning to the office. Jenna had arranged to interview Ella Tate after lunch and a quick glance at his watch told him time was running short. He turned and rubbed Duke's ears in the back seat. Curled up asleep, wrapped in his blanket, the bloodhound opened one dark brown eye to look at him before sighing and burying his head in the soft blue covers. "I'll get you into the office as soon as I can. Although, Maggie is spoiling you and by spring you'll be too fat to keep up with the horses."

His last stop would be about a call that came through the information line from the local mailman, John Wright. He punched the mail carrier's address into the GPS and turned his truck onto the road. Ice crystals had formed around his windows even with the blast of hot air from the heater, and snow piled up on the wiper blades with each pass over the windshield. Saturday in Black Rock Falls was normally busy, with people milling around, but this morning the town was unusually quiet. Apart from the odd bundled up person walking a dog and the smoke from the chimneys, he would have thought the entire town had headed south for the winter. No doubt, the predicted blizzard was keeping everyone at home. He negotiated the blinding white streets and turned into a driveway. Leaving his engine running to keep Duke warm, he made his way with care along the partially cleared pathway to the front door.

His boots crunched on the small patches of ice as he ducked under the icicles hanging from the front porch to peer through the falling snow at the festive wreath hanging on the front door, looking for a bell or knocker. Finding neither, he rapped on the door with his knuckles. The sound of music drifted through the door and the blinking green and red lights of a Christmas tree reflected against the snow-covered windowsills.

The door opened a crack and a young girl looked up at him with big blue eyes, blonde curls tumbling over her shoulders. Her face broke into a wide smile. He smiled back, appreciating the ray of sunshine on a bleak day. "I'm Deputy Kane, is your dad home?"

"I'll tell him." She frowned. "But I have to shut the door. You stay there."

The door closed and a few moments later opened again. A man in his thirties, tall and robust with thick brown hair, peered at him. "Mornin', Deputy, what can I do for you?'

Kane pulled out his notebook. "John Wright? You called in on our hotline about the missing woman?"

"Yeah, that's me." Wright looked at him expectantly.

Kane winced as a snowflake melted and slid down his neck. "I'd like some more information, if you have time?"

"Sure do." Wright stepped back and glanced at his snow-covered coat. "Why don't you leave your coat in the mudroom? We can talk in the kitchen. Jilly has just made a jug of hot chocolate." He waved to a small room filled with coats and boots close to the front door.

"Thanks." Kane kicked the snow from his boots and wiped them clean on the mat before stepping into the house. He removed his gloves, then shrugged out of his coat and found an empty peg on the wall in the mudroom to hang it.

The house smelled of hot chocolate, cinnamon and freshly baked cake. Kids peered at him from around corners. As he followed Wright along the hallway, he glanced into the family room complete with a deliciously warm log fire. A small woman with a mass of blonde curls and the same big blue eyes as her daughter welcomed him as if she had known him for years.

"Come on in, you look frozen." She gestured to a seat. "Sit down. I have hot chocolate and fresh-baked cookies straight from the oven if you're hungry?"

Kane smiled at her. "Thanks, that would be great." He sat down in his appointed chair and Wright sat down opposite.

"This is my wife, Jilly." Wright leaned forward in his seat, cradling a cup between his hands. "She convinced me to call. It sounds a bit trivial but the newsreader did say if we'd seen or heard anythin' unusual to call in, so I did."

Kane nodded in thanks as Mrs. Wright gave him a cup of hot chocolate and pushed a plate of cookies in front of him. As much as he wanted to devour them like the Cookie Monster, he laid his notepad on the table and lifted his pen, then looked at Wright. "What do you have for me?"

"Two things. One might not be much but the other might be important. Being a postal worker, I get to see the daily lives of people more than most." Wright dropped his voice to a conspiratorial whisper. "You heard of a man by the name of Jeff Knox? He is out of Blackwater, drives a pickup on a regular run a few times a week from Blackwater to here at night and has priors. The sheriff charged him with raping a hitchhiker. He never made it to court. I hear the Blackwater DA didn't find enough proof or somethin'?"

Kane made notes, then gave in to the temptation and helped himself to a cookie. "What makes you figure he's involved?"

"I overheard someone talking in the line at Aunt Betty's. They said someone saw Knox carrying a woman into the Blackwater Motel, same night that young woman went missin'. They mentioned his name." Wright gave him a smug smile. "And I just happen to know who that was; his name is Ty Aitken and he opened that fancy bakery in Blackwater, last fall."

The lead was hearsay at best but he wrote down the information. It wouldn't hurt to shake down Aitken and see what fell out. He sipped the hot chocolate. "You mentioned two things?" He bit into a cookie. Not as good as Jenna's chocolate chip, but very tasty.

"Yeah, it is probably nothin' but I often see Doc Weaver on the road up in the industrial area. I pass her on Tuesdays as I'm heading out of town and she's on her way back. I guess she has a patient out that way but yesterday she passed me on the highway heading way too fast and took the turn to the industrial area." Wright shrugged. "Seemed strange considerin' everywhere up there is closed."

I need to dig a bit deeper on Doctor Weaver. A shiver slid across Kane's neck and he lifted his gaze from his notes. "What time do you normally see her?"

"On Tuesdays, around four, but yesterday, I was held up by the snowplow, darn thing goes so slow, I didn't get to my last stop until late, maybe four thirty, or it could have been later." Wright scratched his chin. "I didn't get back to the post office until way after five and my boss was none too pleased."

Kane finished his hot chocolate and closed his notepad. "Thanks, you've been very helpful. If you hear or see anything else, give me a call." He pulled a card from his pocket and slid it across the table, then stood. "Thanks for the drink and cookies."

"Take a few more." Mrs. Wright slipped a few into a paper bag and handed it to him. "You need to eat in this weather."

Still overwhelmed by the generosity of the people of Black Rock Falls, Kane smiled at her. "That's very kind of you, ma'am." But his mind was not on cookies as he headed for the mudroom to collect his coat.

He made his way to his truck and climbed inside, then offered a cookie to Duke. He pulled out his cellphone and called Jenna to update her. "I'm on my way back to the office now."

"Okay. I could send Rowley out to speak to Ty Aitken about Knox this afternoon. His driver's license will be on file. It will be interesting to see if he is the same build as the Axman." She paused a beat as if thinking. *"I'll call Wolfe and see if his FBI friends have discovered anything interesting about Doctor Weaver and if he has any blood test results for Ella."* He could hear her fingers tapping on the desk. *"I don't like this, Kane. She is involved in something, I just know it."*

CHAPTER THIRTY-NINE

Due to the road closures throughout the state, Jenna expected a long delay for a new furnace. She made a call to Mayor Petersham to approve the purchase of heaters, even though disturbing him on a Saturday was not in her best interests. After all, she had an office to run and staff to keep warm. He authorized the purchase without complaint and Rowley had gotten all the local store had in stock. The comforting heat on her legs made her drowsy but she shot to full attention when Kane backed into the office surrounded by the aroma of fresh coffee and carrying bags of takeout with Rowley close behind.

"I figured you'd want to work through lunch before heading out to speak to Ella Tate?" Kane dropped the bags onto the desk. "I brought Rowley up to date with my interview with the postman this morning. Did Wolfe have anything interesting?"

Jenna leaned forward in her seat to peer into the bags. "Not really. He's still waiting on Ella's drug test but if she had date rape drugs in her system, Wolfe figures by now she will remember most of what happened, so we're good to go. The test will just confirm his suspicions and clear her of any involvement." She selected a bagel with cream cheese, her favorite. "What concerns me is our lack of solid evidence. These cases don't follow the usual MO of a kidnapping."

"Yeah, no ransom or demands." Kane sighed. "And we have three people missing without a trace. Our only witness should be the prime suspect at this point and we both know she wasn't involved."

"We might have another witness. Just before, I found an interesting report out of Blackwater on an attack on a motorist." Rowley held the door open with his foot to allow Duke to lumber inside then flop down in front of the heater. "The incident occurred on Thursday night." He pushed a tray of go cups onto the desk then sat down. "I've added the details to the case file."

Jenna took a coffee with her name written on the side and had a sip. "Just give me a rundown. Why is it relevant to the Axman case?"

"I figure the report is close enough to what happened to Ella Tate to be the same person." Rowley reached for a packet of sandwiches. "Levi Holt passed through town on his way to spend his vacation with his folks in Blackwater and came across a pickup, hood up, flashers on. When he stopped to help, a guy climbed out the car and attacked him. Holt escaped and reported the incident to the Blackwater Sheriff's Department on Friday morning. I called Blackwater and spoke to the deputy who took down the complaint. He said he went for a drive-by in the area. He found a few bits of broken glass but the snowplow had been through and cleaned up everything. When I asked him why he hadn't sent us the file as the incident occurred in our county, he closed down. I felt like he was stonewalling me."

"Really? I wonder why. They usually cooperate with us." Jenna accessed the file and scanned the report. "There's no description of the attacker or his vehicle apart from a 'guy in a pickup wearing a scarf.'" She exchanged a look with Kane. "The name on the report is their new rookie, Bates. We need to have a word with Levi Holt and get the whole story."

"His report could back up Ella Tate's statement for the night Sky Paul vanished." Kane leaned back in his seat, sandwich poised in mid-air. "We need to know if the man attacked Holt with a hatchet, for a start."

Jenna glanced at the file again and sighed at the incompetence of the deputy's report. She turned her attention back to Rowley. "Okay, as you're heading out to Blackwater to chase down Ty Aitken about Knox, I want you to drop by and interview Holt then speak to the proprietor of the Blackwater Motel and see if they recall Knox having a woman in his room. I'll call in Webber to ride along with you. Don't go near Knox. From the details on his driver's license, he fits the general description of the Axman. I want to run a background check before speaking to him. If Holt's recollection is the same as Ella's, Knox might be our man." She thought for a moment. "Go see Holt first and see if his account backs up Ella's. I'll be interviewing people all afternoon, so message me straight away if it does and take down a fresh statement from him."

"Yes, ma'am." Rowley reached for his coffee. "Will you clear it with the Blackwater sheriff before we leave? I don't want to be stepping on anyone's toes."

"Sure." Jenna reached for the phone. "Maggie, can you call in Webber for me please. No, he's not at the ME's office, he'll be at home. Tell him I need him for the afternoon." She disconnected, then contacted the Blackwater Sheriff's Department.

Jenna pulled up her hoodie against the bitter cold and slid into Kane's truck. She glanced at him. "I didn't mention it in front of Rowley but I have some good news. The FBI didn't find a connection between Doctor Weaver and the cartel or the reason she ordered a DNA test on me. He's still waiting for the info on what tests she's been doing on the townsfolk."

"That's a relief but I figure she's involved in something illegal." Kane turned in his seat to look at her. "Where to?"

Jenna buckled her seatbelt. "I hope Rowley sends confirmation on Holt's attack before I speak to Ella again. I figure she'd be more forthcoming if she knew the Axman attacked another person. I want to pay Doc Weaver a visit and find out why she was heading out to the industrial area when everything around there is shut down for the holidays."

"She lives over her clinic, so unless she is out on a call, we should find her there." Kane swung the SUV out onto the blacktop and drove through town, took a left turn then pulled up in front of a store with Dr. Weaver's shingle hanging outside. "The lights are on, she must work today."

Jenna zipped up her coat and wrapped a scarf around her face then climbed from the truck. Underfoot, the slippery sidewalk was an accident waiting to happen. As she stepped cautiously toward the door, her insides twisted remembering the scare Weaver had given her at the ranch. She edged her way to the front door, glad when her feet hit the mat. The door chimed as they entered. She scanned the small waiting room; it was empty and no secretary sat behind the front counter. Unlike the usual white, sterile doctors' offices, dark brown walls that made the straight-back wooden chairs appear to blend into obscurity greeted her and from the light hung an ancient strip of flypaper. She walked to the counter and pressed the bell with the sign, "If unattended please ring bell."

A few moments passed before footsteps sounded and Dr. Weaver came through a door. She look over the top of her spectacles at Jenna then shifted her gaze to Kane.

"Sheriff, Deputy Kane, sorry to keep you waiting, my secretary doesn't work today. What brings you out in this weather?"

Unsure why the woman unsettled her so much, Jenna offered her a smile. "We're chasing down people who were in the vicinity of the industrial area out on the highway late Friday afternoon." She caught her startled expression. "I gather you often travel between Blackwater and here on Tuesdays as well. As we've had a few incidents in that area over the last week we are collecting information."

"I visit out-of-town patients on Tuesdays." Weaver frowned. "I can't give you names, I'm sure you're aware of doctor–patient privilege. On Friday, I treated an accident victim out at the meat processing plant."

"Why didn't they call 911?" Kane frowned. "Any industrial accident is required to be written up."

"Not if it's the owner." Dr. Weaver gave him a satisfied smile. "It was minor and he didn't want any fuss."

Jenna pulled out her notebook. "I'll need his name."

"Sorry, I can't give you his name, I've divulged enough already." Dr. Weaver gave her a sickly smile. "Is there anything else?"

Jenna pounced. "Yeah, why did you do a DNA test on me?"

"I did no such thing." Dr. Weaver took a step back in surprise. "Let me see, I did a normal screening and an HLA test."

"That's a DNA test for tissue typing." Kane moved a step closer and his lips flattened to a thin line. "Why was that necessary?"

"Oh, I see you're angry." Dr. Weaver glanced from one to the other. "I'm building a local tissue-typing database. I've been testing all viable patients. So many children die because they need a kidney and so many healthy people live in Black Rock Falls. I wanted to offer them the option of saving a life, is all."

Jenna huffed out a breath, not believing what this woman was saying. "Without consent? That's against the law and there's already a worldwide database."

"Well then I'm sorry." Dr. Weaver peered over her glasses at Jenna. "I guess you'd better arrest me. But I meant no harm."

Jenna looked down at her feet. The doctor did make a habit of treating uninsured people and taking her out of the community would cause hardship for some. The threat of this woman was melting like the snow on her boots. "I won't arrest you this time but I'm confiscating the database, and all blood tests go via the ME's office to be checked from now on." She narrowed her gaze. "I could have you fired for this, you know."

"Very well." Dr. Weaver looked crushed.

"Show me the file." Kane waved a hand toward the computer on the front desk. "Is it on there?"

"No, it's in my office." Weaver led the way. "I have a separate computer for the database."

Jenna took a sheet of paper from the desk and wrote a declaration stating the doctor had given permission for them to confiscate the computer. "Sign this statement."

The doctor complied and Jenna followed Kane out to his truck. As he dumped the laptop into the back seat, she picked up an unsettling vibe from him. "What's up?"

"It's not my place to say, ma'am." Kane slid behind the wheel and started the engine.

Ma'am? Jenna climbed in beside him and turned to look at him. "Spit it out."

"She broke the law and I would have arrested her." He shrugged. "It was your call."

"I have two reasons to leave her be for now." Jenna leaned back in her seat. "She does help people and lives on practically nothing. You can see that too, right?"

"Nope." Kane flicked her a glance. "I see a very dangerous scheming woman, a bottomless pit of contradictions. She uses the kindly doctor façade to fool people. I'm sure of it. So what's your second reason?"

"I still have a bad feeling about her too and want to keep an eye on her." Jenna noted the stubborn set to his jaw. "I want to know the real reason she heads out to Blackwater every Tuesday and see if she was really at the meat processing plant. I figure if I give her enough rope she'll hang herself."

"Hmm, maybe." Kane pulled his hat down over his ears. "Where to now?"

Jenna scrolled through the files on her cellphone. "I think we'll pay a visit to the proprietor of the meat processing plant. I have his details here. Wyatt Sawyer. He lives on Maple Drive and we can go via Stanton Road. If the plant is in shutdown, he could be at home." She punched the address into the GPS.

"Wyatt Sawyer? Didn't the guy at the junkyard have the same last name?" Kane swung the car around and headed back through town.

"Yeah, and he mentioned his cousin Wyatt holds a set of his keys." She leaned back in the seat. "I guess it would be a stretch of the imagination to believe this guy is involved?"

"As the junkyard came up clean, we have no hard evidence against Bill Sawyer or any reason to suspect his cousin. If we start believing everyone is involved we'll just be spinning our wheels." Kane shrugged. "We'll have to keep digging."

"I'm thinking outside the box and considering every angle. Wyatt Sawyer works in the area and will be at the plant during the shutdown on the day they process cattle before Christmas. I'll ask him how often he visits his place of business. He might have seen something." Jenna pulled out her notebook and scanned the pages. "We've no bodies and Sky's car has vanished. I figure the Axman has somewhere close to town to take his victims. It'd be risky moving them too far." She shut the notebook. "We'll interview Knox tomorrow and discover his whereabouts on the nights of the crimes. I know it's like grabbing at smoke at the moment but the Axman will make a mistake soon enough, they all do. Until he does we're all stuck with time-consuming grunt work."

"An isolated place close to town?" Kane made a snort of what could have been amusement. "It would take us years to check all of them. He could have a survival shelter buried under his house or in his yard." He took his eyes off the road for a second to look at her, and frowned. "We could be dealing with a man who keeps his victims alive then sells them as slaves, or someone who likes corpses as friends."

Jenna rubbed both hands down her face in exasperation. She had never been so frustrated about a case before. Nothing seemed to make sense. "The complete lack of evidence is driving me crazy."

"Something will show up. I look at crimes like the shredded pages of a story and we have to find all the pieces and stick them back together to find out what happened." Kane slowed the truck to allow a couple of kids to cross the road to the park with their parents. "The hard part is finding the pieces."

"Really, just figured that out, huh?" Jenna laughed. "How about, 'Confucius says, *Life is like a riddle and we all play a part.*' You'd agree with that, right?"

"Yeah. Seems our part is catching killers." Kane grimaced, then turned into Stanton Road.

CHAPTER FORTY

The beeps coming from the hospital machines roused Olivia from a deep sleep. She gasped and shook herself awake. Had she had a dream to escape the terrible reality of her situation? She swallowed hard, refusing to believe she had imagined walking through the dim corridors and finding nothing but a couple of rooms. *Think. It felt so real, it must have happened.* The last thing she remembered was being in a room with Doug then seeing Jim come through a door and pushing a gurney into Doug but after that, her memory was blank. A wall of fear closed in around her and she fought against the restraints holding her wrists tight against the bars alongside her bed. Pain seared through her as she tore the flesh and blood spotted the white sheets. She let out a scream that vibrated off the walls. "I want to get out of here!"

Tears streamed down her cheeks, tasting salty in her mouth. She sobbed and screamed again. "You have to let me out of here! I can't stand this any longer."

Apart from the beeps and hiss of the machines, it was so quiet. Could she be the only person in the building? She turned and stared at the curtains surrounding her bed. "Doug, are you here? Doug, please answer me."

Silence.

The distinct sound of footsteps, not loud but the soft squeak of rubber-soled shoes on tile, came from the hallway. She turned her head, expecting Jim to walk through the door. Hate rolled over her for the man who treated her as if she was less than human. Heart pounding, she grit her teeth, expecting the worst. The door to the room swished open and the curtains opened. It was not Jim who stood there but the nurse. He looked down at her and shook his head and she glared at him. "Why are you keeping me here? There's nothing wrong with me."

"*I'm* not the one keeping you here." The man's eyes met hers. "I just work here."

Olivia kicked her feet, spilling the blankets off the bed. "Then let me go."

"Can't do that, sorry." He shrugged. "The boss isn't happy with you trying to leave. He hasn't hurt you, has he?" He picked up the blanket and laid it over her. "You should be grateful."

"Grateful?" A shiver of disgust rolled over her. "Have you lost your ever loving mind? He threatened me with a scalpel. I thought he would take out my eye."

"It's what he does to all of them. He has a morbid sense of humor." The nurse examined her wrists and frowned. "He won't be happy you tried to leave and no doubt he'll blame me."

"I don't really care if he blames you. You just stand by and allow him to scare people to death." She glanced over toward the curtains. "Where's Doug?"

"He's right here." The nurse moved around her bed and threw back the curtains. "He's sedated and will remain so."

She raised herself up in the bed and stared at Doug's ashen face. "Dear Lord, what happened to him?"

"He bust a few stitches is all." The nurse turned back and busied himself opening drawers and laying bandages on a tray. "I need to clean up your wrists. The boss will be in later to see you and you must look your best."

Trembling with anger and disgust, Olivia stared at Doug. "Jim did this. He rammed him with a gurney."

"Well, that's none of my concern." The nurse pressed the needle of a syringe into Olivia's drip and his eyebrows rose. "I do know the boss gets angry when people try to leave before they're ready."

A wave of dizziness surged through Olivia. Her mouth went dry. He had drugged her again. Her limbs became heavy and she worked the saliva in her mouth. She needed answers. "How long have I got to put up with this?"

"That's not my call." The nurse unbuckled her wrists and went to work.

Olivia fought the drug. "*Please*, help me escape and my mom will give you money."

The nurse's dark eyes moved to her face. "There is no escape."

CHAPTER FORTY-ONE

Kane pulled his truck into the driveway of Wyatt Sawyer's neat brick home. He lived in the more prosperous end of town. The path leading to the house was clear of snow and salt crystals crunched under his feet as he followed Jenna to the front porch. A stack of icicles sat beside the steps as if recently removed. He had done the same with his own porch to avoid walking into them on his way in and out, so he assumed Wyatt Sawyer was a tall man like his cousin.

He glanced through the frosty window to the family room. Inside, a wide hearth held a roaring wood fire with dancing orange flames that curled smoke up the chimney. A basket of pine cones and logs sat beside the hearth. A large comfortable sofa and two matching chairs surrounded the fire and a polished wood occasional table held an expensive-looking bronze statue of a stag. It looked pristine and resembled the perfect scene in a perfect house. He stood to one side as Jenna pressed the bell and heard chimes echoing inside. The door opened to reveal a tall man in his forties dressed in jeans, a dark blue sweater and slippers. He gave them an astonished look.

"What can I do for you, Sheriff?" Sawyer frowned. "Not a break-in at my plant, I hope?"

"No." Jenna took out her notepad. "Are you Wyatt Sawyer?"

"I am." Sawyer folded his arms across his chest.

"I'm Sheriff Alton and this is Deputy Kane." Jenna's voice gave nothing away. "I believe there was an accident at your plant late Friday and Doctor Weaver attended. Is that correct?"

Kane watched the man's body language and expression but he betrayed nothing.

"Yeah, that's right. Is that a problem?" Wyatt raised one eyebrow.

"As it was an industrial accident, yes." Jenna lifted her chin. "What happened?"

"Nothin' for you to worry about, Sheriff." Wyatt stepped to one side. "You'd better come inside. It's too cold to talk out here." He turned and led the way into a mudroom beside the front door. "Now, why is my injury a matter for the sheriff's department?"

"If it happened at the plant, it needs to be reported." Jenna cleared her throat. "Who was involved?"

"Just a minute. Those rules are if the plant is operational and an injury involves one of my employees. Right now we are in shutdown." Sawyer frowned. "I was doing some maintenance and cut myself. It wasn't bad enough to call the paramedics so I called Doctor Weaver."

"If it wasn't anything to worry about, why not drive into town yourself and see the doctor, or go to the ER?" Jenna pulled back her hood and looked at him. "Are you okay now?"

"I am." He gave Jenna an engaging smile. "Thank you for askin' but at the time I was bleedin' and concerned the cut might have been deeper than I figured." He took a step closer to her and pulled down the neck of his sweater to display a small bandage. "Would you like to see?"

Kane cleared his throat. Sawyer was being way too familiar with Jenna. "Maybe if you explain how the injury occurred?"

"Oh, sure." Sawyer straightened and dropped his hands to his sides. "I'm not sure if you're familiar with the workings of a meat processin' plant but I'd be happy to walk you through anytime." He raised both eyebrows at Jenna as if he was asking her to the movies. "The steers come into the kill floor, get processed, then the carcass is hung on a hook that moves along a production line and goes through many hands before it's packed. I was replacin' one of the block and tackles on the line. The hook swung around and hit me right here." He pointed in the region of his collarbone. "Darn thing cut right through my clothes and gave me a puncture wound. It bled like the devil, so I went to my office, packed it with a bandage and called the doc." He shrugged. "She checked me out, put in a couple of sutures and I was good to go."

"You did clean up any blood and sterilize the area?" Jenna stepped away from Sawyer, wrinkling her nose. "I'm sure you're aware of cross-contamination?"

"Yeah. I've been in this business for years and we have inspectors crawlin' over the place all the time. They'll be there the day we open before Christmas." Sawyer opened his arms and shrugged. "I've never had a complaint. My plant is spotless. I follow the rules. You're wastin' your time here."

Kane narrowed his gaze, taking in his neat appearance, short manicured nails and designer stubble. He portrayed a wealthy businessman and wondered why he'd bother to do the heavy work. "Why didn't you leave the maintenance crew to fix the problem when they got back? I gather the plant is in shutdown over the holidays?"

"Yeah, we shut down for four weeks, sometimes more if the weather prevents the cattle trucks, but I have a small crew who come in to process ten steers from Black Rock Falls the week before Christmas to make sure the local stores have enough supplies to carry them through." Sawyer pushed both hands into his back pockets and leaned casually against the wall. "My maintenance crew have everythin' runnin' smoothly and I have a couple of guys on call should I need them but I didn't bother draggin' them out and payin' them for something I could do alone."

Why not have it repaired before you shut down the plant? Kane rubbed his chin. "So did you just happen to notice it was faulty?"

"Nope." A flash of annoyance crossed Sawyer's face. "When the maintenance crew is in a production area, the workers are off the floor. It's a safety issue. I'd overlooked a report from one of the supervisors on the kill floor that a block and tackle was faulty. I decided to fix it before we did the short run next week."

"Okay, that's all I need for now." Jenna gave Kane a meaningful glance and shut her notebook. "Thank you for your time."

"My pleasure." Sawyer opened the front door and smiled at Jenna. "It was nice meetin' you, Sheriff."

Kane followed Jenna back to his truck and waited for her to buckle up. "What do you make of him?"

"I couldn't pick a hole in his story." Jenna pulled up her hood and shivered. "As he fits the same type as the Axman, I figured I'd push him a bit to see if he showed aggression but all he did was hit on me." She pulled a face of disgust. "I don't really need to know about the cattle-slaughtering process."

Kane started the engine and waited for the snow on the windshield to melt before turning on the wipers. "He likely thought it would interest you. This is a hunting town and most people aren't squeamish about the process of dressing an animal for the table." He backed out of the driveway and headed toward the Pauls' residence. "I did see a flash of annoyance when I challenged him but he employs hundreds of people, so wouldn't be used to anyone questioning him about how he runs his business."

"Hmm, well at least he's given Doc Weaver a reason to be hanging around the industrial area during the shutdown." Jenna let out a long sigh and reached for the Thermos of coffee. "Not that I believe for one minute she's working with the Axman but since she turned up unannounced on my doorstep, I'm convinced she's up to something." She poured two cups of coffee. "I'm drinking this before we speak to Ella. I want you to take the lead in the interview. When you spoke to her last time she wasn't under the influence of drugs, and you'll be able to read her better than me."

Kane looked at her, then returned his attention to the road. "Yeah, she wasn't exactly lucid when we found her on the highway. Date rape drugs would be a good choice if the Axman wanted her to forget what happened." He sighed. "What's not fitting in this scenario is why leave a witness when he had a second chance to take her? It's not logical."

"It's as if he had an insight into our investigation, which is impossible." Jenna sipped her drink. "Maybe he figures we'll believe she's the killer and the Axman is a figment of her imagination?"

Kane processed what she had said then nodded. "If we did believe that, it still leaves us with where she stashed the car and Sky's body. Okay, I guess we only have her word she stayed out in the freezing cold in a blizzard all night, she could have gotten a ride back to the highway and then waved down a truck." He shrugged. "That might make sense if she was involved but then the Axman blows that theory to hell by letting Levi Holt escape. If Rowley comes back from Blackwater and Holt has an identical story to Ella's, we know we're right and she's innocent."

"Unless Holt is involved and he reported the attack as a cover for her." Jenna raised one eyebrow. "That would make sense. If Holt is involved, he could have been in the car with them. I'll give Rowley a call and make sure he establishes Holt's whereabouts at the time of Sky's disappearance." She opened her cellphone and made the call.

The snow pelted the windshield and the wind increased, blowing up great clouds of white across the highway. Kane slowed to avoid a sedan creeping along in front of them. He turned to Jenna. "The weather is closing in. I hope Rowley and Webber make it back from Blackwater without too much trouble."

"So do I." She barked out a laugh. "I don't fancy staying in the motel tonight either. If it gets any worse, we won't get home."

Kane reached for his coffee and smiled. "Don't worry, I'll get you home."

CHAPTER FORTY-TWO

Life was certainly looking up for Rowley of late. The sheriff was handing him more responsibilities. Since Kane's injury and during the sheriff's illness, she had relied on him to keep the office open along with semi-retired Deputy Walters. He'd figured once things had gotten back to normal, he would be back to handling the local squabbles and parking tickets; but his work must have met with her approval. Although driving to Blackwater in the dead of winter with a blizzard on the way was not his idea of fun, the new Yukon sure made life easier. He turned up the music and grinned at Webber. "It's good to get out the office for the afternoon."

"Why don't you turn that noise down for a while and bring me up to speed on what we're doing." Webber tipped back his Stetson and rested one boot on the dashboard. "And no, I'd rather be in the ME's office than out in the darn cold freezing my balls off."

Rowley frowned at the disregard for his new cruiser. "I will as soon as you stop damaging my truck."

"Huh, yours, is it?" Webber grinned and dropped his foot. "Nice ride, you're lucky. I'd have thought old Walters would have been the next in line for a new one. So give me the rundown."

Rowley gave him the details of the attempted assault on Holt and the information Kane had gotten out of the mailman. "Levi Holt is at home and we need to interview him first, then send a message to the sheriff. She wants to see if the stories match and if they do, we have to eliminate the chance the pair are working together."

"Two people working together makes more sense and having Holt make out he was attacked along the same straightaway would be pure genius." Webber opened his cellphone and accessed the online case file. "His statement is practically useless. The deputy who took this down must have had the brains of a monkey."

Rowley took the exit ramp into Blackwater and turned off the music to listen to the GPS guiding them to Holt's residence. He pulled up behind a snow-covered SUV in the driveway to a ranch-style house and slid from behind the wheel. A blast of cold air hit him full in the face. Winter had a smell and a taste, like digging into a freezer for that last quart of ice cream. He led the way up the steps to the porch and pressed the bell. The door opened and a man in his twenties, with ruffled brown hair and a sleepy expression, stood to one side as if he'd been expecting them and waved them through the door. Rowley removed his hat. "Levi Holt?"

"Yeah, that's me." Holt led the way down a narrow hallway and into a toasty kitchen smelling of bacon and coffee. "You'll be deputies Rowley and Webber. Sheriff Alton called earlier to make sure I'd be home. You're here about the man who attacked me." He went to the counter. "Take a seat. Coffee?"

Rowley pulled out a chair. "Yeah, thanks, I'm Rowley."

"How about you, Deputy Webber?" Holt placed three large cups on the table then all the trimmings, before returning with a full pot of coffee.

"I'd be obliged." Webber removed his hat and dropped into a chair. "I read the statement you made to the local deputy and it has more holes than a leaky bucket." He leaned on the table and eyeballed him. "What really happened out there?"

Wondering why Webber had jumped straight to the chase rather than put the witness at ease, Rowley took out his notebook and pen. "How about we start with what time the incident occurred?"

"Late… before midnight, I guess." Holt sat opposite them, poured the coffee and pushed the cups toward them. "It all happened so fast. I was freaking out, I thought for sure the guy was gonna kill me."

Rowley took notes as he explained what had happened. "Can you describe the man? How tall was he?"

"Big, six two, maybe." Holt rubbed his chin and stared into space. "He was white and had dark eyebrows, small eyes. Real intense like Dracula or somethin'. Man, when he came at me with a wrench, I was out of there."

"Did you get a good look at his face?" Webber added cream to his cup.

"Nope, he was wearin' a hoodie with a cowboy hat and had a scarf tied around his face. He was like an old cowboy out of a movie headin' off to rob a bank."

Holt's carefree attitude was setting off alarm bells for Rowley. People who experienced trauma rarely made jokes. It was as if he was being too helpful. "Can you describe his vehicle, the make or color?"

"He had his headlights and flashers on so everything looked orange but I figure it was a late-model white pickup. I'm not sure of the make, a GMC maybe?" Holt shrugged. "I was runnin' for my life, not lookin' at the make of the jerk's car."

Rowley nodded. "Are you sure it was a wrench he threatened you with?"

"Yeah, I got to see it real close." Holt narrowed his gaze. "But I got a hit in. I smashed him hard with my flashlight, hurt him too."

"Where did you hit him?"

"On the right forearm or wrist." Holt shuddered. "Then he came at me again. He smashed my window and put a dent in the side of my door. It's outside if you need to see it. The deputy wrote up a report for my insurance but I can't get it repaired until after the shutdown."

"Yeah, we'll take a look before we leave and take some photos if you don't mind." Webber leaned back in his chair. "Where were you coming from?"

"Louan. I work at Tire and Mechanical and rent a house there. I was on my way home to spend the holidays with my folks." Holt reached for his cup. "I left work, went home, showered and changed. I had my bags packed. I stopped in for a meal then drove straight through."

Rowley looked up from his notes. "Did you leave Louan anytime in the last two weeks?"

"Nope." Holt looked at him with a suspicious glint in his eye. "Why?"

"So you don't go out at night drinking or chasing women?" Webber smiled at him. "I sure do."

"So do I but not in the last two weeks." Holt narrowed his gaze at Webber. "Tire and Mechanical closes down for four weeks and we had to stay back the last two weeks to catch up. People wanted their vehicles ready for the snow and we had them linin' up. I finished up, went home as late as nine and fell into bed most nights."

"Can anyone verify that?" Webber leaned both forearms on the table. "We're checking on everyone who came through Black Rock Falls in the last two weeks."

"Yeah, sure." Holt took Rowley's notepad and wrote down three numbers. "My boss is the top one and the other two are the guys who share the house with me."

"Okay." Rowley indicated toward the notepad. He'd prepared a statement from the Blackwater file and added the extra relevant details. "Read through my notes and if that is a true and accurate account of what happened on the night of the incident, sign and date it." He waited for Holt to read the pages.

"Yeah, that's everything I remember." Holt signed the pages.

Rowley picked up the notepad and stood. "Okay, thanks, we'll take those photographs of your truck then be on our way." He turned to Webber. "You handle the vehicle inspection. I'll chase down these people then contact the sheriff." He headed for the front door.

The weather was closing in when they arrived at the Blackwater Motel. Rowley pushed open the door to find a surprisingly clean foyer and leaning on the front counter in a cloud of perfume was a buxom woman in her thirties. She gave him the once-over and smacked her ruby lips as if she planned to eat him for dinner. "Afternoon, ma'am. I was wondering if I could talk to the proprietor."

"Well, that would be me." She looked up at Webber. "My, they grow them tall in Black Rock Falls." She patted her dark hair. "Are you lookin' for a room?"

Rowley bit back a smile. "Ah no. I was wondering if you'd happen to remember if Jeff Knox had a woman in his room on Friday night?"

"I'm sure I don't know." She eyed him suspiciously. "I don't go spyin' on my residents."

"Residents?" Webber gave her a long look. "Do people live here on a permanent basis?"

"Some do." She smiled at him. "Men mostly. They like a clean room and a hot meal and I provide both. I take in their laundry as well."

Rowley smiled back, hoping being nice and spinning a good yarn would get him a room number. "I need to speak with him. We picked up a woman during an investigation who says she was with him Friday night; she had his wallet and a wad of cash. We figured he might want it back."

"You drove all this way to return his wallet?" She frowned. "How come I find that hard to believe?"

"Knox is her alibi." Webber shrugged. "But we understand if you'd rather not give us his room number."

"I figure he'll need his wallet to pay me. He's in number twenty-six." She gave them a wave as they headed for the door. "Come back soon."

CHAPTER FORTY-THREE

He switched off the TV in disgust and tossed the remote onto the coffee table, then stormed out of the room. Anger heated his cheeks as he shoved open the back door and stood on the porch. Snow battered his bare flesh and sent cold tears running down his face. A deadly chill crawled through his clothes, raising goosebumps on his skin, but he remained motionless, staring at the skeletal trees blackened by frost along the perimeter of his land, and tried desperately to think. Winter seemed to muffle sound as if everything was hiding beneath the blanket of snow, too afraid to make a noise. The usual wildlife was missing today. In fact, everything looked cold and dead. Right now, he needed the quiet solitude to get away from the constant chatter over the radio or TV about the people missing from Black Rock Falls. Why couldn't Sheriff Alton leave well enough alone?

He slammed a fist on the handrail, shattering the icicles and sending them spearing into the snow-filled garden bed below. Dammit all to hell. After driving all over the local counties, picking up hitchhikers and taking them back to his underground hiding place, his laziness had overcome his natural good sense. Kidnapping people anywhere close to home was a mistake and he should have known a woman like Jenna Alton would poke her nose where it wasn't wanted. Most sheriffs didn't give adult missing persons more than a cursory look, especially when he left no evidence for them to find, but leaving Ella Tate alive had been a big mistake and Alton was like a dog with a bone. She had the media making everyone jumpy and her deputies were running all over town chasing down non-existent clues. Now he would have to postpone his plans until spring and then choose a new area to hunt.

Of course, no one could possibly suspect *him* of kidnapping or murdering anyone and the idea of keeping Olivia until the melt flittered into his mind. It would be an option. Doug wouldn't be a problem; he could make him vanish easily enough. He chuckled, filling the air with a cloud of steam, at the memory of Olivia's terrified stare. He still couldn't believe how well things had worked out for him. Who would have thought he'd come across a car wreck complete with a young woman of the right age and type for his needs? But then the sheriff had started an investigation and spoiled everything.

It was just as well he could outsmart Sheriff Alton and had planned each move ahead of time. He'd purposely not touched Ella and the drug he'd given her made her look like she'd lost her mind. She was the last person to see three missing people alive and should be the sheriff's number one suspect but no, Alton was hunting for a mythical axman. Where Ella had gotten the ax idea from he couldn't imagine because he'd hit Sky with a wrench.

Jenna Alton's interference in his business made his blood boil and he wished he had the opportunity to take her out of the equation. Over the last two days the thought of seeing her drugged, helpless and at his mercy had become a fantasy. The idea of feeding Alton into the machine and hearing the satisfying crunch as it ground her bones into mush made him smile. He would send her in alive, maybe tied up and gagged. The sight of her moving slowly into the gaping maw of the machine filled his mind with vivid images. He'd enjoyed watching the machine work its magic many times since he'd created the illusion of a hospital ward. The clinical set-up had been pure genius. It was laughable how calm people became if they truly believed they were safe in a hospital—until he placed them on the conveyor belt.

CHAPTER FORTY-FOUR

Snow hit the windshield in a blinding sheet by the time Kane pulled up outside the Pauls' residence and made a dash to the front door with Jenna close behind him. Sky's mother opened the door with a hopeful expression and Kane gave a shake of his head. "I'm sorry, no news about Sky or Doug but we have every available person working on finding them."

"We came to speak with Ella if she's home." Jenna gave Mrs. Paul a compassionate smile. "We hoped she might be feeling a little better today."

"She's kind of stunned, very depressed and we've contacted the military to try and have her brother sent home for Christmas on compassionate grounds." Mrs. Paul stood to one side. "You can try talking to her, but I've asked her what happened and she seems very vague."

Kane followed Jenna inside the warm house. At Mrs. Paul's insistence, they shucked their coats and followed her into a modern kitchen complete with granite bench tops and aluminum appliances. He inhaled the smells of wood smoke, cinnamon and freshly brewed coffee and took an offered seat at a center island beside Jenna.

"I'll go get her." Mrs. Paul made her way back down the hallway.

Sometime later Ella appeared at the doorway, looking pale, with dark circles under her eyes. She gave him a worried stare, then moved with obvious reluctance to take a seat opposite. Kane cleared his throat and took out his notebook and pen. "I hope you're feeling better now?"

"Not really." Ella gave him a sullen look. "I feel like someone is messing with my head."

"Really?" Kane leaned on the counter. "How so?"

"I keep having nightmares, like when I'm awake." Ella pushed both hands through her untidy hair. "Different versions with the night the man hit Sky and when we saw the wreck."

Kane made a few notes. Often making a suspect believe he was noting every word they uttered calmed them and encouraged them to speak. He lifted his gaze. "What can you remember before seeing the wreck?"

Ella described her discussion with Doug about going to search for Sky, then leaving and heading toward Blackwater. Kane held up a hand to stop her talking. "Think back; you're driving through town and turning onto the highway. Did you notice any signs?"

"Signs, what kind of signs?" Ella frowned. "You mean street signs or stop signs?"

Kane shook his head. "Nope, what about a road closure sign with flashing lights halfway across the access to the highway?"

He watched her closely as she considered his question. The Department of Transport had erected the sign close to midnight. "What time did you leave with Doug to search for Sky?"

"It was going on eleven." Ella wrapped her arms around her stomach and rocked back and forth. "I remember going to meet a guy named Jim. I met him on Facebook, he said he was a medical student but when I went to look for him again, his page had vanished. All our messages are gone as well, as if he didn't exist."

Kane exchanged a meaningful look with Jenna. "If he kidnapped Doug and Olivia, she's the girl missing from the wreck; it's likely he deleted his account." He met Ella's gaze. "Take it slow and try to remember what happened. Did you meet Jim on the highway?"

"I remember seeing his white pickup on the side of the road and his headlights were all cloudy, like there was smoke in the air around him or close by." Ella closed her eyes. "I remember Doug asking me what Jim looked like but when Jim got out of his pickup, he wrapped a scarf around his face." Her eyes sprang open. "He was wearing a cowboy hat over a hoodie."

Kane made notes, then smiled at her. "That's good. How big was he? Could he have been the man who chased you?"

"Maybe, but it was difficult to say with the hat and all." She shuddered and gripped the edge of the counter. "When Doug drove a bit closer, the headlights picked up the wreck and that poor woman hanging out the windshield."

"Was the door to the wreck open?" Jenna leaned forward on the counter. "Did you see the passenger?"

"Yeah, leaning back in the seat with blankets tucked in around her." Ella's eyes brightened. "I saw her move her head. Doug got out and helped Jim carry her into the back of his pickup."

Kane frowned. "In the cargo bed or in the back seat? Did it have four doors or two? Tell me exactly what you saw, step by step."

"They carried the woman to Jim's pickup. It was big, four doors, it looked like my brother's with a big grille at the front so maybe a GMC. Doug slid inside the back seat carrying the woman's shoulders and Jim held the legs. Then Jim shut the door and went around the other side, opened the door and bent in to talk to Doug, then he came to speak to me."

"You didn't go to help?" Kane looked at her and she shook her head.

"No, Doug told me to stay in his truck with the shotgun in case anything went wrong." Ella swallowed hard, then shook her head. "I remember Jim opening the door to speak to me, then the next thing I remember is waking up wrapped in Doug's thermal blankets and seeing the wreck. I was freezing. I'm not sure how I survived." She made a sobbing sound. "Then you arrived. That's all."

When Jenna's cellphone signaled a message, Kane waited for her to glance at the screen. They were expecting an update from Rowley. She gave him a slight nod and he turned his attention back to Ella. "Do you know a man by the name of Levi Holt?"

"No." Ella gave him a long, confused look. "You know I'm not from these parts. How would I know anyone from here?"

Surprised, Kane leaned back in the chair. "I didn't mention he was from here. He is out of Blackwater."

"I still don't know him." Ella gave Jenna a desperate look. "I'm doing my best to remember."

"You're doing great." Jenna smiled at her. "The blood we took from you is being tested. We believe Jim may have injected you with a drug that causes temporary amnesia. The fact you remember what happened now makes me believe this is what happened." She sighed. "What I don't understand is why he took the others and not you. Do you know why?"

"No but right now, I wish he had taken me as well." Tears streamed down Ella's cheeks. "I see the way people look at me as if I did something wrong. Sure I argued with Sky at the roadhouse but we made up in the car before that asshole hit her with the ax—" She looked at Kane. "—*hatchet* or whatever, but I would never hurt her or Doug. I cared for Doug. Sky and me are like sisters."

Kane scribbled in his notebook. "Yet this is the first time you came for a vacation here?"

"Yeah but I share a room with Sky at school." Ella wiped her eyes on a tissue. "Is that all?"

At a signal from Jenna, Kane closed his notebook. "Okay, I think that's enough for today."

"Thank you for your cooperation." Jenna stood and smiled at Ella. "We'll let you know the results of the blood test and I can assure you we're doing everything possible to find Sky and Doug."

*

Outside in his truck, Kane stared at the message from Rowley on Jenna's cellphone.

Holt's story is much the same as Ella Tate's. Checked his whereabouts at the time of the disappearances and he has sound alibis. Will obtain statement and email. Jeff Knox lives in room twenty-six at the Blackwater Motel.

Kane handed back the phone, then started the engine and turned to Jenna. "That rules Holt out of any involvement in the kidnappings and I have a theory why the Axman left Ella behind. He is convinced he is in the clear but is concerned about our investigation. I figure he believes if we catch him, an unstable young woman with convenient memory loss would create reasonable doubt at his trial."

"He's as slippery as an eel and trying to outsmart us." Jenna sighed. "And right now he's doing a great job."

CHAPTER FORTY-FIVE

After making a few enquiries, Rowley drove to the new bakery owned by Ty Aitken and to his relief found the store open. He turned to Webber. "You don't see many stores like this anymore. It's like Aunt Betty's Café. They make everything fresh on site and it's not from a factory like most stores around here. The smell of fresh-baked bread reminds me of my grandma."

"Mine too. She'd bake her own bread and spread it thick with butter." Webber smacked his lips. "Nothing better." He scanned his notes. "So this guy is supposed to have seen Knox carrying a woman into his motel room. This in itself doesn't make him the Axman."

Rowley shrugged. "If the sheriff wants him interviewed, she has an angle. Knox has priors and if the woman fits the description of Sky Paul, he could be a suspect. Right now, we're just treading water. We don't have a shred of evidence and no suspects."

"Okay, I guess we see what Aitken has to say." Webber slapped his hat on his head and climbed out of the cruiser.

Rowley stepped over a mound of graying snow littered with candy wrappers and followed him into the store. The bell chime surprised him. It was as if he'd walked into the 1950s. The young woman at the counter smiled at them. "I'm afraid we don't have much to offer you deputies. Folks have been coming in all day."

Rowley glanced at the remaining cakes, cookies and bread inside a glass cabinet and smiled at her. "We're looking for Ty Aitken. Is he here?"

"I am." A man in his early forties strolled out from the back wiping his hands on a flour-covered apron. "What can I do for you?"

Rowley introduced himself and Webber. "We heard via an informant that you witnessed Jeff Knox carrying a woman into his motel room on Friday of last week." He pulled out his notebook and pen. "Is this true?"

"Come out back." Aitken motioned for them to follow him. "I'll tell you what I know."

They followed him into a room set to one side of the huge ovens and preparation areas. It had a table and chairs in the center. A couple of lockers against one wall and a counter with a sink. Cups hung on hooks beside a coffee machine and a refrigerator hummed in one corner. Rowley took a seat but Webber stood by the door and leaned one shoulder against the wall. Rowley opened his notebook. "Okay, what did you see?"

"I'm usually here between the hours of ten and five overnight. I'm only here now because we received a special order." Aitken rolled his shoulders wearily. "That night I'd mixed the dough and set it to rise, then went to find the order book. I remembered I had an order for a birthday cake but I'd left the details at home. My wife handles that side of the business and it was too late to call her, so I went home. On the way back—"

Rowley held up a hand. "What time was this?"

"Close to three." Aitken rubbed his chin. "I saw him as plain as day. Jeff Knox was carrying a young woman with blonde hair over one shoulder from the back seat of his vehicle to the motel room. She was moving, like wriggling, but not screaming." He frowned. "I know Knox is a lowlife, so I turned off my headlights and cruised to the curb. I could see clear into the room. He dropped her onto the bed. She wasn't protesting, so I figured she wanted to be there and I drove off."

"Are you aware of the people missing between here and Black Rock Falls?" Webber straightened. "It's been all over the news."

"The hours I work, I don't catch the news." Aitken frowned. "Who went missing?"

Rowley looked up from his notes. "A young woman by the name of Sky Paul, blonde, small build, in her early twenties." He noted Aitken's astonished expression. "We believe a man kidnapped her on that Friday night around midnight."

"Do you recall what vehicle Knox was driving?" Webber leaned both hands on the table and stared at Aitken. "You may have witnessed a crime."

"Holy shit! I don't recall the make, and under the flashing lights on the sign over the motel, I'm not sure of the color. A silver, maybe, or white van." Aitken met Rowley's eyes. "Do you figure he's killed her?"

Rowley leaned back in his chair. "We'll need more evidence before we come to any conclusion. The sheriff will likely apply for a warrant to search his motel room. I'll need you to write a statement about what you witnessed. Can you do that for me, Mr. Aitken?"

"Sure." Aitken, visibly shaken, pushed to his feet. "I need coffee first." He went to the counter and pulled down three cups. "I'm dead on my feet."

"Okay, we can wait." Webber flicked a glance at Rowley. "I'll go get a statement book from the truck."

Sometime later, with the statement completed, Rowley led the way to his cruiser with a paper sack of cakes and cookies tucked under one arm. He glanced at his watch. It was close to five and the weather was closing in. He slid behind the wheel. "I hope we make it through to Black Rock Falls. You'd better call the sheriff with an update."

"One thing." Webber peered into the loaded bag of goodies. "We won't starve." He pulled out his cellphone and called the sheriff. "Ma'am, it looks like we have a suspect."

CHAPTER FORTY-SIX

Sunday, week two

Sunday morning arrived and Jenna felt as if she might as well beat her head against a brick wall. It seemed that every time she had gotten ahead in the case, something happened to slow down the investigation. As Knox was considered a resident of the Blackwater Motel, she would need more than the owner's permission to search his room. To avoid any issues if they proved Knox was involved and the case went to court, she needed to obtain a search warrant issued by the Blackwater judge. She would be out of her jurisdiction in Blackwater but wouldn't have a problem seeking assistance from the Blackwater Sheriff's Department.

After emailing the paperwork to the Blackwater judge, he'd refused to issue a search warrant on what he termed as hearsay and requested more information on Knox. It had been pointless to argue with him and she'd set to work searching the Blackwater databases. She hadn't asked for Kane's help but he had worked beside her well into the night hunting down information on the hitchhiker rape case and two cases of violence against women then presenting it in a nice concise file for Judge Eaton. Now they had probable cause but she wasn't sure it would be enough. Judge Eaton was being difficult and to make things worse they would have to wait for him to return home from church before speaking with him again.

They were on their way to Wolfe's house to collect his girls and take them back to the ranch. By the time Wolfe had completed the autopsy on Mrs. Palmer, they could drop the girls back home then approach the judge again with the new evidence. Sunday would be a washout. If the judge agreed to issue the warrant on a Sunday, they would have to convince the Blackwater sheriff to send one of his deputies to assist in the search then try to get through the heavy overnight snowfall to reach Blackwater. Bone weary, she groaned softly but the sound caught Kane's attention.

"Are you okay?" Kane's eyes had not left the ice-covered road but he gave her arm a squeeze. "Or am I giving you the silent treatment again?" He glanced at her then moved his attention back to the highway.

Jenna turned in her seat. The blinding winter light picked out the sharp lines of his face. He was thinner now, without one ounce of spare fat, and carried a haunted look in his eyes that made her heart twist. "It's not you, it's the delay in the search warrant, although I wish you'd talk to me rather than keep what's eating at you bottled up inside. We had gotten to be close friends before your head injury and I miss that."

"I remember." Kane let out a long sigh. "I want that back, Jenna, but I'm so darn angry right now."

Concerned, Jenna frowned. "Angry at me?"

"Not you." Kane barked a laugh. "You're amazing to put up with me. I know I've been a pain in the butt these last couple of months." He swallowed. "It's not being able to join a mission to take out the man who killed Annie that's eating me up inside."

Jenna bit her bottom lip. He rarely mentioned his wife's name. Annie died in a car bombing by a terrorist group in his other life as a special agent. He had been the obvious target and Annie was collateral damage. "There will be no mission. Don't you remember?

Wolfe told you POTUS gave the investigation top priority but the terrorists were like ghosts. If they find any leads, anything at all, they'll handle it and you'll be notified."

"That's not the problem." Kane's hands tightened on the steering wheel and Jenna could hear his leather gloves creak. "Because my memory of the days before the bombing are so clear now, I'm convinced it wasn't a terrorist group at all."

Astounded, Jenna sucked in a deep breath. "Then who would want you dead?"

"Someone on the inside, close to me." Kane's mouth turned down. "Someone I trusted." He looked at her and she could see the cold calculating government assassin looking back at her. "I figure POTUS had his suspicions as well, that's why I'm here with you. If there is a double agent they'll figure I'm dead."

The reasons behind Kane and Wolfe's arrival in Black Rock Falls to join the sheriff's department slid into place. She'd left DEA Agent Avril Parker behind and become Jenna Alton. In witness protection with a new face, she assumed Kane and Wolfe had arrived to protect her but she was wrong. POTUS wanted Kane surrounded by people he could trust because he suspected a double agent was trying to kill him. Perturbed by the implications, she leaned back in her seat and stared out at the miles of frozen scenery considering the options. After giving the problem some thought, she turned back to Kane. "What can I do to help?"

"Nothing." Kane tapped his head with one finger. "It's all in here in bits and pieces. I just need time to fit it all together. I'm replaying conversations in my head and trying to figure out what doesn't add up." He snorted. "It's not going to happen anytime soon, Jenna, it could take months and I'll need Wolfe to run down some information for me as I go, but one of these days I'll find the traitor and make him pay."

Jenna squeezed his shoulder. "*We'll* make him pay, Kane. You're not alone now."

"I know." Kane pulled up at the side of the road and turned to look at her. "You're an incredible friend—in fact the most tolerant and patient woman I've known. I've given this a lot of thought and I'd really like to go back to our movie nights and dinner dates, if that's okay with you."

"Dates, huh?" Jenna poked him in the arm to see if the iceman had finally thawed. "You mean that? Because you've made it quite clear you're still in love with your wife."

"Yeah, I mean it." Kane gave her a slow smile. "I remember how it was between us before the head injury scrambled my brains and I think we're good for each other."

Feeling like she was sixteen again, Jenna met his gaze and nodded. "Baby steps then?"

"Yeah." He touched her face. "Baby steps."

When they arrived at Wolfe's house, Julie and Anna Wolfe rushed out the door to greet them, chattering so fast Jenna burst into laughter. She turned to see Kane swing Anna onto his back and stride through the yard to take a look at the snowman the girls had built earlier in the week. She turned to answer Julie's stream of questions. "Yes, you can ride Lady; she is well named, but only up and down my driveway. Your dad has given us strict instructions not to allow you off my land."

"Anna won't be able to ride Dave's horse, it's way too big." Julie frowned. "Maybe she can ride with me?"

"Anna is riding with me." Kane loomed up behind them grinning like a baboon. "After the ride you get to eat Jenna's cookies."

"Not too much sugar." Wolfe appeared in the doorway smiling. "I have to live with them and this behavior, right now, is normal."

Jenna followed everyone inside and Kane went back to his truck to grab Dr. Weaver's computer for Wolfe to examine. When the girls took off to collect their things, she turned to Wolfe and dropped her voice to a whisper. "Try and make time over the next couple of days to speak with Dave. I can't give you any details but he needs to speak with someone in confidence."

"Sure." Wolfe frowned and his eyes showed concern. "Are you worried about his head?"

Jenna shook her head. "It's not his injuries, it's something else."

The front door opened and Kane came in carrying the computer.

"Where do you want this?" Kane looked at Wolfe.

"In my workroom." Wolfe led him away down the hallway and into a room.

"Hi, Jenna." Emily strolled toward them and gave her a hug. "How are you feeling?"

"I'm great." Jenna laughed. "I'd be better if I could solve this case; it's keeping me awake at night."

"Dad will have some answers for you in a couple of hours and he mentioned the blood test on Ella Tate should be in by now as well." Emily pushed her long blonde hair over one shoulder. "I didn't get the feeling Ella was involved in Sky's disappearance. She seemed genuine to me. You know what I mean, stunned and a bit disorientated. I've studied various types of behavior and she acts like a victim of trauma."

Over the past couple of months, Jenna had come to appreciate Emily's friendship and their discussions on crime. She nodded. "Yeah, but a killer can act exactly the same as well, especially after a crime of passion. I'm not talking psychopath, they can fool the best of us, but most normal people who kill for whatever reason are in shock and traumatized to some degree."

"So I should never jump to the first conclusion?" Emily sighed. "It's more difficult than I imagined."

"Not really." Kane strolled up behind them as quiet as a mouse. "Often your gut instinct will help, and as you go along your intuition and ability to read a person gets stronger. You are doing just fine. Learn all the angles and everything will fall into place."

Jenna turned as the girls came bounding back down the passageway bundled up in coats, hats and gloves. "I see you're ready to go." She turned back as Wolfe strolled toward her. "Give me a call when you're done and we'll bring them home. If we obtain a search warrant we're heading out to interview Knox in Blackwater."

"If you're doing a forensic sweep of the room, try to obtain a DNA sample from Knox as well. I'll get a full forensics kit together and you can pick it up when you drop the girls home." Wolfe rubbed his chin. "Find out when the room was cleaned last; if he is a resident, it might have been a while. We may hit pay dirt."

"That's a great idea." Jenna turned to go. "Come on, girls, the horses are waiting."

CHAPTER FORTY-SEVEN

Under the sedation, Olivia fought to stay awake. Gripped in fear, she shook her head, willing her drooping eyelids to remain open. A tremble of terror shuddered through her and the adrenaline coursing through her veins brought her awake. She gulped in huge deep breaths and turned her head to look at Doug in the next bed. His pale face rested peacefully on the stark white pillow. A large bruise extended from temple to cheek. He had tubes attached all over, including one coming from his mouth. The machine beside his bed made a breathing sound and she bit back a sob. The crazy people here had put him on a ventilator, which could only mean he could no longer breathe on his own. The memory of their attempted escape drifted into her mind in pieces. She remembered finding the exit out of this hellhole and Doug lifting his hands to fight. Oh Lord, Jim had rammed him with the gurney then hit him with something heavy and Doug had collapsed in a heap on the floor.

Panic gripped her at the sound of voices from the hallway. She kicked her legs, wanting to run away, but the restraints held her firmly in place. She took a few steadying breaths, then shut her eyes, leaving them open a slit to peer out under her lashes. The only way she had a chance of discovering Jim's plans would be to pretend to be asleep and listen. The machine had picked up her racing heartbeat and she willed her body to relax. The doors swung open and Jim and the nurse strolled inside.

"Why is her heartbeat so fast?" Jim came close to the bed and she could smell him. "What does that mean?"

"You keep her drugged all the time, her blood pressure is way too low and she's dying of starvation." The nurse placed an oxygen mask over her face. "How much longer are you planning on keeping her?"

"Not long." Jim cleared his throat. "Although I would like to keep her a bit longer."

"She'll die soon." The nurse went about adjusting drips. "I'm turning off the meds for a while. Her organs will start to deteriorate, then she'll be no use to anyone." He moved to Doug's bedside and Jim followed. "Are you really willing to risk losing all those orders?"

"Her organs will be fine." Jim snorted. "As long as her heart is pumping, she is viable as a donor." He leaned over Doug. "This one is gonna make me a fortune."

What did he say? I'm not an organ donor. Horrified, Olivia clamped her jaw shut in an effort not to scream. Trembling with effort, she kept her breathing slow and steady. *Oh, dear God, they're going to harvest my organs.*

"Doug's surgery will be scheduled on Tuesday and we'll do Olivia when I can confirm the orders." Jim's voice became sullen. "Damn cops are everywhere and I can't risk bringin' any new subjects here for a while. With the media hype everyone in town is under suspicion, so we'll have to lay low until the melt." He headed for the door. "When Olivia leaves, I want this place emptied and bleached from top to bottom. They have nothin' on us and I'm not plannin' on them findin' anythin' should they get it into their heads to search my premises."

As the footsteps faded, Olivia tore at her restraints until her bandaged wrists bled. She thumped her head on the pillow and screamed until she was hoarse. The door to the room opened and Jim strolled inside and stared at her. She swallowed the fear and scowled at him.

"What's wrong, Olivia?" He moved closer and grinned. "Just found out we're gonna cut out your kidneys without anesthetic?"

Anger raged through her. She whipped her head around, lifting her shoulders off the bed. "You murdering son-of-a-bitch." She spat at him and watched the spittle run down the front of his hospital scrubs.

"There's nothin' you can do, Olivia." Jim's eyes had turned into dark slits. "I'll enjoy watchin' you taken apart piece by piece, then I get to have my fun." He chuckled. "Spit at me all you like. I'm not plannin' on killin' you yet. You have at least another day to enjoy my company but it's coming soon, Olivia. I have a buyer for just about all of you. You're worth your weight in gold."

Shaking with terror and disgust, Olivia glared at him. "I hope you rot in hell."

"Darlin'—" Jim swaggered to the door. "—I'm already there."

CHAPTER FORTY-EIGHT

Jenna handed Anna up to Kane and he tucked the girl against his chest and smiled down at her. "Be careful. Are you sure you should be riding bareback with her?"

"Yeah." Kane held Anna around the waist and clicked his tongue. "See you in a little while." His horse moved off down the dirt road with Julie riding Lady by his side.

The cellphone in Jenna's pocket chimed and she hurried up the front steps and into the warmth of her house. The cookies in the oven filled the house with a comforting aroma and she accepted the call and walked into the kitchen. "Sheriff Alton."

"Oh, this is Daisy Lars out at the Two Trees Ranch. My husband Stan called me before and mentioned seein' the local tow truck driver, Chuck Burns, headin' through town last Friday night around one with a yellow car hitched to his truck. As the man on the TV insisted any information was confidential, I decided to call as Stan won't be back in town for a few days yet, been held up with the weather in Helena."

Jenna grabbed a pen and notepad from beside the landline and made notes. "How come he didn't call you before?"

"He didn't know about the missin' people until I mentioned it. He's been on the road for a week now. He drives a truck for Mackenzie." Daisy cleared her throat. *"I was tellin' him how nobody's safe around here anymore and he remembered seein' the car."*

"I understand. Do you have a number where I can reach your husband, Mrs. Lars, and your contact details as well?"

Mrs. Lars related the information and Jenna took it down. "Do you know Chuck Burns?"

"He isn't the type of person we would associate with, Sheriff. I know he owns the junkyard in town." Mrs. Lars drew a deep breath and hesitated as if not sure to continue. *"I'm not sure I should say anything more, I don't want him showing up on my doorstep all riled up."*

Jenna would have given a month's pay to find out the gossip on Chuck Burns. There was no way she was letting this go. "What the media is saying is correct. I promise your name will never come up. In any reports, I'll refer to you as my CI. That's how we refer to a confidential informant."

"Okay." Mrs. Lars's voice became low and conspiratorial. *"I hear tell he is an ambulance chaser, you know, out cruisin' the streets looking for an accident. His store sells recycled parts like the one owned by Sawyer out on the highway but I don't figure he worries too much about where they came from, if you know what I mean?"*

"Yeah, I understand." Jenna leaned against the kitchen counter; Kane and Rowley had visited both junkyards and found zip. "Are you saying he is running a chop shop? Because my deputies searched his junkyard last week and everything seemed to be in order."

"His junkyard is beside an old garage, the one that still has the 1940's gas pumps out front." Mrs. Lars' excitement came through the earpiece. *"Burns owns the entire block of buildings. Stan told me he often sees Burns waving vehicles through the old rusty doors of the garage late at night. Strange, seeing the place has been closed for fifty years or more."*

Jenna pumped the air, pen in hand, then grinned. "Thank you, Mrs. Lars, you've been very helpful. We'll contact you if we need any more information."

"No trouble at all." The line went dead.

After letting out a whoop of excitement, Jenna ran down the passageway and took a quick look out the front window to check on Kane and the girls. Kane had everything under control and was moving slowly along the dirt road, holding firmly on to Anna and chatting to Julie. She turned and made her way to her office, where she had a list of the owners of the properties in her county. Since arriving in Black Rock Falls, she'd discovered local gossip could be a goldmine of information. Sliding into the seat at her desk, she located the file on her computer and scanned the pages. Sure enough, Chuck Burns owned the junkyard, the adjoining property, listed as a derelict gas station, and another building currently used for storage by the owner. If Chuck Burns was involved in a chop shop like Mrs. Lars had intimated he might have a criminal record.

She accessed the local databanks and soon found he had priors. He'd spent jail time for kidnapping in Wyoming and received a fine for dealing in stolen property. She made up a file and would present it to the judge first thing in the morning to obtain a search warrant of his properties. Although the junkyard wouldn't be open on Sundays, a wild spark of urgency made her want to head out right away to see if the old garage had any windows they could peer into to see if Sky's vehicle was inside. She took a deep breath to get back on track. Right now, her proof against Burns was hearsay and she had to concentrate on obtaining evidence against Knox.

As Jeff Knox was their main suspect, she needed everything she could find to induce the Blackwater judge to issue a search warrant for his motel room. She wasn't convinced the charges of assault they'd found would be enough to sway a judge from a different county, especially as he had refused her first request. After entering Knox's name in the statewide database results filled her screen. She gaped in astonishment. The DA in Deep Valley County had also charged him with raping a hitchhiker. Just like the case in Blackwater, it never went to trial. *Two for two.* She chewed on her bottom lip wondering how come two women had him charged with rape then dropped the charges. Had he threatened them? She needed to speak with the victims to find out why they refused to give evidence.

She entered the women's names into the search engine and swallowed hard. Both women had missing person's files. It was if they had driven into the Bermuda triangle and vanished just like her three missing persons. She added all the information to the file and emailed it to Judge Eaton in Blackwater. Surely, now she would have enough probable cause to convince him to issue a search warrant for Knox's motel room.

The noise of someone banging on her front door and the sound of the two girls calling her name, Jenna closed the files and headed for the door. The girls, with rosy cheeks and excited chatter, met her as she opened the door. "Come inside in the warm." She helped them with their coats and hung them on the pegs beside the front door. "I have cookies in the kitchen and Dave says I make the best hot chocolate in town."

"He's taking care of the horses." Anna beamed up at her as they made their way to the kitchen. "He said we should be helping him because that's how you say thanks to a horse for riding it but he said he would thank them for us because we were shivering."

Jenna glanced at the clock and frowned. The time had flown. "No wonder you're cold, you've been out there for an hour."

She had them settled in front of the fire watching TV by the time Kane walked in the front door, removed his coat and kicked off his snow-covered boots. She took him into the kitchen and brought him up to date. "I've emailed the file to Judge Eaton. Now I guess we wait until after lunch to call him."

"Yeah, I figure we give him plenty of time to read the file." Kane nibbled at a cookie. "Wolfe should be calling soon. We could drop the girls home and do a drive-by of Chuck Burns' junkyard. I doubt it will be open today but if it is, we could make some excuse to have a look around and see if he has a yellow car in there."

Jenna reached for a cookie. "A slow drive-by, maybe. I don't want to spook him. If he thinks we're on to him, he'll destroy any evidence." She sighed. "I'd rather wait until we have a search warrant."

"That sounds like a plan. We could drop by Aunt Betty's for lunch. It will give me time to read over the info you have on Knox."

Jenna grinned at him. "Your tank is always empty. Are you ever *not* hungry?"

"It's the long hours." Kane reached for another cookie. "I need a lot of fuel to keep up with you."

Jenna laughed. "Okay, we'll wait it out at Aunt Betty's. It will be warmer than opening the office and I do need to eat. I'm exhausted and the cold weather isn't helping." She sighed. "The thought of driving to Blackwater this afternoon to execute a search warrant on a potential kidnapper isn't my idea of a perfect Sunday."

"I had a ball riding with Julie and Anna." Kane turned his cup around on the table and sighed. "I wanted to have kids. They're exhausting but I'm kind of jealous of Wolfe. I know he lost his wife too but she left him with three beautiful daughters."

"I figure we're lucky." Jenna pushed words out over the lump in her throat. "He has adopted us as family and we get to enjoy his kids for a couple of hours at a time, then hand them back." She shrugged. "The hours you put in on the job, you wouldn't have time for kids."

"I guess not." Kane sighed.

Jenna's cellphone chimed. It was Wolfe.

"Autopsy showed Mrs. Palmer died in the wreck, nothing suspicious, and the blood test for Ella Tate came back positive. So it seems she was telling you the truth. The amount she still had in her system would have knocked her out and messed with her mind."

A wave of relief lifted a weight from Jenna's shoulders. "That's good news. Are you finished for the day?"

"*Yeah. I'm home now.*" He cleared his throat. "*Another thing. Doctor Weaver's computer confirms she was making her own HLA typing database. I figure we need to question her about her motive. My gut tells me she is up to something.*"

Jenna frowned. "I have the same feeling but the kidnapping takes priority right now."

"*Sure. Have my girls behaved themselves?*"

"Perfect as always and they'll sleep well tonight." Jenna smiled at Kane. "They rode for about an hour."

"*Great. Will you be able to drop them home now? Emily is making lunch.*" Wolfe's voice lowered to a whisper. "*I'd ask you to stay but I wouldn't advise it.*"

Jenna chuckled. "Sure, we'll be there in half an hour." She disconnected and looked at Kane. "We're good to go. Mrs. Palmer's death was accidental and Ella's blood test came back positive for the date rape drug I suspected."

"That's one less murder to investigate." Kane pushed to his feet. "I'll go and get changed into uniform; if the search warrant comes through I guess we'll be heading out to Blackwater." He glanced down at Duke curled on the rug. "Do you mind if I leave him here? He's tuckered out."

"Of course not." Jenna reached for her cellphone. "I'll give the Blackwater sheriff the heads-up we might need one of his deputies this afternoon. If there is any evidence at Knox's motel room, we'll need him there for any jurisdiction issues."

CHAPTER FORTY-NINE

Much to Jenna's surprise, she received a call from Judge Eaton as she finished lunch at Aunt Betty's, to inform her he had signed the warrant and a deputy from Blackwater would meet her at the Blackwater Motel within the hour. She had spoken at length with Wolfe and he'd advised them to seal the room if they found anything significant and leave the forensics to him. Jenna agreed; it would be easy enough to have the Blackwater deputy take Knox into custody and hold him for questioning.

The drive-by of Chuck Burns' junkyard yielded zip. He had the place locked up tight and the rusty pull-down door to the garage looked as if it hadn't opened in years. The windows out front had a thick coating of grime and Jenna had no other option than to wait until the following morning to pay him a visit with a search warrant in hand.

The sun was dropping low in the sky by the time they turned onto the highway to Blackwater, with Kane behind the wheel as they headed down the straightaway. Her dislike of driving in the snow picked up pace as they headed down the first hill. Snow thrown from the snowplow created huge banks on each side of the highway and the blacktop wound away ahead, resembling a luge track etched out of the countryside. She turned her attention away from the steep decline and peered through the side window. Ice sparkled in patches and the last rays of the winter sun colored the wide expanse of snow across the grasslands in orange.

As they traveled through the miles of open plains, leaving the vast forests behind, they passed a few ranches, roofs piled high with snow and surrounded by fences buried to the top wire. In the distance, an elk pawed at a cleared driveway, searching for a meal, then bounded through deep snowdrifts toward a small wooded area. "I'm surprised animals survive in this weather."

"They are more adaptable than you think." Kane glanced in the direction of the elk. "It's unusual to see them away from their herd in this weather. I figure they stay together to keep warm. You seem very tense." He turned on the radio. "Am I driving too fast?"

Jenna laughed but it sounded false. "No, it's fine, I know I'm safe with you. It's a weird feeling of dread I get since I spun out and landed on the roof of my cruiser last year. Driving long distances in these conditions isn't something I enjoy, especially with sundown so close." She waved a hand at the spectacular views. "Although, I have to admit the snow-covered plains look beautiful. Lethal but very pretty."

"I usually figure the snow looks picturesque for the first day, then I wish it was spring." Kane glanced at her. "Tell me more about Jeff Knox. What do you make of him?"

Understanding he was attempting to take her mind off the journey, Jenna pulled out her notes and flicked through the pages. "Apart from his priors, we only have what Aitken has alleged to have seen. Knox's past and the sighting of him carrying a woman into his room make him a person of interest. The description on his driver's license puts him in the size range of the Axman."

"We could speak to Levi Holt again and offer him six images of men around the same size and see if he picks him out as a possible suspect?" Kane slowed to take the off-ramp into Blackwater. "Did we confirm what vehicle he drives?"

Jenna took a deep breath of relief as the town came into view. "Yeah, a white pickup and a van." She shuddered. "I can't imagine why people drive white vehicles in the snow. They become invisible in seconds."

"That may be the point." Kane slowed to drive through town. "At night he switches off his headlights and he becomes invisible but he'd be able to see the blacktop quite well; even in the dark it sticks out against the snow."

They drove into the parking lot at the Blackwater Motel and pulled up beside a deputy's cruiser. Jenna scanned the area. Only a few vehicles had parked outside the rooms. The motel was tired-looking and needed renovation. The old paint had started to peel off the walls and potholes littered the cleared driveway. She glanced at him. "I guess not many people stay here in winter."

"I'm not sure I'd stay here at all." Kane slid from behind the wheel, pulled his cap down over his pink ears and turned to her, puffing out a great cloud of condensation. "The walls look paper-thin and that roof is a few more snowfalls away from collapsing. I figure it will be freezing inside."

A blast of cheap perfume accosted Jenna's nostrils as she led the way into the motel reception area and nodded to the Blackwater deputy leaning against the counter chatting to the receptionist. She recognized Deputy Blake. "Thanks for coming out on a Sunday."

"The sheriff called me after he'd gotten a call from Judge Eaton and I dropped by his house for the warrant. I'll serve it and then you can do your thing." Blake frowned. "Do you figure Jeff Knox is involved with the kidnappings along the highway?"

"He's a person of interest." Jenna turned to the receptionist. "When did you last clean the room?"

"Two weeks ago, I guess." The receptionist wrinkled her nose. "He's a resident. I clean the place when he asks me to, which isn't often."

That's good. Jenna nodded. "Is Mr. Knox in his room?"

"As far as I know." The receptionist patted her blonde hair and smiled at Kane. "Would you like me to show you the way?"

Jenna rolled her eyes and headed for the door. "We'll be fine, thank you, ma'am." She glanced over her shoulder at Kane. "Room twenty-six."

CHAPTER FIFTY

Chuck Burns paced up and down, unsure what to do. The sheriff's department had paid him another visit, the second in less than a week. His heart had pounded so fast he thought he might suffer a heart attack, seeing the deputy's big black truck stop outside his yard again. He'd frozen inside the old garage and turned off the light. To anyone passing by the place looked deserted. He pulled out his cellphone and turned off the ringer just in case the sheriff had a mind to call him. What the hell did they want now? He pulled the door to the storeroom shut to conceal the filled shelves of car parts he'd salvaged from the cars his benefactor had given him then moved to the door and listened to them chatter about visiting someone in Blackwater.

He enjoyed the "no questions" agreement he had with his anonymous partner. All he had to do was to pick up a vehicle, strip it then crush it. The man wanted nothing in return but his silence and the deal had become lucrative but since the deputies started sniffing around his yard, he smelled a rat. He heaved a sigh of relief as the black truck drove away, and found the man's number on his phone. The only time he called was to confirm a pick up and the man had made the rules quite clear. He hit the call button and waited.

"Yeah." The voice at the other end was as calm as usual.

"I've had the sheriff here checkin' out my yard twice this week. I figure they're lookin' for that yellow car."

"You should have crushed it by now." The man's annoyance came down the line. *"Our deal was to strip the vehicles and crush them as soon as possible."*

Burns cleared his throat. "Yeah well, I would if the deputies hadn't arrived and searched my yard. I stripped it down but I haven't been able to crush it in case someone sees me. It's all over the news, don't you know?"

"When did the sheriff drop by?"

Burns rubbed the back of his neck. "'Bout five minutes ago. I overheard them talkin' about Blackwater and they took the highway south."

"Get rid of that damn car and leave the sheriff to me." The line went dead.

CHAPTER FIFTY-ONE

A cloud of condensation formed around Jenna, Kane and Blake as they crunched through the salt-laden parking lot of the Blackwater Motel to reach room twenty-six. She stood to one side with one hand on her weapon as Kane knocked on the door. The sound of a man cursing came through the thin walls and the door opened. A wave of unwashed male and stale food wafted out around him in a miasma of nasty. The man who stood before them had mussed-up brown hair, and dark blue circles hung under puffy eyes. He straightened to about six feet tall and glared at them. A noisy truck went by on the main street and Jenna raised her voice. "Mr. Knox?"

"You know darn well who I am. Leastways he does." Knox pointed a finger at Blake. "What you doin' wakin' a man at this hour? I work nights and you're disturbin' my rest. Sunday is my only day off." He attempted to close the door and gaped as Kane's large hand pushed the door wide open. "What do you think you're doin'?"

"We have a warrant to search your room." Blake pressed the warrant into Knox's chest and pushed his way into the room. "Stand over against the wall. Do you have any weapons you want to tell us about?"

"Yeah, my rifle and a Ruger LCP." Knox paled. "I ain't done nothin'. It ain't illegal to own a gun in these parts."

As Kane placed the forensics kit on the table inside the door, Jenna exchanged her thick leather gloves for latex and moved inside the room. She covered her face with a surgical mask, not willing to breathe in the toxic air. "Any knives?"

"Yeah." Knox gave a bark of laughter. "You kiddin' me, Sheriff? This is Blackwater. Maybe you've mistaken the motel for an apartment on Fifth Avenue."

She made her way into the middle of the room and Kane moved to her side. She lowered her voice. "You start in here, I'll see if I can sweet-talk him into giving up a DNA sample and ask him a few questions."

"Roger that." Kane snapped on gloves and went to work.

After pulling out her notebook and pen, she approached Knox. He gave her a long salacious look that made her skin crawl. Although she was aware Knox owned a white van and a pickup, she wanted confirmation. "Mr. Knox, I'm Sheriff Alton from Black Rock Falls. I would like to ask you a few questions, so Deputy Blake will read you your rights." Jenna waited a moment, then lifted her chin. "Do you wish to have a lawyer present for questioning?"

"Nope." Knox grinned at her. "Unless bein' a stud is a crime."

"Mr. Knox, this involves you being implicated in a kidnapping." Jenna raised her eyebrows. "It is a serious crime."

"I have no idea what you're talkin' about." Knox chuckled. "I don't have to kidnap women to get them in my bed."

Jenna glanced at the grubby sheets and suppressed a shudder. She couldn't imagine any woman walking into his room willingly. "You mentioned working nights. Do you have an employer?"

"Yeah, I work for Brightways as a delivery driver. They're a wholesale distributors. Groceries mostly. I deliver them late at night." Knox shrugged. "My run is from here to Deep Valley and back through Black Rock Falls."

Jenna made notes, surprised he'd offered so much information. "What do you drive?"

"The vehicles outside." Knox indicated with his thumb toward the parking lot. "I drive the van unless the roads are bad or it's a small delivery, then I take my truck."

Jenna lifted her gaze. "Why at night and can you give me an idea of the times you're on the highway?"

"Ah, because that's when the stores want to restock their shelves with fresh produce for the mornin'." Knox gave her a long stare as if she was an idiot. "I leave Brightways around ten-thirty 'n' get back here sometimes as late as six. It depends on how many stops I have to make. If it's just a few deliveries into Black Rock Falls I can do the trip in an hour or so in good weather."

"I gather you would have been traveling on the highway around midnight the Friday before last?" Jenna attempted to gauge his reaction but he just looked at her with the same contemptuous expression.

"Yeah, that would be right." Knox rubbed his chin, then frowned. "It was an early run. I'd gotten back here around two, maybe three, I don't rightly recall."

Jenna wanted him to admit he'd taken a woman to his room. If he wasn't involved in Sky's kidnapping, the woman Aitken saw him carry into his motel room would give him an alibi. "Is there anyone who can verify that you arrived here between two and three on Saturday morning?"

"Nope. I didn't see anyone. It was late and most folks around here are tucked up in bed." Knox didn't move his intense stare from her face. "Anything else?"

"Yeah." Jenna ignored his hostility and glanced back at her notes. "I'd like to see your right forearm."

"How did you know abou—" Knox shook his head. "Never mind." He rolled up his sleeve, displaying a dressing. "Yeah, I injured it opening a crate last Tuesday packing my truck."

The same day someone attacked Levi Holt. Interesting. "So if you hurt yourself on Tuesday did you complete your run that night as usual?"

"Yeah."

I have him. "So the highway closure wasn't a problem for you at all?" Jenna cleared her throat. "I believe a truck overturned and spilled its load, closing the highway for eight hours or more. How did you get through and back, Mr. Knox?"

"I took a backroad." Knox gave her a triumphant grin. "It goes through the Strong Ranch. It bypassed the closure. It's a dirt road and they keep the snow well cleared. I'm not the only driver aware of it."

His confirmation of being in the area could go both ways. Either he was sure the victims had not recognized him or he was innocent. Jenna took in his self-assured attitude and the way he looked at her, moving his eyes up and down her body, and decided the former. "What about Thursday evening, what time did you drive to Black Rock Falls?"

"I had one delivery in town so it was a quick turnaround. I got back here before one, I guess." Knox glared at Kane and shook his head. "I don't like people messin' with my stuff. I ain't done nothin' wrong. This is police harassment."

Jenna glanced at Kane. He was removing the sheets from the bed with care and stuffing them into plastic bags. They exchanged a meaningful look. She figured Kane had found evidence, but he said nothing and added the bag to the pile he had collected on the table. She turned her attention back to Knox, ignoring his outburst. "Did you have car trouble on Thursday night?"

"Nope." Knox shuffled his feet. "It seems real strange speakin' to you behind that face mask. What's wrong, scared you might catch somethin'?" He moved a step closer, grinning.

"You need to mind your manners." Blake stepped in front of Jenna. "You're speakin' to a lady, not your stripper girlfriend."

Jenna shot Blake a look she hoped conveyed her annoyance and moved around him. "Stand down, Deputy. I am quite capable of handling Mr. Knox." She lifted her chin. "Did you have a woman in your room, Friday before last?"

"If I did—" Knox grinned at her, "—as a gentleman I wouldn't tell."

"Ma'am, may I have a word?" Kane moved to her side.

Jenna followed him outside and shut the door. "What have you found?"

"What could be blood on the sheets." Kane shrugged. "A few blonde hairs on the carpet, some red hairs. The room is a DNA cocktail." He removed his gloves. "The blonde hairs could belong to the receptionist so we'll need a sample of her hair for Wolfe to compare. I've bagged the sheets. They stink as if they've been on the bed for months." He held up a set of car keys. "I'll check the pickup as that was the vehicle Aitken mentioned in his statement. If there's blood inside, and it's a match for Sky Paul, we may have our Axman."

"*If* you find some and it's a match." Jenna removed her gloves and mask, then bundled them into a ball. "I have him in the location of all three incidents at the right time; he drives a white pickup but not regularly and has an injury to his right arm. It sure points to him but many people drive white pickups and use the same road regularly at night for deliveries. Unless Wolfe finds some trace evidence, we don't have one chance in hell of convincing Judge Eaton to sign an arrest warrant. He'll say it's circumstantial evidence at best." She sighed. "He seems so unconcerned, it's unnerving."

"Yeah, but we shouldn't discount him yet." Kane leaned one shoulder against the wall and huffed out a cloud of steam. "He displays narcissistic tendencies and is so sure he hasn't left any DNA, that's a red flag in itself." He rubbed his chin. "We've dealt with his type before. They believe they can outsmart us and without a trace of the missing persons, no bodies, we have zip right now. If Knox is the Axman, he has the upper hand and knows it. I figure we should dig a little deeper into Mr. Knox."

Jenna tossed her gloves into a trash bin. "He hasn't convinced me he isn't involved."

"Blake obviously knows the woman he sees. Maybe we need to get a name and check out her story." Kane removed his gloves and mask. "If she's the woman he carried into his room, he'll be in the clear for kidnapping Sky at least."

Jenna straightened. She still had to sweet-talk Knox into giving a DNA sample. "Okay, you process the pickup and van then go speak to the receptionist, see if she'll volunteer to give you a hair sample. I assume she is the one who cleans his room and if not we need a name. I'll wrap it up with Knox."

She pushed open the door and took the few steps across the small room to speak to Knox. "Mr. Knox, are you willing to take a DNA test to exclude you from our list of suspects? Then we'll leave you alone."

"Sure." Knox wet his lips. "Trust me, I never leave my DNA anywhere it's not wanted."

Ignoring his smart mouth, Jenna turned back to the table and opened the forensics kit. The idea of getting close to Knox made her want to gag. She tossed a pair of gloves to Blake then gave him a test kit. "I'll leave that to you, Blake." She turned to Knox. "Thank you for your cooperation." She noticed him open his mouth to reply, but put her back to him and collected up the evidence bags, then opened the door, glad of the rush of fresh cold air on her face.

She waited outside for Blake to join her, then added the DNA kit to the large bag of evidence and looked at him. "Do you know the name of the woman you mentioned? He could have been carrying her into the motel room."

"Nah, she's a redhead." Blake snorted. "One of the dancers who works at the titty bar." He flushed to his ears. "Sorry, ma'am. I meant the local strip club."

"Okay, I'll need all the information you can get me on Knox. I'll clear it with your sheriff." Jenna tapped her bottom lip. "Someone will know his friends and who he hangs out with, bars he goes to, so see what you can find out about him. He is way too overconfident. Most people freak out when the cops search their homes. I'm worried if the woman Aitken saw him carrying into his room was Sky Paul, where is she now?"

CHAPTER FIFTY-TWO

Despondent from the lack of progress in the missing persons' cases, Jenna trudged through the fresh snow to Kane's truck. During their time with Knox, the sun had slipped away and now colored flashing lights from the gaudy motel sign reflected in the icy parking lot. The world had turned from a winter wonderland to every shade of gray in minutes, much like her mood. The facts surrounding the disappearances gnawed at her. When people went missing in similar circumstances, either of two things usually happened: the kidnappers sent a ransom note, or they found bodies, but some cases were never resolved. She let out a sigh filling the air around her in a cloud of white. *Where the hell do I go from here?*

She met up with Kane at the truck and heard Blake jogging up behind them. They turned to greet him. "Problem?"

"Nah." Blake smiled at her. "It's just you might want to hold off leaving for half an hour or so. The snowplows drove by just before. They'll be clearing the highway and spraying brine, so you might want to give them a head start?"

Jenna stowed the evidence bags in the back of Kane's truck and nodded. "Thanks. I could do with a strong coffee before we head home."

"Can you suggest a good place to get a steak?" Kane gave Blake an optimistic look. "We might as well eat before we leave. I won't feel like cooking by the time I've gotten home."

"The Turf and Surf Grill is opposite the park." Blake waved a hand in the direction of town. "Good food, nice clean place."

At the mention of steak, Jenna's stomach growled. She glanced at Kane. "That will do fine, thanks." She pulled open the door to Kane's truck, then paused to pull a business card from her pocket and handed it to him. "Call me if you find out anything about Knox."

"I sure will, ma'am." Blake took the card and made his way to his cruiser.

An hour or more had passed by the time they reached the highway and headed back to Black Rock Falls. Snow pelted the windshield like confetti, slowing the wipers and turning the highway into a scene from a Christmas globe. With no traffic on the highway, the blacktop loomed before them in a tunnel of the truck's headlights. Glad not to be alone, Jenna leaned back in the seat relaxing and listening to the chatter on the radio. It was unusual for Kane to be so quiet but as he needed all his concentration to drive, she decided not to discuss the case. Instead, she glanced at him, wanting to know more about his secret past. "Have you ever wondered why the three of us ended up together in Black Rock Falls?"

"At first, I figured this was the end of the line, put out to pasture job. I had a degree of memory loss covering the time before the car bombing, so I guessed it was because of my injury." Kane shrugged. "Until I worked alongside you. I know agents and you had so many tells, I could only imagine I'd been sent here to protect you." He barked a laugh. "An obvious mistake."

Jenna grinned. "What about Wolfe? I know we need his expertise as an ME and his IT skills are crazy but why send him?" She reached for her go cup of coffee. "He isn't in witness protection, is he?"

"Nope, no need." Kane flicked her a glance. "As far as anyone knows he left the service, worked in IT for a while, then stayed at home to nurse his wife. That's all true but he built a secure room to use for communications. I would imagine he handled a few agents before me. When I realized you were an agent, I made enquiries. That caused enough ripples for POTUS to send Wolfe here. He is my communication to HQ should I need it because unlike you, I'm not in witness protection, I'm officially off the grid."

Jenna pondered his words. "So do you figure they sent Shane here to keep an eye on us?"

"Nope." Kane glanced in his mirror and frowned. "I guess they wanted someone here I knew I could trust. If I get a message to inform me I'm back on active duty via him, I'll know it's true, but after the damage I sustained last fall, I don't figure that will be anytime soon if ever." He looked in the mirror again. "I'm sure I caught sight of a vehicle following us before and it just vanished."

"Maybe it's a ghost truck that haunts the highway late at night." Jenna chuckled and stared into the side mirror. "I can't see anything."

She noticed the tightening of Kane's jaw and the ticking of the muscle in his cheek. His attention flicked from the mirror and back to the road. Jenna turned in her seat to peer behind them. Her scalp tingled and her belly quivered with the unnerving feeling someone was watching them. The road behind appeared empty and only the blacktop snaked away around the previous bend.

"Turn back around and watch out the side mirror." Kane's voice was low and calm. "I caught a glimpse of something glistening when the moon came out from behind the clouds just before we took the last bend."

Instinctively Jenna went for her weapon and laid it across her knees. She turned to look at Kane. "Do you think it's the Axman? Maybe we have gotten too close and he wants to take us out?"

"Maybe but my truck is unmarked, so how does he know it's us? Unless it's Knox, he might have seen our vehicle but I didn't notice him peer out the window at the motel." Kane frowned at her Glock. "You'll need both hands to hang on if he makes a move."

"Okay." She holstered her weapon and moved her attention back to the mirror. "I can't see anyone."

As they rounded the next sweeping bend, an engine roared behind them and as if out of thin air, the menacing crash-bar-covered grille of a vehicle appeared in the side mirror coming fast. Jenna clamped her jaw tight and hung on. "Oh, my God, watch out!"

"Shit!" Kane accelerated across the highway then slammed on the brakes and his truck slid sideways for fifty yards on the fresh covering of snow road before coming to a rocking halt.

The white pickup flashed past in a blur, missing them by inches, and fishtailed up the road then slowed to stop four hundred yards away on the sweeping bend as if waiting. Jenna's heart pounded as Kane moved his truck back to the right lane then stopped in the middle of the road.

"Did you get a plate?" Kane's gaze hadn't moved from the speeding white truck.

"No, it was covered in mud. I figure he's planned this and probably followed us from town." Jenna swallowed hard. It was like being stuck in a horror movie. The white pickup's lights came on in a flash of brilliance. It spun around and faced them, steam billowing from under the hood and the engine revving like a raging bull. The dark windows gave the pickup an eerily robotic appearance as the vehicle lifted up at the front and shook with power. Unnerved, Jenna gripped the seat. "What's he doing now?"

"Playing chicken and he sure picked the wrong guy."

A sense of foreboding dropped over Jenna. God help them. One look at Kane and she knew he'd dropped into combat mode. She took in his determined expression and noted the pulsing vein standing out in his neck. "You'd risk our lives on a stupid game on an icy road. Have you lost your mind?"

"You need to trust me, Jenna. No one wants to die. He'll fold then lose control on the bend and end up in the ditch." He glanced at her. "He wouldn't be doing this without wearing a seatbelt, so we'll play his stupid game, then drive over and arrest him."

Angered by his overconfidence, she turned on him. "I'd rather you stopped acting like a teenager and shoot out his tires. You never miss, do you?"

"And if he's just a kid in a high-powered truck playing chicken? I shoot out his tires and he rolls and dies in the wreck." Kane didn't take his eyes off the white pickup. "You willing to risk that, Jenna?" He revved the engine as if in reply to the challenge. "No? Then hang on tight." He hit the gas.

The truck's tires spun, then gripped the blacktop, and they shot forward at speed. Jenna dug trembling fingers into the seat, her gaze fixed on the white truck hurtling toward them. The space between the two cars narrowed and, blinded by the headlights, she held her breath. Her heart pounded fast in her ears and her stomach cramped so tight she wanted to vomit.

The next moment the bright lights of an eighteen-wheeler rounded the bend in front of them, air-horns blasting in warning. Jenna bit back a scream. If they swerved to avoid the white pickup, they would crash head on into the truck, but Kane didn't flinch and held his course. At the last second, the white pickup swerved in front of the oncoming truck. She waited for a loud bang and the scream of tearing metal but only the truck's air-horns continued to screech into the night.

Panting and speechless with fear, she waited for Kane to slow down and stop beside the road, then leaped out the door and vomited. She turned to see him standing in the middle of the highway staring into darkness. "You. Are. Insane." Her voice sounded shaky. "We could have been killed."

"Not a chance, he started moving over the line to avoid us way before we'd gotten close. I figured he was going to use the truck for cover." Kane held out a bottle of water and shrugged. "He must have nine lives to have gotten away with that."

Legs trembling, Jenna took the water and washed out her mouth, then bent over, hands on thighs, trying to slow her panicked mind. "It's pointless pursuing him. He knows this strip of highway and could be holed up anywhere."

"At least we have a good description of his truck." Kane pulled his hat down over his ears and rubbed his hands together. "White, blacked-out windows with a mark on the passenger-side door, like the outline of a sticker."

Jenna gaped at him as she made her way back to the truck. "You saw all that in a split second?"

"Just doing my job, ma'am."

CHAPTER FIFTY-THREE

Monday, week two

It took some effort for Jenna to climb into Kane's truck the following morning without shaking the memory of the previous night. The winter weather was in full force and the roads more dangerous by the hour. As they would be working alongside each other all day, it seemed good sense to leave her cruiser and take a ride with him to the office. After being mad all evening after he risked their lives in a movie-like stunt, she'd run through the scenario a thousand times and realized that, stuck out in the middle of nowhere and twenty minutes away from backup, they'd had no other choice. Kane had made a split-second decision, summed up the situation and acted with confidence—as usual.

"I filed a report about last night's incident." Kane turned into town and slowed to join the line of traffic moving at a snail's pace behind the snowplow. He glanced at her and raised an eyebrow. "Are you holding a meeting today as usual?"

Jenna had held a Monday staff meeting at nine since she became sheriff, but of late they needed meetings to update everyone more frequently. She nodded. "Yeah, I called Rowley yesterday and asked him to run down more info on Chuck Burns. I figure we've enough probable cause for a search warrant but the more we can sweeten the pot with the better. It'll be interesting to see what he found. I'll update everyone on Knox and our 'incident'." She held up two hands and made quote marks. "If that was the Axman, we might be looking at homicide for Mrs. Palmer."

"It sure would be a way of pushing someone off the road without leaving any trace evidence." Kane pulled into his spot outside the sheriff's department. "I'll give Ella Tate a call and see if she remembers anything about the white pickup. She didn't mention the tinted windows or the sticker mark on the door."

Jenna paused, one hand on the door. "So we can rule out Knox. You searched his vehicle but didn't mention dark windows or a sticker."

"It had dark windows but it had a logo across the door." Kane shrugged. "It didn't look like a sticker but maybe the Blackwater deputy could take a closer look. It could be a magnet. He owns those vehicles, not Brightways."

"I'll call him." She slipped from the vehicle.

The wind had picked up, swirling the snow and biting through her clothes. She glanced down the sidewalk at the people bent over, heads down, battling against the weather with scarves wrapped around their faces and wearing sunglasses. The look struck her as comical for a moment but then she remembered the furnace. Even with the small heaters, the office would be freezing until they resolved the problem with it. She brushed away the snowflakes resting on her eyelashes and followed Kane inside the building. When a blast of warm air hit her, she stared at Maggie on reception in surprise. "How come it's so warm in here?"

"I had a call early yesterday morning from Shane Wolfe. He said he'd found someone to replace the furnace. He didn't want to bother you, seeing as you were lookin' after his girls." Maggie frowned. "I came down and opened up. I waited here until they'd finished. I didn't want them poking their noses into things that don't concern them."

"You're a gem, Maggie." Jenna bit back a grin. As usual, Wolfe had called his government contacts and fixed the problem. "That's wonderful news. I'll be sure to thank him." She made her way to her office.

After calling Deputy Blake in Blackwater, she updated her whiteboard, then strolled down to the kitchenette to fill the coffee maker. Kane and Rowley were busy and didn't look up as she passed. She collected a container of chocolate chip cookies and headed back to her office. At eight fifty-five, the room filled with her deputies and Kane placed a cup of coffee on the desk for her before taking his seat. She thanked Wolfe for organizing the furnace and brought them up to date with the Knox interview, then looked expectantly at Wolfe. "Have you had time to look over the evidence we collected from Knox's motel room yesterday?"

"I haven't had time to reach any conclusions. The DNA tests will take a few days." Wolfe rubbed his chin. "I can tell you the marks on the sheets are blood. I typed the sample and it's the same blood type as Sky and Knox, so it's inconclusive at this time." He frowned. "What worries me is your incident occurred along the same stretch of road as the Palmer accident and possible abduction. I re-examined the photographs of the scene and if Mrs. Palmer had swerved to avoid a collision with an oncoming vehicle, the result would have been the same. As we found no evidence of a collision, we assumed she lost control on the ice taking the bend and slid off the road. It happens frequently at this time of year."

Jenna leaned forward in her seat. "So have you changed your finding?"

"I'm leaving it an open verdict for now." Wolfe reached for his coffee. "When you catch the Axman, I'll see if his tires match any of the other sets we found."

"I have Deputy Blake out of Blackwater chasing down any known associates of Knox, especially women." Jenna took a sip of her coffee. "I had the feeling he was lying or covering up for someone. He carried a blonde-haired woman into his motel room the same night as Sky Paul went missing. Blake knows the townsfolk and we'll have to hope Knox talked to one of his friends. He likes to boast, so I can't see him keeping a secret." She turned her attention to Rowley. "Okay, now on to the report from Mr. Lars about Chuck Burns. Have you found any additional information?"

"Everything she told you about him appears to be true enough." Rowley flicked through his notes. "We have spoken to him before when we checked out the junkyards. We didn't find anything suspicious." He flicked through his notes then lifted his head and looked at her. "As you know, Burns owns the old garage next door to the junkyard and a storage area adjacent to the garage. It's a collection of red brick buildings. He frequents the road between Blackwater and here, looking for abandoned cars or wrecks, and owns a white pickup used for towing. He's an ambulance chaser and owns a scanner. I gather he collects abandoned vehicles valued under $500 so he can crush them without verifying ownership." He frowned. "Not many of the townsfolk were forthcoming about him running a chop shop but unless the recycled parts have identifying numbers on them, as in some parts of vehicles, he could be selling them through his yard."

Jenna smiled at him. "That's all we need. I'll add that information to the warrant for you to take over to the judge. I want you to stress the importance of serving it this morning and wait for a reply."

"Yes, ma'am."

"Okay." Jenna pushed to her feet. "The moment the warrant arrives, we'll move out." She glanced at Wolfe. "Do you want to be involved?"

"Not at this stage." Wolfe indicated to Webber. "I need to work on the Knox evidence. I can spare Webber for backup."

"Good, then that's all for today." Jenna exchanged a look with Kane and he hung back as the others filed out. "Do you figure Chuck Burns will cause any trouble?"

"I'm not sure. He was wary and defensive but he gave us permission to search his property. He didn't have too many wrecks there at all and nothing even remotely late model. We just gave it a quick sweep and left." Kane shrugged. "Of course at the time I wasn't aware he owned other buildings close by."

Jenna chewed on her bottom lip. "If he has Sky's car hidden somewhere else, he wouldn't be worried about you searching his yard." She leaned one hip against her desk. "Burns is looking more like a suspect by the second."

CHAPTER FIFTY-FOUR

Anger raged through him with each step from the parking lot and between the red brick buildings. He used his key to open the hidden entrance to his secret rooms. The freezing fingers of melted snow running down his neck did not cool his temper. No one had ever gotten so close to destroying his business. He reached the next door and thumbed in the password on the keypad. He grunted as red lights flashed his error. "Dammit all to hell."

The nosy sheriff was sticking her nose into too many places. She was smarter than he had given her credit for and the deputy always at her side had a stare that cut into a man's soul. He snorted, recognizing a killer. When he looked into the mirror, the same truth reflected back at him. *It takes one to know one.*

Deputy Kane was hiding a secret just like him. His reaction on the highway when he challenged him was unexpected and showed Kane was a certain type of man—one who doesn't fear death—which made him a threat. He thumbed in the password slower this time and the door clicked open. Smashing the metal door against the wall, it echoed down a passageway lit only with small downlights. After removing his coat and boots, he shoved them into a locker containing his spare coat and the male nurse's clothes then dragged hospital scrubs over his clothes and wore a hat and face mask as a disguise. He would never risk anyone seeing his face just in case one of his victims escaped. It was going to be a rush; he had so little time to complete his orders and didn't want his reputation for delivering on time shot to hell because of Sheriff Alton. Due to her interference, he would have to cease operation until the smoke cleared and it would cost him millions.

His temper hadn't cooled by the time he came up on the male nurse he'd cajoled into working with him. In truth, he wanted to feed the wimp into the hogger machine and watch his eyes as the machine slowly shred him into little pieces but right now, he needed him. *Maybe later.* "You've watched the doc harvest organs so I need you to work on Doug alone because we're runnin' out of time and I have business to attend to in town."

"No way." The nurse stopped washing Olivia and peered at him over his face mask. "Watchin' is one thing and I assist but doing a number of complicated procedures is another matter. If I made one mistake and cut too deep, the sample would be useless." He raised both eyebrows. "Then your reputation won't be worth a dime." The nurse cleared his throat. "Another thing—you'll have to pull back on the drugs before shipment, you're givin' Doug enough meds to bring down a grizzly."

A wave of frustration gripped him at the sight of Olivia's terrified stare but he'd no time to indulge in his fantasies, he'd need to leave soon to convince the doc to drop everything and complete the next shipment. "Okay, drop him down some but keep him strapped to the bed. He'll be first when I can get the damn doc here."

"What about Olivia?" The nurse met his gaze.

He shook his head. "We'll get to her later. Is she on the zombie drug?"

"Yeah but it won't last long, maybe another ten minutes or so." The nurse picked up the bowl and towels and left the room, leaving them alone.

It took an effort to control the rush of excitement. Unlike Sky, she'd be alive when he fed her into the hogger, and watching the machine do its job sated his desire. He'd once preferred to strangle them. Stabbing left too much evidence behind. He had to admit leaving their bodies to rot beside the highway had been a waste but all that had changed now. Now, nothing went to waste.

CHAPTER FIFTY-FIVE

Caught up in Jenna's exuberance, Kane slid behind the wheel and waited for her to fasten her seatbelt before peeling out of the parking space and heading to the outskirts of town to Chuck Burns' junkyard. The tires gripped well on the newly brined blacktop, and he accelerated leaving the decorated main street behind. "I sure hope we find something substantial this time."

"Time has been our enemy, not getting the report from Mrs. Lars until yesterday then waiting for the judge to sign a search warrant, we've given Burns plenty of time to dispose of evidence." Jenna waved the document. "I wish we'd had this yesterday."

Kane shrugged and pulled his truck to a halt outside the junkyard with Rowley's cruiser close behind. "Then Knox could have slipped through the net. He looked the most suspicious and he's still on our list. How are you playing this?"

"We'll go see Burns. I'll send Rowley and Webber round back of the old garage in case he tries to run." Jenna climbed from the SUV and issued orders then led the way into the office. "Mr. Burns, we have a warrant to search your premises."

"Sure, I said before you could look around." Burns wiped greasy hands on a stained rag. "I ain't got nothin' to hide."

"The warrant extends to all your premises, including the old garage and storage areas you own in this location." Jenna slapped the warrant on the desk. "If you have keys it would be wise to open the doors or I'll give my deputies instructions to break them down."

Kane tried to avoid the rancid smell of male sweat and dirty motor oil and rested one hand on his weapon; if Burns planned to escape, he would try in the next few seconds but the man's face paled and he leaned heavily against the wall. It was as if all the life had drained out of him. "Hand over the keys, Mr. Burns."

"Okay, sure." Burns' eyes shifted from him and back to Jenna then he went for something below the counter.

Don't go for a weapon. I don't want to kill you. We need answers. Before he finished the thought, his Glock was in his hand. "I wouldn't do that if I were you."

"One more step and Deputy Kane will blow your fingers clean off." Jenna had her Glock aimed at Burns' chest. "Hands on head. Step away from the counter." She exchanged a meaningful glance with Kane.

Kane moved around the counter and pulled open a drawer. Inside he found sets of keys and whistled at the sight of a Smith & Wesson 500. He holstered his Glock and pulled on a pair of latex gloves, then lifted the pistol out the drawer. "You weren't planning on shooting me, were you, Burns?" He smiled at the quivering man. "And just for the record, I wasn't aiming for your hand, I was aiming right between your eyes and I never miss." He unloaded the gun, letting the bullets tumble back in the drawer, then slipped the heavy weapon into his jacket pocket.

"Show me the keys for the garage." Jenna held her weapon steady. "Then cuff him, Kane. I don't want any surprises." She read Burns his rights. "Let's go."

"Move." Kane gave Burns a little push in the back and marched him out the door and to the old garage next door.

"Oh, lord. Don't go in there." Burns' head hung down on his chest and his shoulders slumped. "You don't understand."

"Oh, I understand just fine." Jenna slid the key into the padlock on the garage door. "Do you have something to tell me, Mr. Burns?"

She gave him an enquiring look. "No? Well then I guess we take a look for ourselves." She bent to slide up the door.

The door moved without the grating sound Kane would have expected for an old rusty door. He took a hold of Burns' arm and the man's muscles trembled against his palm. Light flowed into the dark interior and hit the polished finish of a late-model yellow sedan. The car was little more than a shell and Burns had stacked parts on shelves complete with labels giving the make, year and model of the vehicle. The exact same car owned by Sky Paul.

He heard Jenna ordering Rowley and Webber to return, then she turned to face Burns.

"Where's Sky Paul?" Jenna holstered her weapon. "This is her vehicle. Best you tell us now before my deputies tear the place apart."

Burns trembled but said nothing.

Kane squeezed Burns' arm just hard enough to let him know he meant business. "Where's Sky Paul?" He glared at him. "The DA will go easy on you if you cooperate."

"I don't know anyone by the name of Sky Paul." Burns lifted his head and a determined expression crossed his face. "I found the vehicle abandoned on the side of the road up near the industrial area out on the highway."

"Why didn't you report it?" Jenna stood hands on hips and her eyes bored into him. "It's been all over the news we were looking for this car."

"I ain't sayin' no more." Burns turned his head and spat on the ground at Jenna's feet. "I know my rights, I want a lawyer."

Just then, Rowley and Webber came jogging back through the snow toward them. Kane pushed Burns toward Rowley. "Escort Mr. Burns to the back of your cruiser."

"Yes, sir." Rowley took Burns' arm and led him away.

"Right." Jenna raised her voice. "Let's tear this place apart. Check for root cellars. Webber, I want evidence. There should be blood in the car. The seats are over there, check them as well." She pointed to the beige car seats leaning against one wall. "Kane, check the other buildings."

Kane waited for Rowley to return, then grabbed the set of keys hanging from the padlock. "Show me the storage area." He followed Rowley down a dirt road recently cleared of snow. "This looks promising. Burns took an effort to clear this area. I sure hope we find Sky Paul alive." He bent to examine tire tracks. "Hmm, I make out three maybe four tracks here. It'll be difficult to isolate one."

"Something big came through here and ripped the branches clean off the trees." Rowley stared down the row of naked western larch. "There's a clear track here. A delivery van maybe?"

The image of the confident Knox flashed into Kane's brain. They hadn't considered it could be a group of people involved in the kidnappings. He grimaced at the thought. "I hope it's not sex-slave traders." He brushed away the snowflakes from his cheeks. "Tracing the victims would be impossible."

The dirt road led to a massive separate red brick building with a small parking lot at the back. An alleyway divided two buildings and Kane led the way, taking in what resembled air conditioning units attached to one side. Someone sure wanted it cold inside that building. He approached a metal door and fitted a number of keys in the lock. After a few tries the door clicked open. He glanced over his shoulder at Rowley. "Watch my back." He stood to one side and swung the door open.

Inside was pitch black and Kane swore under his breath. It seemed every time he investigated a missing person, he ended up venturing into some eerily dark place or another, and it didn't get any easier. He used his flashlight alongside his weapon to light the way and edged slowly forward with Rowley close behind, his breath sending great clouds of condensation into the air. It seemed entering the dark unknown wasn't Rowley's job of choice either. Further along the hallway they found an empty inner office covered in a thick coating of dust and another door. The door opened onto a long dark passageway. He ran the beam of his flashlight over the wall to find a switch. Only small inset lights, like those in the floor of an aircraft, illuminated the way. "Sheriff's department. Is anyone in here?"

Nothing.

Heart pounding, Kane pushed down the creeping unease crawling up his spine and reached down deep for his professional façade. Something about this place made his skin crawl and the unpleasant odor seeping from the damp walls played tricks with his mind. Flashes of past crime scenes danced through his subconscious in a warning. Keeping to the wall, he led the way down the dim corridor to another metal door with a keypad set in the wall next to it. He moved forward to examine it and recognized the type. It was a familiar brand and not very secure. He had the technology to open it without a problem but his gut told him he wouldn't like what was on the other side.

"Now what?" Rowley moved up beside him, aiming his flashlight on the contraption.

Kane holstered his weapon and pulled out a decoder, as small as a cellphone, from his pocket. "I never leave home without this; it's very useful."

Moving with speed, he attached wires to the box and numbers flashed on the screen. After a few seconds, the numbers stopped on the decoder and the door clicked open. A cloud of sub-zero air escaped, bringing with it the metallic smell of blood. He wanted to slam the door shut and glanced at Rowley's suddenly ashen face. "That doesn't smell good."

"Jesus, that smells like... oh, shit." Rowley's eyes widened, looking like black orbs in the dim light. "Not bodies again. Should we just call Wolfe?"

Kane shook his head. "We have to take a look." He slapped Rowley on the shoulder. "You should be getting used to this by now."

"I'll never get used to seeing murder victims." Rowley's mouth turned down. "At least I don't puke as much as I used to."

Unease slid over Kane as he pocketed the decoder and slid the Glock from its holster. Walking into a dark abyss filled with the smell of death brought back memories he'd rather forget. The sightless eyes of past victims flashed into his mind in fast-forward reruns and he ground his back teeth. *Not again.* "I'm going in. Make sure the door remains open."

"Roger that." Rowley placed his back to the door, held his weapon along his flashlight and gave him a less than confident nod. "Ready when you are."

Taking a deep breath, Kane eased through the door and, senses on full alert, moved inside one step at a time. The smell of blood surrounded him and before he could drop into his professional safe zone of calm, his flashlight illuminated a headless skinned body hanging on a giant hook. The hair on the back of his neck bristled and his mind continued to play tricks on him. Heart pounding, he lowered his flashlight; sure he had seen the shapely back of a woman then turned to catch Rowley's pale face and wide eyes in his beam. "What was that?"

"A deer maybe." Rowley's Adam's apple bobbed up and down as he swallowed. "The door is six inches thick. I figure it's a freezer."

Kane shone his light over the door and surrounds searching for a handle. Above the door, he found a rod to keep the door open and slotted it into place. "See if you can get the lights on."

Moments later the room flooded with light. Kane shook away the macabre images inside his head and scanned the room before him. Frozen carcasses of elk and deer hung in lines. It was unusual to see so many in one place. Hunters in Montana field-dressed their tagged kills, left them to cool then took them home or donated them to charity. Seeing so many in storage made him suspicious. He would contact Fish, Wildlife and Parks and give them the heads-up. Taking care to avoid touching anything, he walked the walls of the freezer, checking each line of carcasses. There was only one entrance, yet the building was vast. There must be another way into the place. He strolled back to Rowley and they headed back out and into the watery sunshine.

"What was that all about?" Rowley scratched his head under his woolen cap.

Kane shrugged. "I'm not sure. Poaching perhaps. I'll get the FWP to look into it but right now our priority is finding the missing persons." He pulled the outer door shut, locked it and led the way around the building.

After an extensive search, they'd found nothing but a bunch of empty rooms. Disappointed, Kane exchanged his gloves for something warmer than latex and sent Rowley to do another search of Burns' office and yard. He made his way back to Jenna and explained what they'd found. He noticed Jenna's excitement and the pile of evidence bags sitting on the counter. "What have you got?"

"We have enough here to bring Burns in for questioning." She smiled. "Blood evidence in the vehicle and on the seats. Also, we found Ella Tate's cellphone. Sitting right on the bench in clear view."

Kane frowned. "Wolfe had no luck searching for her phone. You sure it's Ella's?"

"Oh yeah, but the battery and SIM are missing." Jenna held up an evidence bag. The pink phone had "Ella" on the cover in rhinestones. "Just like the description she gave Wolfe." She smiled. "We have enough evidence here to book him." She pulled out her cellphone. "I'll call Wolfe." She made the call, then lifted her gaze to Kane. "He's on his way, we'll wait."

"Ma'am." Rowley came jogging back. "The snow is a foot deep around the vehicles. Nothing has disturbed them since we were here. The office doesn't have a cellar. I can find no trace of Sky Paul or the others."

She turned to Webber. "Wrap it up. We'll wait for Wolfe to arrive now." She turned to Rowley. "Take Burns back to the station and put him in a cell. He can cool his heels until we get back then I'll call his lawyer. We'll be along as soon as Wolfe has completed his examination of the scene."

"Yes, ma'am." Rowley tipped his hat and strode toward his cruiser.

Kane walked out of the oil-polluted atmosphere and into the crisp winter morning. He took a few deep breaths and looked at Jenna. "I wonder if he'll talk. We still have three people missing." They crunched through the snow back to his truck. "I'm starting to wonder if there are more people involved in this crime."

"How so?" Jenna rested one hand on the door of his truck.

Kane shrugged. "A gut feeling. There's too much going on for one person to handle." He waved a hand toward the junkyard. "If he's working with Knox, for instance. It would make more sense. Knox kidnaps the people and Burns disposes of the vehicles. The only part of this that worries me is where Doug Paul fits into his MO. If it's a killer we're dealing with, unless Doug was collateral damage, and he mistook Levi Holt for a woman, the motive doesn't make a whole lot of sense." He leaned against his truck. "Kidnappers who aren't interested in collecting a ransom or selling their victims usually do it to rape, murder or both. I've never heard of one who deals in spare car parts and frozen poached meat on the side." He snorted. "They're usually way too smart to keep a victim's car in their possession."

"So you're not convinced we have our man?" Jenna's brow crinkled into a frown. "It all adds up to me. Especially if Wolfe finds evidence that Burns disposed of the bodies in the crusher."

Kane shook his head. "It will be hard to prove he is involved in Doug or Olivia's disappearances, especially if the vehicles he used to conceal the bodies have already been recycled." He blew out a huff of steam. "That's if he murdered the other victims. Burns doesn't fit the profile I'd expect for a killer escalating so fast. He was quaking in his boots when I had hold of his arm and didn't try and sweet-talk his way out of trouble."

"The evidence is stacked against him, Kane." Jenna folded her arms and stared at him. "What do you see that I'm missing here?"

Kane shrugged. "Oh, he's involved but he doesn't have the street smarts to do this alone." He waved a hand toward the garage. "What's his motive?"

"He could have raped the women." Jenna stared into space. "I figure the chop shop would be lucrative."

Kane nodded, then mimicked her pose and folded his arms. "Sitting out on the highway hoping to kidnap a woman and steal her car seems a bit extreme, when he'd have the ability to steal one from a parking lot. To be perfectly honest, it would be difficult to rape someone outside in this weather. He must have taken the women somewhere other than here. We've searched this place and there's no sign anyone's been in the other building for some time. And the junkyard office hasn't got more than a spare foot of space." He kicked at a wedge of snow with the toe of his boot. "Then we have to factor in Doug Paul. He plays hockey for the Larks so he'll be fit. How did Burns subdue him, drug Ella, then get Olivia out of the wrecked car all on his lonesome?"

"All good points I'll consider after Wolfe has examined the premises." Jenna brushed snow off her jacket and opened the door to Kane's truck. "I think Burns is guilty as hell. The evidence is right in front of us."

Kane met her gaze. "Well, I figure Burns is just the tip of the iceberg."

CHAPTER FIFTY-SIX

Doug woke to the sound of arguing, his head pounded and his tongue was stuck to the roof of his mouth. The memory of Jim ramming the gurney into him was the last thing he remembered apart from the searing pain in his head before he blacked out. From under his lashes, he watched the nurse and Jim come toward him. He lay very still and tried not to flinch as the nurse moved close then touched him.

"He won't last much longer if you keep damaging him." The nurse peered down at him. "His organs will be worth zero if they're bruised. "Look at him. What will they say about his condition?"

"I don't care what they say." Jim slammed down a fist on the side cabinet, shaking the utensils. "They work for me just like you do and be here first thing to complete the orders. I'm going to see her now and make the final arrangements, then I'll be back to finish up outside. Pack up everything we don't need and I'll store it somewhere safe when I return." He turned on his heel and charged out the door.

Doug clamped his jaw shut as the man washed him and changed the dressing on his wound but neglected to fasten the restraints. His heart pounded at the thought of escape and the monitoring machine kicked up the beats, but the nurse was too busy with Olivia or didn't care. He attempted to move and discovered his limbs worked just fine. Moving with slow measured movements, he eased the needle carrying the drip from his arm and pressed down hard to stop the flow of blood. Then he pressed the needle into the mattress. The effort made the machine beep faster and he heard the nurse curse under his breath. Doug pushed his arm under the blanket, leaving his right arm on top.

The curtain swished open, then closed, and the nurse peered down at him.

"I told him the drugs would kill you. Too late now. I'm not letting you suffer." The nurse adjusted the drip, then turned to look at him closely. "Oh, great, now you're sweating. I bet you have a fever." He bent over the bed to attach the restraints.

Using every ounce of strength, Doug balled his fist and slammed the nurse in the temple, then hit him again. The man fell across him, stunned, with his mouth opening and closing like a fish out of water. Doug ripped the needle out of the bed and jammed it into the nurse's jugular. He held him down until he went limp. "There. How do you like it?" Agony ripped through him and he lay back panting.

"What's happening?" Olivia sounded as if she'd been crying. "Are you okay?"

Doug leaned over, ripped the curtain from the railing and looked at her tear-stained cheeks. "I'll do." He rolled the nurse away from his legs and staggered to his feet. "You don't look so good. Let me get you out of there." He made it to her bed and unstrapped her wrists. "Do you know if Jim is here?"

"He was… before but he had to go organize something in town. He was in a real bad mood. Something has gone wrong. I figure the cops are onto him. He wants to harvest our organs then get rid of us before they find this place." Olivia blinked away tears and looked up at him. "What's the point trying to escape? Jim will bash us again and drag us back here."

Doug turned and unclipped the swipe card from the nurse's scrubs, then patted him down and found a set of keys in one pocket. "This time, we have a card to open the door and car keys." He placed the items on the cabinet and looked at her. "Help me get him on the bed. We'll tie him down and gag him."

"He must have outside clothes here. We have to find something to wear or we won't survive outside." Olivia grabbed the nurse's feet and lifted them onto the bed. "Grab an arm. You're in no condition to lift him."

The monitors beeped in panicked alarm as they heaved the man up on the bed. In agony, Doug pulled the tubes and wires from his body. Then tied and gagged the nurse. He dragged the blankets from the bed then turned to her. "We don't know when Jim will return, we have to risk it. Grab his shoes, they'll fit you. I'll wear the rubber boots in the corner over there. Hurry!"

He shuffled out the door listening intently but it was all quiet. The office was empty and so was the room with lockers and a shelf packed with surgical scrubs. They pulled on pants and tops, wrapped the blankets around them and moved as fast as possible down the dark hallway and into the large room with the door to freedom. He glanced around for a weapon, then thought better of it; being so weak, he would be useless in a fight. The pain had drained him and it was becoming hard to breathe. He leaned one hand against the wall, panting, then swiped the card and the door clicked open. They moved outside into the bitter cold and he spotted a locker. "Bingo." He dragged out two heavy coats and handed the smaller one to Olivia.

"I found gloves and a hat in the pockets of mine—check yours." Olivia shrugged on the coat and buttoned it up, then pulled on the gloves and hat. "Now we just have to find his vehicle."

Sweat trickled down Doug's neck from the effort of dressing. It was as if cotton filled his head and his vision blurred. He shook his head violently, then staggered after Olivia. She turned a corner and he followed. At the end of the passageway, they encountered another door. It opened without a problem but the moment he peered cautiously outside a blast of arctic air and snowflakes smacked him in the face, followed by a horrendous stink. He blinked, blinded by the snowscape before him. They were in an industrial area. Red brick walls loomed up high on each side and ahead he made out snow-dusted machinery.

"There's no one here." Olivia pulled on his arm. "Hurry, he could be back any second."

Half dragged down a laneway by Olivia, Doug shielded his eyes allowing them to adjust to the light before scanning the area. "There's a truck over there in the parking lot." He pointed the key fob at the vehicle and the lights flashed. "Do you drive?"

"Yeah." Olivia's reply came out in a puff of steam. "I know you're hurting but we must get in that truck now."

They slid and slipped across the icy roadway, negotiated the chain fence then climbed into the SUV. Before Doug had clicked his seatbelt, Olivia had the engine running. She glanced at him. "How long should I idle the engine before we leave? I don't want it to break down."

"Drive it real slow. The engine will warm up by the time we hit the highway." He turned up the heater, then searched the vehicle for a cellphone. "Why doesn't he have a cellphone?"

"I'd say he doesn't want to be traced." Olivia had crawled the truck out the parking lot and made her way down a long road, keeping it in the tire tracks of another vehicle. "I doubt harvesting organs from kidnapped people is legal."

They reached the highway and Doug placed a hand on Olivia's arm to prevent her making the turn to Black Rock Falls. "We have plenty of gas. Head to Blackwater. I don't want to run into Jim on his way back. We'll tell the sheriff what happened and he'll contact Sheriff Alton."

"Sure." Olivia accelerated along the highway. "I want to be as far away from that creep as possible."

Doug leaned back in the seat. "I won't let him get away with this." He smothered a moan of despair at the thought of what his sister Sky must have suffered at the hands of Jim. "If I have to, I'll hunt him down like the animal he is, then tear him apart with my bare hands."

CHAPTER FIFTY-SEVEN

The smell of freshly brewed coffee and donuts greeted Rowley as he walked back into the office after delivering Burns to the cells. He made his way to the small kitchenette at the back of the room and helped himself. In the background, he could hear the demanding voice of a woman and Deputy Walters' calming monotone. Not wanting to be involved, he slipped behind his desk to write a report.

He had finished the donuts and was leaning back in his seat enjoying the coffee when Walters came blustering toward him looking like a thundercloud. "Anything wrong?"

"Maybe, maybe not but I went to school with Beatrice Paul and I don't take too kindly to being screamed at as if I am some doddery old fool." He sat in Kane's chair and pushed a hand through his gray hair. "She claims to have seen someone wearin' her granddaughter's sweater in town just before and seein' as the young woman is missin' I called the sheriff and she told me, you should haul tail out there and get a photo of the alleged sweater. She said to hunt down where it came from then call her immediately."

Rowley glanced up to see an elderly woman marching down toward them with a determined expression on her face. He pushed to his feet. "Can I help you, ma'am?"

"You sure can." She pointed a finger at Walters. "This old fool won't listen to me. I saw Doctor Weaver wearing Sky's sweater not twenty minutes ago."

Rowley dropped his voice to a calm steady tone. "How can you be sure it is the same sweater?"

"Because I made it for her." She lifted her chin. "I gave it to her last winter. It is one of a kind. It's yellow and has a red heart right in the center. It's a big size. Sky wanted it big so it would fit over layers of clothes and it comes down to her knees." She glared at him. "She would have had it with her. Don't you understand? If Doc Weaver has it, whoever gave it to her must have taken it from Sky."

Rowley's heartbeat picked up as he considered the implications. Doc Weaver had a vital clue to Sky's disappearance in her possession. "Did you ask her where she obtained the sweater?"

"Of course I did." Mrs. Paul's cheeks flushed deep red. "She informed me her boyfriend picked it up at a yard sale." She gave an exasperated sigh. "And before you ask, no she didn't know who had the yard sale but I can tell you, there aren't many at this time of year."

Rowley frowned. He needed to move on this clue immediately. "Okay, give Deputy Walters all the details and I'll speak to the sheriff."

He stepped out of earshot and called Jenna to explain the situation. She didn't hesitate to send him to hunt down Dr. Weaver and get photographs of the sweater. After dragging on his coat and hat, he headed downtown to Dr. Weaver's clinic, found a parking space and headed inside. He nodded at the people in the waiting room and went straight to the desk. "I need to speak with the doctor."

"Oh, is it a medical emergency?" The receptionist blinked at him over her glasses.

Rowley shook his head, sending ice crystals in all directions. "No, a police matter."

He waited for the door to open and the patient to walk out, then, before the receptionist could open her mouth, walked inside the doctor's office. "Doctor Weaver, I'm sorry to bother you when you're so busy but I need to know about the sweater you're wearing." His attention went to the sweater. It was yellow with a red heart. "May I take a photograph of it please and where did you get it?"

"If you must." Dr. Weaver came from behind her desk and stood in front of him. "I already told the crazy woman, my boyfriend purchased it at a yard sale in town. It's just like new and although a little snug, is very warm."

Rowley used his cellphone camera to take the images. "What's your boyfriend's name and where can I find him?"

"You only just missed him." Dr. Weaver smiled at him. "He's heading back out to the fertilizer plant. He has some maintenance work to do outside in the yard, so he'll be easy to find. I'd say he left about twenty minutes ago."

"Okay." Rowley rubbed his chin. "What's his name and contact details?"

"Wyatt Sawyer. He owns the meat processing and fertilizer plants outside of town." She smiled at him. "Did you know all the waste, the bones and the like from meat processing, end up in blood and bone fertilizer? It's made right next to the meat processing plant." She looked up at him, eyes sparkling with obvious pride. "That's why he buys things at yard sales, he hates waste."

"I see. And I'll need his phone number?"

After she rattled off the number, he thanked her and headed for the door. He would have to take a ride out to the plant and speak with Mr. Sawyer. From the sheriff's case notes, he'd been cooperative during his last interview and Rowley doubted he would cause a problem. After calling in his destination to Maggie in the office, he headed out in the falling snow to the industrial area. He turned the radio to his favorite country and western station and sang along to ease the boredom of the drive.

The scenery changed with every season in Montana. The snow had flattened the landscape, turning the grasslands into a frozen tundra. A few elk sheltered in the spattering of pines but it seemed eerily quiet and he realized how frightened Ella Tate must have been, alone in this wilderness. He'd felt sorry for her the day he'd picked her up and was glad the blood test cleared her. She must have gone to hell and back.

He turned into the snow-covered road leading to the industrial estate and followed the icy blacktop to the processing plants, following a well-worn path through the snow. He found the fertilizer plant without difficulty—he could have followed the smell to it anyway. From the stink, the process of crushing and cooking the waste carried on even during the shutdown. He rolled into the parking lot in time to see a man walking toward him, cellphone in one hand and a shovel in the other. Dressed in a dark hoodie, matching pants and steel-capped working boots, he stood close to six feet, with wide shoulders. He eyed Rowley with suspicion. When the man pushed the phone into his pocket and gave him a smile, he slid from his cruiser. "Mr. Sawyer?"

"That's me." The man stopped a few yards from the vehicle and leaned on his shovel. "What can I do for you, Deputy?"

The case and the questions he needed to ask came to the front of his mind and Rowley took a step toward him. "I wanted to ask you about the sweater you gave Doctor Weaver." He remembered he'd neglected to report his arrival to Maggie and held up a hand. "Just a minute, I forgot to call in."

As he turned to climb back into the cab, the sound of a gong inside his head broke the silence and his brain exploded in pain. Confused, he staggered and fell against his truck. What had happened? He turned slowly to peer through blurred vision at Sawyer and caught the cold look in his eyes and the way his mouth had set in a thin line. Shaking his head, he went to say something, but Sawyer raised the shovel again, advancing like a rattler. He moved so fast, Rowley didn't have time to defend himself. Agony slammed into him, the blow sending shockwaves through his teeth. His stomach rolled and the too-bright parking lot moved in and out of focus. *Holy shit, he's going to kill me.*

CHAPTER FIFTY-EIGHT

Agitation slithered over Jenna at Wolfe's shake of the head. "What do you mean, 'no blood'? There has to be trace evidence here. It's the middle of winter and Burns had to dispose of the bodies. The crusher makes sense." She jammed her hands in her pockets. "It's not as if he could dig a hole in the frozen ground, is it?"

"Nope, but assuming the victims *are* dead, and I've yet to discover any evidence to prove that theory, he could have stashed them somewhere." Wolfe gave her a condescending look. "It's not as if they are going to be found until the melt and moving frozen bodies would be easier than rotting corpses." He sighed. "He would have at least three days before they defrosted and plenty of time to drop them down a mineshaft once the roads cleared."

"Jenna." Kane touched her arm. "Do you want me to go get Duke? If there are any bodies around the property he'll find them."

"Not necessarily." Wolfe removed his gloves and mask. "The snow is great for tracking because we can follow footprints or whatever but Duke isn't cadaver-trained. The dogs learn to recognize the scent of decomposition and when a body is frozen and covered with fresh snow, it becomes an almost sterile environment. There are no scents for the dogs to smell."

"What makes you believe they're dead, ma'am?" Webber gave her a long look. "The blood in the vehicle is consistent with the one blow described by the witness. According to Ella, Sky was alive after the attack. Have you considered the sex-slave trade? That would make more sense than murder."

Annoyance rippled over Jenna. There should have been blood evidence and now Webber was trying to undermine her authority. "Of course I have but those monsters usually want their merchandise much younger and in good condition. They prefer teenagers or younger and Doug Paul would be more of a problem than he'd be worth." She glared at him. "I'm convinced this is a homicide case and I'm treating it as such until proved otherwise."

"I can't consider it a homicide without substantially more evidence." Wolfe's mouth flattened to a thin line. "I'm sorry, Jenna. There's just not enough evidence."

Jenna's phone chimed. "It's Maggie. I'd better take it."

"Seems someone found what looks like a tooth in a bag of fertilizer this morning. They found it when they were potting up bulbs in their garden shed." Maggie sounded apologetic. *"I have it right here. I figure the ME needs to take a look at it, it sure looks like it has a filling to me."*

Appalled, Jenna swallowed hard and touched Wolfe's arm to get his attention. "Do they have the packaging the fertilizer came in?"

"Sure do, it's sitting right here on the counter and it stinks. It's from the local plant right here in Black Rock Falls."

"Okay, place it in an evidence bag and seal it. Wolfe will come by and collect it." She disconnected and explained the situation to Wolfe.

"It's probably an animal tooth with dirt in it but I'll swing by on the way back to the office and take a look." Wolfe rubbed his chin and glanced back at the junkyard. "To put your mind at rest, I'll come back after dark and douse the crusher with luminol in case I've missed anything but I've swabbed every inch of it and it comes up clean." He glanced at his watch. "I'll have time to run tests on everything else we've found this afternoon. If I find anything from here or if the tooth is human, I'll call you."

"Okay, thanks. We'll head back to the office." She turned her attention to Kane. "Lock up the place. I don't want any complaints if Burns walks." Trying to clear her head of the conflicting views from her deputies and put everything in order, she leaned on Kane's truck to wait and surveyed the area.

Tucked away on the edge of town, the old red-brick building had once been a gold exchange for the miners but although gold-mining was still profitable in her county, the local mines yielded little now and the risk wasn't worth the effort. She cast her gaze along the street and apart from the men walking around behind her the only noise came from the cracking of frozen branches. It was quiet in Black Rock Falls in winter but not a void of white. The abundant wildlife in the area surprised her and even the alpine birds seemed to adapt to the cold weather.

The cellphone in her pocket chimed and she glanced at the caller ID and frowned. It was the Blackwater Sheriff's Department calling her. The new sheriff's name had slipped her mind, although she had seen a memo sitting on her desk from Maggie about him. "Sheriff Alton."

"This is Sheriff Buzz Stuart out of Blackwater." Stuart cleared his throat. *"I'll get straight to the point. I have two of your people here, Douglas Michael Paul and Olivia Kate Palmer. They say a man kidnapped them and held them prisoner up in the industrial estate next to the highway not a half-hour from Black Rock Falls. I assume these are the people you mentioned in the BOLO and the media releases?"*

Stunned, Jenna waved Kane toward her then put the cellphone on speaker. "Yes, those are two of the missing persons. What shape are they in?"

"Mr. Paul is in need of immediate medical assistance due to a wound on his side and Miss Palmer has a head injury. Mr. Paul won't leave here and is hell-bent on speaking to you. I've called Black Rock Falls Hospital and they're sending paramedics. They should be here within the hour."

Heart racing, Jenna exchanged a look with Kane and smiled. "Put him on."

They listened in amazed silence as Doug told his story. Disgusted and alarmed, Jenna stared at Kane, watching the emotions move over his face. She straightened. "You say this man's name is Jim? Can you describe him?"

"Yeah, solid, about six feet, dark hair, white. He'll have a cut on his chest too. Olivia stabbed him with a scalpel. I figure it would have needed stitches." Doug's anger radiated down the line. *"He's strong as a bull and the nurse called him 'the boss'. I figure he owns the place. The hospital room is under the fertilizer plant and the entrance is right beside a big machine, like a shredder of some kind. We tied up the nurse and left him on one of the beds."*

Anxiety crammed Jenna's belly. "What about Sky?"

"I don't know." Doug took a ragged breath. *"I figure she's dead. From what we heard, Jim has been running an organ-harvesting racket for some time. I have a bad feeling they already took one of my kidneys."*

Jenna caught Kane's horrified expression before he walked away, pulling out his cellphone. She frowned and went back to the conversation. "Okay, we'll head out there now. Go with the paramedics to the ER and I'll have a deputy waiting to meet you. We'll come and speak to you at the hospital later. I'll make sure you are in a secure ward, so no one can get to you." She disconnected and called Deputy Walters and explained what she needed, then stared at Kane's pale expression. "What's up?"

"Get in the car." Kane threw himself behind the wheel and started the engine, then took off at speed. "So this Jim they mentioned could be Wyatt Sawyer, the owner of the fertilizer plant. Earlier, I heard Rowley call in and say he was heading up there to speak to him." He gave her a grim look. "I just called him and he's not answering his cell. We need to warn him about Sawyer."

"I sent him to see Doc Weaver about Sky's sweater." Jenna swallowed hard. "What's he doing at Sawyer's fertilizer plant?"

"I heard him tell Maggie that Weaver had gotten the sweater from her boyfriend, Wyatt Sawyer. Rowley went to speak to him." Kane's face was grim. "Buckle up."

Heart thumping, Jenna snapped on the seatbelt as the truck fishtailed down the road and drifted around the corner. Kane darted down backstreets to avoid town, and shot out like a bullet onto the highway. The engine roared as he engaged lights and sirens and accelerated. He had turned into a military machine again, his face a mask of determination. It was as if Deputy Kane had left the building and a black ops agent had taken his place. He drove like a man possessed, and not afraid of dying.

As they left the town behind, the snow-covered grasslands flashed by in a white blur. Breathless with anxiety, she reached for the radio. "He might be out of range. I'll try to reach him on the radio, then call Maggie and get an update. He would have called in when he arrived at the fertilizer plant."

After frequent calls to Rowley's cruiser yielded no response, Jenna radioed Maggie with their destination and requested backup. When Wolfe came on the two-way, she glanced at Kane. "Yes, Wolfe, what did you find? Over."

"It's a human tooth. We're on our way, over."

"I've got a real bad feeling about this." Kane's fists gripped the steering wheel as he pushed his truck faster over the icy roads. "With a human tooth in the fertilizer, we know how he disposed of Sky's body and her vehicle. There's a nurse involved and to harvest organs he must have a doctor on his team as well."

Unable to imagine the horror Sky must have endured, Jenna tried to keep her mind set on the case. "My money is on Doctor Weaver."

"Oh, it's her for sure. Her boyfriend is Wyatt Sawyer and he gets off on seeing his victim's sweater on his girlfriend. He is a smooth talker and was too smart to use his cousin's yard to dispose of Sky's vehicle. I'm wondering how long this has been going on." Kane snorted in disgust. "SOB bashes and then drugs his victims to keep them quiet, then sells their body parts. I figured I'd seen some of the worst killers in my time but this one beats all." He flicked her a cold stare. "We need to get there before he starts working on Rowley." He slammed his foot on the gas.

CHAPTER FIFTY-NINE

Dazed but still on his feet, Rowley ducked the next blow and the metal shovel clanged on the door of his cruiser, the sound echoing against the red brick walls. He shook his head, not able to comprehend the situation. Why was Sawyer trying to kill him? He went for his weapon but Sawyer had him pinned down in the truck's open door and the next blow sent screaming agony up his arm as the shovel slammed into his elbow. Fingers numb, his Glock dropped to the ground and spun away into a snowdrift. His cellphone vibrated in his pocket. Help was a call away but he had not one chance in hell of answering the call. When Sawyer raised the shovel again, Rowley lifted his arms to protect his head. *I have to get away from my truck and into the open before he finishes me off.*

After ducking the next blow, he took a step forward but Sawyer pushed him in the chest with the shovel and laughed at him.

"You're mine now." Sawyer's eyes flashed menace. "You don't have a chance against me and I'm so gonna love killin' you."

A wave of desperation and fear gripped Rowley but he pushed it away, determined not to allow this lunatic to win. One on one, he'd have a chance, but stuck between an open door and the cab, Sawyer had the upper hand. A couple more blows to the head would finish him. Right now, he was out of options, it was move or die. Then he remembered his tracker. Wolfe had supplied them all with an emergency beacon; it used the same technology as a satellite phone. He reached across his chest and pressed the stud beside his badge.

Soon Jenna and Kane would be able to hear every word he uttered and know his position. He just had to survive long enough for them to get to him. The chances of surviving had fallen to just above zero, then, as if someone had heard him, Kane's advice drifted into his head. *When cornered, attack.* Grinding his teeth, he glared at Sawyer's amused expression and lifted his chin. "Do you give yourself extra points for attacking an unarmed man, Sawyer? You're nothing but a yellow-bellied coward."

"Oh, listen to the brave deputy." Sawyer took a few steps back and grinned. "Okay, let's make this real fun. The truck is stoppin' my swing anyways." He beckoned him forward. "Show me what you got."

Rowley had trained for this type of situation. He turned to one side, then lashed out with his foot once, twice, three times, but Sawyer deflected the strikes with the handle of the shovel. Giddy and hurting, he took a couple of unsteady steps away from the cruiser but kept his attention on Sawyer. The man stood, eerily confident and with a slight smile on his face, swinging the shovel as if waiting for his next move. He was playing with him, like a cat with a mouse.

"That all you got?" Sawyer laughed. "What are you? A black belt in stupid?"

Not willing to give in, Rowley straightened and stared him down. Although his right arm was practically useless, and agony cut through his head like a knife, he took a fighting stance. No way was he going down to this maniac. Help would be coming and he needed to transmit as much information as possible. "You can't win, Sawyer. Backup is on its way. The sheriff knows you own the fertilizer plant and is heading here now."

"I don't think so. You forgot to call in, didn't you, and how long do you figure it will take me to disable your radio?" Sawyer gave him a maniacal grin. "I've taken down bigger men than you and you're injured. You won't last long. I've seen hogs bleed less than you."

A rush of warmth trickled down Rowley's cheek and bright red spots splashed the snow at his feet. *I'm bleeding.* He stared at the crimson flow in disbelief and tried to concentrate then aimed another kick, this time at a Sawyer's knee, but landed a feeble blow to the man's thigh. "You may have damaged one arm but I still have my feet."

"Not for long." Sawyer grinned in a flash of white teeth, raised the shovel and brought it down in a whoosh of air.

Oh, Jesus. Slowed from the head injury, Rowley had no way of avoiding the blow. Searing pain shot across his right knee and he buckled, falling face down in the snow. "I'm down." He hoped Kane could hear him.

Another crushing blow to his head sent shocking agony rocketing down his nerve endings and white stars danced across his vision. Sawyer's low chuckle and the fear of dying in the snow shot adrenaline through his veins, pushing away the red-hot pain. He blinked blood from his eyes and rolled away, kicking at Sawyer's legs with every ounce of strength he had. "Now you've made me mad."

He landed a kick on Sawyer's knee but to his horror, the man absorbed the blow and just stood there grinning down at him. Panic welled and he gulped down freezing mouthfuls of air. Under him, the ice-packed snow, crimson with his blood, blurred. His muscles trembled and it was as if he floated on the edge of reality. He shook his head, desperate to stay alive; help was coming and he had to remain conscious. Digging his fingers into the ice, he inched away to get some distance between him and Sawyer. Too late. With a triumphant grunt, Sawyer came down on him hard with both knees. Air left his lungs in a rush of steam and in seconds, Sawyer had pulled zip ties from his back pocket. Rowley fought hard but Sawyer was incredibly strong and, moments later, had him trussed up. He stared up into Sawyer's black unyielding eyes and hoped Kane or Wolfe could hear him. "I'm down, need assistance."

"You sure do but you don't have no radio on you, now do you?" Sawyer gave him a satisfied grin. "Did I hit you too hard and scramble your brains? Don't pass out on me now or you won't enjoy the next bit." He slapped Rowley hard across the face.

"Oh, Jesus." Rowley ground his teeth against a rush of searing agony.

"Jesus can't help you now." Sawyer bent over him and stared into his eyes. "I'm so gonna enjoy watchin' you get all chewed up in the hogger."

Cold hit Rowley's back as Sawyer lifted his feet and dragged him with ease across the parking lot, heading toward the hogger machine. The stark horror of what Sawyer intended to do hit home. Fighting to keep conscious, he tried to reason with him. "It's not too late. You can walk away now. I won't say anything."

"Oh, you'll say plenty and by the time you die you'll be cryin' for your mommy." Sawyer dragged him into the courtyard. "When I have the conveyer belt runnin' and you're headin' down into the grinder, you'll scream and no one will be able to hear you but me." He chuckled and kept moving closer to the machine. "I love it when they scream."

CHAPTER SIXTY

Jenna gripped Kane's satellite phone in both trembling hands and listened to the horrific attack on Rowley. Sick to her stomach, she glanced at Kane. "We won't make it in time."

"We will." Kane moved his fingers restlessly on the steering wheel. "Jake will fight back. Listen to him. He might be injured but he isn't down yet."

Terrified for Rowley, Jenna stared at the screen, willing him to survive for just a few more minutes. She wished he could hear her. "We're coming, hang on. Come on, Jake, fight back."

The sickening thuds and gasps made her stomach cramp. Her hands shook with every word Rowley uttered. Hearing a friend fighting for his life was tearing her apart. She looked at Kane. "Go faster; we have to get to him. *Please*, Kane, we can't let him die."

They shot past two eighteen-wheelers and Kane aimed the beast into the middle of the highway, wheels straddling the centerline. The motor roared and the hood raised as the powerful engine threw Jenna back in her seat. Ahead the road was clear into the distance, but even Kane wasn't invincible. If they hit one patch of ice they would slide into the ditch at full speed. She gripped the seat. "Oh, shit."

"The middle has less ice at the moment and every second counts." The nerve in his cheek twitched as trees flashed by in a blur of brown and white. "Hang on."

Jenna held her breath as Kane slid the truck around the corner and it fishtailed on the ice before he gained control and they charged down the road leading to the fertilizer plant.

In her hand, Kane's cellphone relayed the horror Rowley was suffering. His voice came through the speaker in almost a whisper now.

"Sawyer is dragging me to a machine he calls the hogger. It's a massive shredder." Rowley panted out each word. *"I'm not going to make it out of this. Get this SOB for me, Wyatt Sawyer is the Axman."* He sucked in a deep breath and his voice came out calm, almost resigned. *"It's been a pleasure knowing you all."*

Fighting back tears, Jenna's chest constricted and she bit back a sob. "Oh, my God."

"There's Jake's truck." Kane bypassed the parking lot and squeezed his truck down a sidewalk toward the building. Ahead, Jenna could see a man dragging Rowley by the feet toward a huge piece of machinery. She slotted the phone into its bracket and pulled out her weapon. She was out the door and running by the time the truck slid to a halt in front of a concrete post dividing the walkway. The snow underfoot bogged her down and she slipped on the ice-covered pathway. Glacial air cut deep into her lungs. Seconds later Kane was at her side in a cloud of steam, Glock drawn. She kept running. "Sheriff's department! Stop what you're doing."

To her horror, Sawyer ignored her and lifted Rowley onto the conveyer belt as if he weighed nothing. He glanced at them and shrugged, then calmly walked to the machine. Jenna kept running— she had to save Rowley. "Stop or I'll shoot."

When Sawyer grinned and gave her the finger, she did not hesitate. "Take him out, Kane."

Two shots rang out and blood spurted from Sawyer's shattered knees but before he fell, he stumbled forward to press a red button on the machine. The massive grinding machine sprang to life and the conveyer belt shuddered, then moved slowly toward the sharp grinding teeth flashing menacingly inside a large hole. For the first time in her life, she heard Rowley swear as he wriggled around in a desperate attempt to roll off the wide conveyer belt.

Lungs bursting with effort, Jenna holstered her weapon and sprinted the last few yards at speed, then threw herself at Rowley in an attempt to roll him off the machine. They spun sideways but remained stuck. The machine made a terrible grinding noise and she had a close-up view of the deadly sharp blades turning inside, ready to shred them to pieces. Feet and hands slipping on the greasy belt, she couldn't pull herself free. Panic made her hands shake. In seconds the belt was going to drop them inside the gaping maw. She turned to see Kane running toward them. "Kane, do something."

His face was a mask of concentration as he raised the pistol in both hands. Another shot rang out and the red button on the machine exploded into a shower of red plastic. Time seemed to stop as the stinking machine came within a few inches of swallowing them alive before the engine whined, shuddered and died. Heart thundering, Jenna heaved a sigh of relief, then pushed herself up and looked down into Rowley's blood-soaked face. "I'm sure glad Kane never misses."

EPILOGUE

Friday morning, week two

It never surprised Jenna how many criminals rolled over on their partners for a deal. The DA attacked the weakest link, one Geoffrey La Rocca, the nurse, and he soon gave up the entire horrific team. Wyatt Sawyer, the rapist sex addict, had boasted about killing women in other states as well and leaving their bodies to rot beside the highway. The Roadside Strangler, after a ferocious twelve-month killing spree in Wyoming three years previously, had been unmasked.

The Sawyer interview had been interesting, conducted in a hospital room with both hands cuffed to the bed. It seemed like poetic justice. After his lawyer convinced him the jury might go easy on him if he talked, Sawyer went from angry to boasting about how he had outsmarted everyone his entire life. He gave Jenna a slow smile, then admitted to coming close to killing her and Kane. After examining Sawyer's white pickup with the sticker mark on one door, Kane identified it as the vehicle that played chicken with them on the highway.

Jenna had listened intently as Sawyer went on to tell the story of how he stumbled onto the idea of organ harvesting after meeting the unworldly Dr. Weaver and convincing her he could help the less fortunate by supplying the desperately needed organs if she performed the surgery. He had the money to set up a small clinic and by paying substantial amounts to the right people soon gained access to the black market. The trade in illegal organs was widespread and with so many young people advertising their whereabouts on social media, kidnapping a few potential donors wasn't too difficult.

He'd chosen women as the majority of his victims because they'd fed his need to kill and admitted that unless they died under the knife, he fed them to the hogger machine alive. The men he processed swiftly, selling off their organs and disposing of them within a couple of days. He owned both the meat and fertilizer plants, so used refrigerated trucks from the meat processing plant for organ transportation and the hogger machine in the fertilizer plant for disposal of the remains. Adding the bodies to the waste from his meat processing plant and turning them into fertilizer was easy and undetectable.

Sawyer had discovered people would do anything for money. A disgraced nurse was easy to come by, as was the ambulance chaser Burns who he used to pick up the vehicles of the people he kidnapped. The story made Jenna sick to her stomach. It was as if he was proud of his ingenious scheme and told his story with relish. When asked where he kept the cash from the sale of the organs, he informed them payments went into an offshore bank account. The FBI had searched but found no trace of the account or Sawyer's list of contacts.

Jenna had to admit arresting Dr. Weaver had given her a modicum of satisfaction; although the woman had intimidated her to some degree, her gut instinct had been right. After searching the underground clinic at the fertilizer plant, they discovered the computer in the office held the same organ-matching data Dr. Weaver had collected. The database gave them an insight on how big Sawyer had expected his scheme to grow. Had he planned to pluck a matched donor from town when an order came in?

The DA charged Dr. Weaver for performing illegal organ harvesting on living people and murder in the first degree. The doctor had refused to say anything, not giving a clue to how many victims they had murdered. At least they had the tooth and if Wolfe could extract any viable DNA from it, they might be able to solve another missing person's case. The problem was that so many people just up and vanished without a trace all over the USA.

It was with some degree of relief, when Wolfe confirmed his original findings on Dr. Weaver's history. After an extensive search of Dr. Weaver's background and contacts over the last ten years, the FBI had found absolutely no connection between her and Viktor Carlos or the cartel. At last, Jenna could breathe easy again and likewise Kane.

Jenna had assisted Kane by listening and making notes as he delved into his new memories of the time immediately before the car bombing. Not long after, he'd passed all his suspicions to the office of POTUS. Jenna was aware Kane desperately wanted to be involved in the capture of the men responsible for his wife's death, but obviously POTUS thought otherwise. However, when Wolfe gave him the report of the deaths of the men responsible, he'd taken the news in his usual professional manner then vowed not to speak of it again. It sure was good to see the burden lifted from his shoulders. Maybe now, he could move on with his life.

Jenna walked into the hospital room and took the seat beside Kane and Wolfe. She smiled at Rowley. After seeing him safely to the ER, she'd been so busy with arrests she hadn't had time to visit him, but had called him and listened to Kane and Wolfe's daily reports. "I'm so sorry I've not been in for a visit before now. How are you feeling today? You don't look ready to go home. Have you been hiding your injuries from me?"

"I'm just fine, ma'am." Rowley looked at her through bloodshot eyes peering out from a bruised and battered face. "Like I told you, I have a chipped elbow and a bruised knee. The rest of me is fine."

"Let's not mention the severe concussion, twelve stitches in his head and a cracked rib." Wolfe frowned. "It's just as well you arrived when you did."

"The tracker you gave me saved my life." Rowley smiled a crooked grin. "But I figure it was the sheriff's flying tackle that broke my ribs." He chuckled, then met her gaze. "I'm joking, ma'am, you put your life on the line for me and I'll never forget it."

"Thank you." Jenna smiled. "One thing I have to ask." She turned to look at Kane. "Why didn't you take out Sawyer?"

"He wasn't armed." Kane shrugged and stretched nonchalantly. "I figured you'd want him for questioning and your order was in the heat of the moment."

"Yeah, we sure found out a lot about Mr. Sawyer." Jenna nodded and turned her attention to Wolfe. "What about the tooth?"

"I've sent the DNA profile out to all agencies and we'll see if we get a match. I've left the case open and turned everything over to the CSI unit in Helena." He smiled. "I dropped in to see Olivia and Doug and they're doing okay considering Doug had a kidney removed, but they'll need counseling. The doctors told Doug he'd be in the hospital for at least another week."

"Oh, something else." Kane smiled at her. "After hearing about our interest in Knox, the Blackwater Motel receptionist called Maggie and admitted she was the blonde Knox carried into his room." He chuckled. "She would have come forward sooner but didn't want to ruin her reputation."

"I should have her charged with withholding evidence." Exhausted by the stressful case, Jenna sighed. She just wanted to go home, sit by the fire and relax for a while. Kane was monitoring the 911 line and she turned to him. "Has anything urgent come in for us to attend to today?"

"Nope. I figure we go get a tree and maybe buy some presents." Kane smiled at her, took her hand and gave it a squeeze. "I figure we all deserve some downtime, don't you?"

Jenna shrugged and stared down at their linked hands in amazement, he'd never as much as touched her in front of the others. She glanced up to see Rowley and Wolfe grinning like baboons. She untangled Kane's fingers and cleared her throat. "I do have a few things to do at the office."

"Nothing that can't wait." Kane's eyes twinkled with mischief. "Don't forget we're having Christmas with Wolfe and the girls."

Is it that time already? Jenna blinked. "When is Christmas?"

"Tomorrow." Kane chuckled. "Ho, ho, ho."

A LETTER FROM D.K. HOOD

Thank so much for choosing my novel and coming with me on another thrilling adventure with Kane and Alton in *Where Angels Fear*. If you enjoyed it and you'd like to keep up to date with all my latest releases, just sign up at the link below. Your email address will never be shared and you can unsubscribe at any time.

www.bookouture.com/dk-hood

It is wonderful continuing the stories of Jenna Alton and Dave Kane and having you along. I really appreciate all the wonderful comments and messages you have all sent me during this series.

If you enjoyed my story, I would be very grateful if you could leave a review and recommend my book to your friends and family. I really enjoy hearing from readers so feel free to ask me questions at any time. You can get in touch on my Facebook page or Twitter, or through my blog.

Thank you so much for your support.
D.K. Hood

DKHood_Author

dkhoodauthor

www.dkhood.com

dkhood-author.blogspot.com.au

ACKNOWLEDGEMENTS

I must give a shout out to Veronica Slater and Jason for wearing images of my book covers on their T-shirts and promoting me in my hometown and beyond.

A special thank you to Noelle Holten and Kim Nash for the fantastic online promotion, they are part of the incredible Bookouture team who work so hard behind the scenes to publish my books.

11-23
cmw

Made in the USA
Middletown, DE
08 April 2023

28502150R00172